THE SUMMONING

Recent Titles by F.G. Cottam

BRODMAW BAY
THE COLONY
DARK ECHO
THE HOUSE OF LOST SOULS
THE MAGDALENA CURSE
THE WAITING ROOM
THE MEMORY OF TREES *
THE SUMMONING *

* available from Severn House

THE SUMMONING

The Shadow World: Book One

F.G. Cottam

Severn House

This first world edition published 2014
in Great Britain and the USA by
SEVERN HOUSE PUBLISHERS LTD of
19 Cedar Road, Sutton, Surrey, England, SM2 5DA

British Library Cataloguing in Publication Data

Cottam, Francis, 1957
  The summoning.
  1. Excavations (Archaeology)–Scotland–Fiction.
  2. Scotland–Antiquities–Fiction. 3. Fantasy fiction.
  I. Title
  823.9'2-dc23

ISBN-13: 978-0-7278-8350-6 (cased)

All Severn House titles are printed on acid-free paper.

Severn House Publishers support the Forest Stewardship Council™ [FSC™],
the leading international forest certification organisation. All our titles that
are printed on FSC certified paper carry the FSC logo.

Typeset by Palimpsest Book Production Ltd.,
Falkirk, Stirlingshire, Scotland.
Printed and bound in Great Britain by
TJ International, Padstow, Cornwall.

For Emmeline Cottam

ONE

A dam Parker liked Grayling. He supposed everyone on the dig liked the professor. Archaeology was painstaking and sometimes the fragility of what they stumbled upon in their excavations made it stressful too. It was not difficult to miss clues and destroy valuable evidence and artefacts. It was frighteningly easy, in fact.

But Grayling ran a relaxed dig. He wore his expertise lightly. He was witty and considerate, a fair-minded man happy to share his knowledge and the practical tips accrued through years of experience.

He had gained that experience searching in desolate and remote places, often beneath a brutal sun or a deluge, always driven by his need to find a truthful answer to some ancient and stubborn mystery Adam thought him an easy man both to warm to and to respect. He actually thought him something of an inspiration.

It was why he was so confused now. The object he had found the previous day had been intact and extraordinary. That much was immediately obvious to him as he brushed the soil from its elaborate metal detail, literally unearthing it, exposing it to light and scrutiny for the first time in what he thought might be many hundreds of years.

He held the thing he had discovered in the palm of his hand and tried to calculate what metal would weigh quite so much. He reckoned it was heavier than lead. Was it bronze? He didn't think so. It felt weightier and denser in his hand than even gold or platinum would. It was carved or cast into the shape of some kind of mythic creature.

He held it close to his face and blew on it, shedding more soil fragments, revealing detail that almost made him drop it, shocked at the feral cunning so finely depicted in the features of the artefact.

He put it into his finds tray, careful to mark the exact spot from where he had taken it. He looked around. It had started to rain; he could hear the raindrops pattering softly and then more rapidly on the leaves of the trees around him with the gathering strength of this latest shower.

The rest of the team – most of them – were out of sight at a spot a hundred yards to the north of him, working eight or nine feet down in the deep excavation. He could hear their muffled banter, cheerful despite the conditions.

It rained a lot in Scotland. They were equipped with the right sort of clothing for the weather. Daylight was better than lamplight to see in, but they were used to working, on this dig, under plastic sheets when they needed to. It was what they were doing now.

Adam hesitated. An instinct, imprecise but very strong, told him that he should not take the thing he had found to Grayling on the tray. It should not be exposed to the risk of full public scrutiny. It was too remarkable, he thought. It in no way matched their expectations of what they were likely to find here.

It might confuse people. It might distract and disturb them, as he felt it was now in some curious way disturbing him. The rain was splashing on it, cleaning its contours, revealing more detail as it sat there at the centre of the tray.

And Adam began to feel that the more of it he saw, the more difficult it became to look at. There was something unsettling about the find. Actually, he thought there was something awful about it, as though it were some contagious relic of a cruel, barbaric age. Close study of the object almost provoked a shiver of dread in him.

He picked it up from the tray and put it carefully into one of the bellows pockets sewn into the leg of his combats. It was safe from the rain there and also out of sight. He was very aware of the weight of it, of its gravid pull against his belt.

He dusted his hands on his thighs. The trees around him were oak and downy birch, ash and alder and willow. And he was conscious of how ancient a place this was. Once, the whole of the Scottish lowlands had been covered in just such dense, deciduous woodland. Now, the Forest of Cree was part of a scarce and protected wildlife heritage, but it was still substantial enough a wilderness to get easily lost in, still a place that wrapped its mysteries in silence and seclusion.

He hesitated, listening to the drip of the strengthening rain through the branches. He unfolded his waterproof poncho from its pouch on his belt and put it over his head.

Adam felt that he faced a moment of some enormity. He was

nineteen, a second-year student on the archaeology course at his university. He greatly appreciated the sacrifices that had been made to enable him to study his chosen subject. He valued the friendship in particular of two of his fellow students among the group who were digging and bantering under the waterproof sheet in the deep excavation a stone's throw away from where he stood, stirred into excitement by the discovery of gnawed animal bones marked with the charring of cooking fires and odd shards of Bronze Age pottery.

If the thing in his pocket was not a deliberate fake, it was the find of a lifetime. But it wasn't a fake, was it? No one had planted it there out of mischief.

An archaeologist might spend an entire career searching and never find anything so finely wrought and extraordinary. He suspected it might be priceless and unique, and that its study might reveal something new and profound and unknown about the past in this venerable place.

Adam's intuition about all of this was pretty certain. And he wondered, with a sinking heart, if it was what he really needed at this stage of his life.

This find represented the pinnacle of his archaeological career. It had come before he had exited his teens, before he had even qualified as an archaeologist proper by completing his coursework and taking his finals. It had happened entirely by fluke at a location he hadn't chosen and in a way for which he could take no genuine credit.

I could put it back, Adam thought. He looked around. There was no one yet above the ground to see him. *I could put it back and rediscover it in five or ten years when my own mature research could quite reasonably compel me back to this spot.*

But he couldn't do that, could he? It wasn't even the risk that someone else might stumble across it in the meantime; he could hide it obscurely where they wouldn't. It was the potential significance of the find. He could not cheat Professor Grayling or his fellow students or himself or archaeology out of that. Not for an interval of another five to ten years, he couldn't. He couldn't in all conscience delay it for a day.

The thing had been unearthed. He had discovered it. And it was wonderfully intact and complete. For better or for worse, a mystery was about to be created or solved on the strength of the artefact in his pocket. If he concealed it from study, he betrayed everything he believed in and all that he aspired to become.

Adam went over all this again and again in his mind in the pub in Newton Stewart. He was four miles from the site of his find and a full day had elapsed since he had taken it to show to the professor. There had followed no triumphant announcement or revelatory moment of scholarship in the field.

He had stood in the spacious tent, in the clearing where they had set up, while the object sat on the card table Grayling used as a desk and the professor studied it by lamplight with his arms folded across his chest. Rain drummed on the fabric roof of the tent. It had grown torrential in the ten or so minutes since his discovery. His poncho dribbled on to the earth floor.

The professor was about the same height as Adam, but had this silver-headed air of intellectual authority that seemed to enhance his actual size. Years of subsisting on field trip rations had given him a lean, well-toned physique. His features were lean too, under his clipped salt-and-pepper beard. He looked capable and serious and at that moment Adam thought his expression particularly severe.

He looked as if he was about to give someone a serious dressing-down rather than a congratulatory pat on the back. The object sat squat and baleful on the table. Professor Grayling looked anything but delighted at its presence there. Eventually he went across and zipped up the tent flap, his signal that he was not, for the duration, to be disturbed by anyone outside it.

'What is it that you think you've uncovered, Adam?'

Adam took a deep breath before replying. 'Something pre-Christian, from a part of the world with no trade links with northern Britain. It might have some religious significance. I think it is possibly Etruscan, or even Persian in origin.'

The professor grunted, but the sound was non-committal. 'Not bad guesswork,' he said. 'But wrong. How would you describe it? Its character, I mean.'

'It's ugly. It's a bit sinister too. It's meant to be a living creature, but looks like no animal copied from life. I think it's a representation of a demon or a god. My money would be on a demon.'

'Would you care to estimate its age?'

'Carbon dating would tell us when it was carved, or cast. I wouldn't be surprised if it was three or four hundred years BC.'

'Yet it has survived in the ground intact.'

'I'm not a metallurgist, Professor. I'd stick with that estimate until proven wrong.'

'You're a bright young man,' Grayling said. 'Your assumptions are informed and your preliminary conclusions reasonable. But I think the results of carbon dating might surprise and even confound you.'

Adam didn't reply. He felt nervous and more deflated than he thought he should, in the circumstances. Shouldn't he feel thrilled or exultant? Shouldn't he at least feel inspired by the mystery thrown up by his find? Perhaps it was a forgery after all. Maybe that was the reality the professor was gently breaking to him.

'What if I told you it was not symbolic, that object,' Grayling said. 'What if I were to tell you it was an accurate depiction, taken from life?'

Adam swallowed. 'The animal it most resembles is a wild boar,' he said.

The professor nodded. 'Agreed.'

'But wild boars don't have the claws of a reptile. And I've never seen one with two heads.'

'Would you care to guess again as to its function, Adam?'

'I'm sticking with religious. But it could be anything from a good luck charm to a toy,' Adam said. 'It could be a piece of art. Or an elaborate paperweight.' He was thinking forgery again. 'It's pretty gruesome, though. What do you think it is, Professor?'

'I haven't the remotest idea,' Grayling said. He added nothing further. He stroked his beard again and his eyes remained on the object on the table as the rain gurgled, dripping from the tent fabric over their heads.

And Adam started to suspect that actually, the professor knew more than he was prepared to say. Grayling's sombre mood seemed to be provoked by something more than the current dismal weather that was laying siege to them. The weather was very changeable in Scotland in the autumn. The clouds would eventually lift.

'Give me twenty-four hours to consider this, Adam,' Grayling said. 'Have your explorations in the town taken you as far as the Black Horse?'

'Yes.'

'They serve an excellent pint of bitter, do they not?'

'They do.'

'And they do a very decent platter of stew.'

'I'll have to take that on trust, Professor.' *The condemned man ate a hearty repast,* Adam thought. He didn't know why he thought it

'I'll see you in the saloon bar at eight o'clock tomorrow evening. Please mention this find to no one in the meantime,' Grayling said.

'I won't, Professor,' Adam said. The request didn't greatly surprise him. He'd suspected since the securing of the tent flap that they would likely part on that instruction.

They'd been digging for two weeks. For most of the team, it was their first proper work in the field. It had been planned as an austere start, meagre and unglamorous. They had found none of the tell-tale black wax from those sacrilegious ceremonies which plagued the more celebrated archaeological sites from Stonehenge to Melrose Abbey. No one thought of the Forest of Cree as a mystical or black magical hotspot.

The aims of the dig were pretty much anthropological, Adam thought. The forests had once covered all of the land. Who, then, had lived here? How had they lived? And what had sustained them? It was mundane stuff and deliberately so. Shards and bones and bones and shards, and if they were dead lucky, an iron arrowhead or a bronze sandal buckle, would provide their evidence. And then, two weeks in, he had found this.

What had he actually found? It was a thing fashioned from some heavy metal that could fit easily into the palm of an adult hand. It was exquisitely wrought and it was profoundly ugly too. It was entirely unique, in Adam's shallow experience. And it was an abomination, he thought, in the language his mother would have used to describe it.

The professor placed a glass of beer on the table and sat down opposite him. He was exactly on time. Adam had been five minutes early and was three consequent inches into his own drink. But whatever else they were destined to argue over, he had to agree with Grayling's earlier claim that the Black Horse served a sublime pint of bitter.

'You're an only child?'

'Yes.'

'Your mother widowed?'

'Not exactly, no. My father left when I was eleven years old. I believe he's alive, somewhere. My mum finds the idea of death easier to deal with than the fact of abandonment.'

'That's understandable. Do you possess martial accomplishments?'

Adam sipped his beer. 'That's not a question I understand. I'm not in the Territorial Army or anything like that. I was never even a Scout or a Sea Cadet. I'm not a great one for joining in.'

'Have you ever studied the martial arts?'

'No. I boxed as a schoolboy. I fenced too, foil and épée. No ninja stuff. Why?' Adam noticed that Grayling hadn't yet touched his drink.

'Were you any good? At your fencing and boxing, I mean. Modesty apart, Adam.'

Adam saw no point in dishonesty, even if the nature of the interrogation baffled him. 'Very,' he said. 'I've an aptitude for sport.'

'But not team sports?'

Adam shrugged. 'Like I just said, I've never been much of a joiner-in.'

Finally, Grayling took a sip from his drink. 'Have you any notion of quite how good-looking a young man you are?'

'My mum always told me to count my blessings but to remember that there's always someone who exceeds you in every department. That would include looks, Professor.'

Grayling was silent for a moment. 'Don't you like what you see in the mirror?'

'Not particularly, no. A mirror image is the obverse of the truth, isn't it? It's a distortion. It isn't what other people see when they look at you. At least, I hope it isn't. This is a pretty oblique line of questioning, Professor Grayling.'

'Bear with me. Be patient. Where do your course mates think you are?'

'I didn't say and they didn't ask.'

'Might they not come in here and discover us?'

Adam sipped from his glass and grimaced. 'No. They'll be in the Bell, where the draught lager only costs two quid a pint and there's half-price shots till ten o'clock and a couple of decent pool tables.'

'The enduring imperatives of student life,' said Grayling.

'You've had time to take a proper look at my find, Professor. Have you come to any conclusions about it?'

But Grayling ignored the question. He said, 'I want you to describe to me the exact circumstances of the find. You were digging at a speculative location some distance from the main area of excavation.

No one witnessed what occurred. Take me through yesterday morning, from the moment you got to the site. Leave nothing out.'

So he did think it was a forgery, a plant, a bit of mischief. Adam sat back and sighed. 'Well, I was up early yesterday morning, obviously, because at car boots you've got to be there at the crack of dawn to have any chance of finding a bargain. My eye was caught by a tray of bric-a-brac, some Victorian stuff, Gothic-revival mostly. I singled out my ugly little front parlour mantelpiece ornament, gave the bloke a fiver for it and the rest I'm sure you can reconstruct for yourself.'

Grayling smiled. His eyes did not waver. 'I wish that scenario were true. If it was, this is something we could both just quietly forget about. But the thing you discovered is all too genuine, I'm afraid.'

And to Adam, at that moment, the professor himself looked genuinely afraid.

'Tell me truthfully and accurately about the circumstances in which you found it. Tell me about what impelled your movements. Tell me what was on your mind.'

Jane Dobb had been principally on his mind. She had a mane of red hair and a generous mouth. She had a gorgeous figure and a filthy laugh and she smoked too much. She was clever in that careless way only women ever were, in Adam's slightly envious experience. He was speculating on what kissing her would be like. But three wasn't divisible by two and he thought that she had her eye on Martin Prior. He couldn't blame her. Martin made women laugh. He did it effortlessly. It was a very attractive attribute.

She was there now, standing at the lip of the main excavation, sipping something with steam rising from it from a metal flask cup that was dull in the matt morning light against the ruby pucker of her lips. She was laughing at something Martin, standing next to her, was saying. Of course she was. She stood there, sipping and laughing, looking sexier than anyone had any right to in a plastic poncho and a pair of rubber boots. She was tall and lithe and she rested her head on Martin's shoulder in amused empathy at something he had just said.

Adam walked away. It was all a bit tragic, really. You didn't expect to be hit by the hopelessness of an adolescent crush at the age of nineteen. It didn't really seem particularly fair. But maturity was one of those wobbly attributes, wasn't it? It tended to desert him in times of crisis. And the crises tended to be provoked by attractive girls. Jane Dobb was the most attractive girl he had ever encountered. He couldn't compete with Martin's wit or Martin's classic Mercedes sports car. Martin was sophisticated and rich. The fight for Jane's affections was a battle lost before it had even been fought.

He retreated and walked away. He sensed that their eyes were on his back, which really was adolescent, wasn't it? It was the sort of self-consciousness fourteen-year-olds inflict on themselves because they assume they are the principle point and natural focus of the world that surrounds them. Next, he'd be thinking that they were talking about him.

Were they? He turned and looked. But they were remote now and out of sight, already below the ground and busy sifting for the jigsaw puzzle pieces of the past. He carried on in the same direction he had been travelling, walking backwards for a few steps before stumbling on a surface root and stopping to gather some composure.

He was a foot beyond the lip of a slight depression. The depression had exposed the root on which he had just snagged a heel. The way in which the root had been exposed was slightly suggestive of sagging in the ground, of gentle subsidence. He was on the edge of a very shallow bowl, about twelve feet across and maybe eight inches lower at its centre than at its perimeter. He didn't know what this circle of ground resembled; perhaps, slightly, a baked cake that had failed to rise.

What it didn't resemble was a patch of earth concocted by nature. The circularity was too neat. Nature was more ragged and imprecise. The depression was very subtle, though. He owed his noticing it at all to the snagged root and to something else; which was the low angle of the autumnal morning sun. It had only just broken through a skein of cloud. Any higher, and it would flatten out the subtle contour of depression. With cloud cover, you wouldn't notice the geometric perfection of this slight feature at all, covered as it was by the random forest litter of fallen leaves and broken twigs.

He walked the perimeter of the depression. He could think of only two things that left perfect craters in the earth and they were the impact of meteorites and the explosion of high velocity artillery shells. The concave shape he studied now seemed far too slight to have been caused by either.

Adam was aware that a silence had descended upon the moment

and the place, and stillness also. There was an atmosphere he was aware of but could not have easily described. There was something confidential about it, he told Professor Grayling at their table in the pub. And the mood was odd.

'The mood was odd in what way?'

'There was urgency,' Adam said. 'The air almost crackled with it. The forest is a serene location, you know that yourself. But the mood in that spot at that moment was anything but serene. It was as though something dramatic and urgent impended there.'

'What prompted you to dig?'

Adam became conscious of the trowel hung on his belt because its blade tinkled audibly against the keychain hanging next to it. It was as though the shining metal sang to him. The wind hadn't shifted it because there was no wind, and neither had his movement, because when it happened, he was standing still, staring at the ground. He felt the vibrating thrum of the trowel blade, of its energy against his leg.

He looked to the centre of the depression. And he saw something dimpled and infirm in the spread of leaves at the spot, as though signalling something concealed, a weakness in the sub-structure of the soil itself – a flaw caused by some ancient damage done to the fabric of the earth. He sensed the violation of the ground caused by digging, by burial. And he walked across to the spot, slid to his knees, then took his trowel and began to dig himself.

'Most unusual,' Grayling said, dryly. 'Ancient damage done to the earth doesn't generally leave traces of violation on the surface for millennia.'

'I know it doesn't,' Adam said.

With the back of his hand, Grayling wiped traces of beer from the bristles above his top lip. 'Go on.'

'I dug. The earth was giving.'

'Collusive,' Grayling said.

But Adam ignored this. 'I found it two feet down, loose in the soil. I fingered it out. It never felt the sharp edge of the trowel. I suppose it must seem in some way that I knew it was there. Maybe in some sense I did. I can't really explain the find otherwise.'

'Did anything else strike you as strange?'

'Don't you think it strange enough already?'

'I can't judge. I don't think you've described the whole event,' Grayling said.

Adam thought hard, trying to remember the exact detail of the experience he'd undergone in the clearing the previous morning. 'I thought I heard music,' he said eventually. 'The silence of the forest was breeched, at least in my mind, by music. I heard it distinctly at the very moment of the find.'

'What manner of music was it?'

'It was trumpets. They were shrill and deafening. That was what I heard when I groped through the soil. I heard music that was harsh and loud. For a moment, my mind was filled with it.'

'And that's everything?'

'I think it is. That's except for the object itself, Professor. You have that.'

Grayling pushed his pint away and stood up. The spell of his story broken, Adam looked around the bar. It was dimly lit, smoky from logs that hadn't yet properly caught in the big grate of the fireplace over to his left. There were no other customers in the bar. No one had eavesdropped on his curious account.

'You're going?'

'We're going. We're going to the site.'

'But it's dark.'

'And there are enough lights on the Defender's rig to illuminate a rock concert. That is unless you've other, pressing business?'

The torrential rain gave the streets of the small town a glossy look in the darkness. The interior of the Land Rover smelled of diesel and loam and vinyl seat covers and damp canvas, and this cocktail of odours was a comfort to Adam, because it was familiar and normal. He needed comforting, he realized. He was nervous about this unscheduled visit to the site.

He didn't know why, but recalling the circumstances of the find, reliving the moment, had been an ordeal for him. When he thought of the object itself, he felt something close to actual horror. Grayling switched the engine on and the wipers started to swish across the screen. 'Fasten your seat belt, Adam,' he said.

They travelled the four miles to the site in silence, encountering no other traffic on the road. As they left the tarmac, Grayling engaged the four-wheel-drive and they bumped along forest path with the headlamps dimmed and the visible world just a shallow crescent of yellow forest growth unfurling before them.

Adam thought about the Bell in Newton Stewart. He looked at his watch. It was just after nine. Martin Prior had another hour to work his cut-rate seduction magic on Jane Dobb. Not that cost was really an issue with Martin.

He saw one of the dig markers emerge into view through the windscreen and was able to orient himself. 'A degree or so south,' he said to Grayling. The professor turned the wheel fractionally and put the headlamps on full beam. 'The spot is framed by the two large trees straight ahead of us,' Adam said, after a minute. 'It lies just beyond and between them.'

Grayling brought the Land Rover to a halt. He put the shift in neutral but kept the engine idling because it would power the flood-lights on the rig mounted above the cab. Above the engine noise, Adam could hear rain heavy on the canvas that covered the rear of the vehicle. Rain on taut canvas was usually a comforting sound, he thought, suggestive of dry and cozy shelter from the elements. But not tonight; tonight was an exception.

Grayling flicked on the lights. A white dazzle bathed the scene before them in bleached shapes and deep black shadows. They pulled on their ponchos and climbed out and down to the sodden ground. Waterlogged soil and leaf mulch squelched under their boots.

'Jesus!' said Grayling.

Were they carrion crows? No, Adam decided. These birds were too big. They were not crows but ravens. And they clustered and fought, tugging at the entrails of something pale and dead at the place where he had dug the previous day. They hadn't been alarmed by the bright electric light. Perhaps their eyes didn't equip them to be aware of it. But they must be aware of the approach of the two poncho-clad men. Either they were bold by disposition, or the thing they scavenged was a feast so tasty it made them reluctant to leave. Adam and the professor were almost upon them before they flapped and scattered, cawing, tearing upward at the night sky in a tatter of dark wings.

They left their prize behind. It was a lamb. It did not, to Adam, look more than a few days beyond birth. Its entrails were pink and immature. Its eyes were sockets, pecked out, empty. It lay on the precise spot where Adam had knelt and dug out his find.

'It's called a Clarion Call,' said the professor, his voice soft, beside him in the rain. 'The first mention of it occurred in the eleventh century. It's a call to arms.'

'What are you talking about?'

'The trumpet sound you heard. They were shriller, then, less accommodating to the ear. Their place was not the concert hall, but the battlefield. They had to be heard, you see, above the tumult. It's said the angels were the first to sound them. But that's a Christian myth.'

Adam gestured at the small carcass on the ground. 'How do you think it got here?'

'A Sea or Golden Eagle would be a plausible explanation,' Grayling said. 'The breeding of both species has been encouraged in recent years. They're indigenous, of course. Both are predatory and either one is big enough. And neither, dropping this from the sky above us, would have been able to recover it. Eagles don't really do forests. It's a matter of wingspan, you see.'

He walked forward. He had with him something he had taken from the equipment rack in the back of the Land Rover. He walked to the centre of the clearing, shifted the lamb carcass with his boot and swept the loose leaves from the surface of the ground, then put it down. He crouched to look at what it displayed. It was a spirit level. Adam thought its use pointless. He could see for himself that there was now no dip in the ground where he'd described one. The ground here was wet and muddy and almost billiard table flat.

They were back in the Land Rover cab and out of the rain before either man spoke again.

'What is it, that object I found in the ground yesterday?'

'I honestly don't know.'

'You know something, Professor.'

Grayling switched off the searchlights and flicked on the wipers, then put the Land Rover into gear. He turned them around before he spoke. 'Through decades of hard work and very occasional moments of inspiration, I've achieved a modest reputation in my chosen field.'

'Come on, you're a legend.'

'You hear stories, over a career as long and varied as mine has been. You see things. The best preserved sites are always the ones left intact by fear, where breaching hallowed ground or opening the door to somewhere long considered sacred and forbidden invites punishment.'

'That thing I found? I think you know something about what's going on here and it's only fair to ask you to share the information.'

Grayling brought the Land Rover to a stop. 'You'll be familiar with the old saying about a little knowledge being a dangerous thing, Adam?'

Adam didn't reply.

'I had a tutor back in my own undergraduate days, a man I greatly respected. He's long retired now, in his nineties, I should think, but still intellectually vigorous and his memory has not yet departed him. He lives in Brighton, in retirement. I think you ought to talk to him.'

'There's nothing you can tell me now?'

'What scant information I might possess would probably alarm rather than enlighten you. I wasn't certain until I saw what we both saw back there just now, but having seen it, I am. You need to speak to Doctor McGuire. I'll call him tonight. Men of his age don't require a great deal of sleep and he'll still be up when we get back. You can take a train from Carlisle in the morning. I'll give you a lift to the station.'

'It's sixty miles to Carlisle from here. You think it that urgent?'

'I do.'

'Because I discovered that object in the ground, where it was not supposed to be?'

'Not because you discovered that object, Adam. But because it discovered you.'

He was hungry when he got back to the town. The rain had finally stopped. He didn't really want the professor dropping him off outside the hostel, where someone might see him climb out of the Land Rover. But neither could he really afford the gastro-pub platter the professor had so heartily recommended, not with a return rail ticket to Brighton to have to stump up for in the morning. He got Grayling to drop him on his own route back to his dinner at the Black Horse, then found a chippie and ate steak pie and chips seated on a wet bench on the high street.

In theory, Adam was sharing a room with Martin Prior, but Martin had paid for his own accommodation at the hostel, muttering something about how he'd done enough sharing of night dorms at prep school. So Adam had a double room to himself.

He walked back to the hostel after his dinner in the rain thinking that Martin would probably have no need of the room he'd paid for tonight. They would be discreet about it. There was nothing cheap or cheesy about either of them. But Jane and Martin would be an item soon, if they weren't one already. The thought was a despondent one, accompanying him through the empty darkness of the streets on the route back.

He'd agreed a cover story to explain his abrupt departure in the morning: he had to courier a set of valuable documents back to Cambridge for the professor. Unique and priceless, they were not documents that could be trusted to any means of transportation other than personal delivery. It would be seen as sucking up to Grayling. He might get some stick for it from the others. But it was a more practical story than the truth. Revealing the find was out until Doctor McGuire had spoken to Adam and, more importantly, examined the artefact.

When he reached the hostel he went straight to the kitchen, because the salt on his chips had made him thirsty and he wanted a glass of water before turning in.

Jane Dobb was seated at the kitchen table. Alone. She was listening to a transistor radio. On whatever station she had tuned into, Fleetwood Mac was playing – Stevie Nicks singing one of her gypsy ballads. A Coors Light sat halfway gone in front of Jane. Beside it was an open pack of Marlboros. She had an unlit cigarette in her right hand and was rolling it between her fingers.

'What are you doing?'

'It's more a case of what I'm not doing,' she said. 'I'm trying not to go outside and smoke in the rain. The Scottish weather really brings home the humiliation of addiction on a filthy night like this. Anyway, I'm trying to quit.'

'I thought you were a live fast, die young sort of person, Jane.'

'Well, there you go,' she said. 'It's a life of surprises.'

What he actually thought, was that she was the most beautiful woman he had ever seen. The overhead lighting in the hostel kitchen was not kind, but it proved no handicap in her case. Her lips were ripe and full. Her eyes were a green as vivid as sunlight on the sea. And though she was naturally redhead pale, her skin was even, with a creamy lustre over strong bones.

She was staring at him. He prayed he was not beginning to blush. 'You should grow your hair,' she said. 'Really, you should. You'd look like one of those Grail Quest knights in a painting by Arthur Hughes.'

'Bloody good reason for keeping it short, I should think.'

'The looks of Sir Galahad,' she said, 'undermined by the soul of Victor Meldrew.'

That made him smile.

'Join me,' she said. And so he did.

'We were talking about you this evening.'

'Really?'

'You're surprised?'

'It's a bit adolescent to go around thinking that people are ever talking about you. Thankfully, I stopped thinking the world revolved around me when I was about fourteen.'

'We think you're up to something. Well, Martin thinks so anyway. He thinks you might have found something or found out something that you're keeping to yourself. You've been elusive, the last couple of days.'

'Maybe I'm just giving you two some room.'

'What does that mean?'

'It means exactly what it says. I like you both. I enjoy our being friends. But sometimes I sense the need for privacy. There's this . . . awkwardness.'

Her expression had changed. Adam couldn't read it; it seemed frozen. Then she blinked and shifted forward and tilted her face to him. 'Kiss me,' she said.

'What?'

'Just do it, Adam. Jesus. I didn't bring the manual. Just kiss me.'

And so he did.

He got into the Land Rover the following morning carrying only a small rucksack containing a change of underwear and his toothbrush and a book to read on the train. He saw his artefact straight away. It had been placed on one of the rear seats in a cloth drawstring bag, probably wrapped in tissue paper, he thought, looking at the soft, indistinct shape it made against the fabric of the bag.

There was a first-class return rail ticket awaiting him at the Carlisle Station booking office, Grayling told him. He was staying overnight at a Brighton hotel where Grayling sometimes stayed himself. He was not to concern himself with the cost of any of this. The college was paying, Grayling informed him blithely. The college could certainly afford it and Grayling thought it better for him to arrive in Brighton fresh. So comfort on the journey was only a sensible precaution.

Adam nodded but did not comment. He thought that the book in his rucksack had probably been needlessly packed. It was a novel that had come highly recommended. But he didn't think he would have the concentration or the enthusiasm to follow a fictional plot. Events in his real life had taken an intensely interesting and completely unexpected turn. Not even the baleful object on the back seat of the Defender could spoil his euphoric mood.

He hadn't slept with Jane Dobb. He had wanted to, of course. They had shared a final kiss outside her bedroom door. He had sensed her struggle at that moment with her own desire. She had wanted them to share her bed as much as he had. But she was a woman who felt the need to be earned. And he knew he had never been paid a greater compliment in his life.

'Even by your rather taciturn standards, your conversation this morning lacks a certain sparkle, Adam.'

'Sorry.'

'Also, your hair smells of Shalimar perfume. It's a classic, of course. But not a scent you habitually wear.'

'No.'

'I would advise against studying that object on the journey. You might be tempted. Seclusion is sometimes a feature of first-class travel and you might find yourself alone in a carriage with a long run between stations. But I'd caution against taking it out of the bag until you are with Doctor McGuire in his study. I'm aware I can't forbid you from looking at it, and I remember how strong an impulse curiosity is in the young, but I'd counsel discretion.'

Adam nodded. He thought that the professor had chosen his words with forensic care. A week ago, the notion that an object could possess malign powers would have made him laugh out loud. But he had not seen the bestial figure squatting on the seat behind him then. Grayling, who knew more than he was letting on, had let slip a couple of things. Adam had not discovered the object. The object had discovered him. And he had heard at the moment of discovery the clarion call's angelic summons to arms.

He would listen to what this elderly professor in Brighton had to say about the artefact. He would do so with an open mind and genuine interest in what the old man might reveal. Then he would return to Scotland and give it to Grayling. He could have it as Adam's gift on the condition that the true circumstances of the find could never be disclosed.

Adam had resolved to ignore the weird portents, the shrill trumpeting, the lurid business with the ravens and the lamb. He wanted no part of any of it. His life had just become vastly more intriguing and worthwhile and he was not about to jeopardize its new possibilities.

In the station car park, he took the bag from the back seat and put it into his rucksack, struck by the thought that what it contained had grown larger in the time since he had last seen and handled it. It can prompt irrational judgment, he thought, as well as provoke dismay. Maybe he should just fling it from the end of Brighton Pier. But something told him he would be punished if he did that. And not just by Grayling.

The artefact really did provoke irrational thinking. He was aware of that fact after he had said farewell to the professor, pacing the platform with a latte in a paper cup, waiting out the ten minutes until the arrival of the nine a.m. express, unable to shake the uncomfortable conviction that someone there on the station was watching him all the while with eyes that were hostile and keen.

TWO

His carriage aboard the train was quiet, the artefact discovered in the Forest of Cree safely out of sight in his rucksack on the luggage rack above where he sat.

He thought about Jane Dobb. He had wondered what it would be like to kiss her. And then he had done so, at her invitation. It didn't seem real to him now, that moment in the hostel kitchen under the harsh fluorescents with Stevie Nicks warbling on the radio. He had not seen it coming at all. Had it really happened? Had he not just dreamed the whole experience?

A text signal sounded on his phone. He took it out of his pocket and read the message. It was from Jane.

Last night was delicious, it read. *You were delicious. Come back soon.*

As soon as I can, he replied. He signed off with a kiss.

It had happened. It really had. And there was more of it to come. He really couldn't wait to see her again.

Jane was posh. It was all relative; everyone was posh compared to Adam, but Jane was from one of those flamboyantly posh families that got written about in glossy magazines. Her mum was a famous fashion designer who campaigned on environmental and human rights issues.

Her dad was possibly even more famous. He was an architect, quite old to have teenage daughters, Adam thought. But despite his age, he was very radical in his building theory and design and therefore remained a somewhat controversial figure.

Unusually for an architect, he was also a bit of an intellectual all-rounder. He had written a book about the Restoration architect Nicholas Hawksmoor, which had been highly praised. And he had come up with a theory about the origins and true purpose of Stonehenge which had eventually been the basis of a two-part television programme.

Adam had seen it. He had been sixteen at the time and thought it interesting and quite convincing, too. But even at sixteen, he had thought the mysteries of the Salisbury Plain megaliths beyond any modern-day explanation. He did not think the ancient past could be neatly rationalized by the standards of the present. He suspected it to be both alien and strange in a way that modern thinking simply could not grasp

Jane and her twin sister Dora had been brought up all over the world. Adam envied her this. It should have played havoc with her education, but she was really clever. She learned stuff with a careless ease. The lack of a routine hadn't mattered. Martin said she spoke three or four languages fluently.

Even if she wasn't so easy on the eye, Jane would be likeable, Adam thought. She was friendly and funny and cheerful. But she just happened to be gorgeous too. And she was interested in him. She was attracted to him. They were about to embark on a romantic adventure.

He sighed. He sensed the weight of the baleful item of luggage he carried in the rack above him. And then he folded his arms and did what any student would do, faced with a long train ride, occupying a comfortable seat. He fell asleep. He didn't dream. Or, if he did, he did not recall the dream. And he didn't wake up again until the train slowed on its approach to Euston station.

Carrying his prize in his bag on the underground proved an uneasy experience. Descending the escalator from the Euston concourse to his Victoria Line platform, he had become acutely aware of the weight and sheer malevolent strangeness of the object in the pack on his back. It seemed to swell between his shoulder blades, as though gaining in strength the deeper it travelled downward through the tunnelled earth.

The looks on the faces of his fellow passengers took a lurid turn and Adam felt trapped and claustrophobic in the confines of his underground carriage as he never had before. The sound of the train on its rails was loud, less like a mechanical noise than the maul through the tunnel of some groping beast.

His discomfort must have showed somehow on his face. A fellow passenger broke with London custom and asked him if he was feeling okay. The question came from a woman in a smart business suit in the seat next to his. He smiled and said he might be suffering a bit from travel sickness having come up from Scotland that morning, and she nodded and gave him a sympathetic smile.

He felt that all the eyes in the carriage were on him, curious and appraising. He couldn't shake this feeling until he emerged into afternoon daylight at the entrance to Victoria.

On the Brighton train, he looked at his watch. There was no chance of missing his station. Brighton was where the train terminated. He was due to arrive there at around three-thirty. His appointment with Doctor McGuire was not until six p.m. He thought that there were probably worse places than the famous south coast seaside resort to kill a couple of hours.

But he was basing that judgment on what he had heard about the city. He'd never visited this part of the country before. There hadn't been the money for childhood holidays, and when his growing interest in archaeology had started to prompt his independent travel in his mid-teens, it had taken him and his tent and his trowel and metal detector to the south-west. He had naturally been drawn to the enigmatic England of standing stones and pagan myth. He had gone to Wiltshire and Dorset and Devon and Cornwall.

He would tell Jane, he decided. When the moment came, he'd tell her about the forest find. Everything he learned from McGuire, he would eventually confide in her. He would even tell her about the odd business with the ravens and his surreal recent experience on the London underground.

Partly he resolved to tell her because he wanted to be honest, and to keep the whole business of the find secret would be deceitful and patronizing. But in part, his motive was selfish, he knew. He believed that a problem shared was a problem if not exactly halved, then at least reduced in size – and his instinct kept insisting ominously that the object in his rucksack was going to prove to be a problem.

He was looking forward to showing her the artefact. He wanted to see how she reacted to it; whether it provoked in her the same unsettling emotions it did in him and had seemed to even in Professor Grayling.

McGuire lived in an Art Deco mansion block on the promenade, about half a mile west of the pier. It was a distinctive building, according to Grayling, and should be very easy to find since almost every other facade dated from the Regency period.

Adam walked through narrow lanes towards the shore with the scent of the sea growing stronger in his nostrils all the time. Then he emerged on to the promenade and saw the sea, vast and sullen under a sky growing pink at its western extremities. In the descending sun, the foam cresting the breaking waves was the colour of candy-floss. He found the apartment block he was looking for and then with the secure knowledge of its location, decided to walk the length of the pier in search of something entertaining to do in the time until his appointment.

The weight of the rucksack he carried seemed to have increased. He was aware of this as soon as he set foot on the pier. He adjusted the straps so that they would not dig so viciously into his shoulders. When he inventoried in his mind what the little pack contained, it seemed ridiculous that it could burden him so uncomfortably. It felt large and leaden and unwieldy, increasingly so with every step. He stopped. He was over the water now, could see it toil and sway pinkly in the twilight in the gaps between the wooden planking under his feet, twenty feet beneath him.

It was the artefact, of course. It had increased in apparent weight when he had descended with it beneath the ground. It was reacting in the same way to being conveyed out over the water. It was a response to elemental change, a protest, or a warning that it would not be interfered with.

It suspects I'm going to throw it into the sea, he thought. *I pictured doing that in my mind and the sly little beast knows I did. It's digging its feet in, protecting itself. How much further before I feel the grip of its claws in the meat of my back, or the prick of its tusks, or the power of its bite?*

Adam stopped. He was sweating now, though the approaching evening was cool and blowy and he was out there thoroughly exposed in it. He thumbed sweat out of his eyebrows and wrestled off the rucksack. He looked at the various stalls flanking the central walkway of the pier with their flags and banners and candy-stripes, their gaudy displays of rock and giant lollipops and balloons and crappy toys.

And he saw what he was looking for. He saw the detached expression of terminal boredom that signals a student in casual employment. He recognized it. He'd worn that face himself enduring a dozen indifferent part-time jobs.

This particular student was selling a selection of souvenirs: key fobs and T-shirts and fridge magnets depicting Brighton Pavilion. Except that he wasn't selling anything just then, he was merely manning the stall in the event of a sale. Adam walked over to him and gestured at the rucksack, hanging from his hand now with a weary, impossible weight. He had money in his wallet. He'd visited a cash point before buying his fish and chips the night before in the expectation of funding the journey Grayling and the college had paid for.

He nodded towards the amusement arcade at the end of the pier. 'Could I dump this with you for an hour, mate, while I go and play the machines? I don't want it nicked while I'm distracted winning the jackpot.'

'You'll be lucky.' Not a local accent. Lancashire, maybe Preston or Chorley, somewhere in that region, Adam thought.

'It's worth a fiver to you.'

The student grinned. 'So long as there's not a bomb in it,' he said. 'I'm not being blown to pieces for five quid.' He reached for the rucksack, swinging it back over the display in front of him as though it weighed nothing. He didn't look exceptionally strong. He was only slightly built. He put it in the corner of the stall, behind him, out of sight.

'Cheers,' Adam said.

'No worries.'

Adam wished that were true. Relieved of his burden, he felt weightless himself. There was Wurlitzer music pumping out of the amusement arcade ahead of him. It didn't sound like a real organ. This was the seaside; everything here was cheap and contrived and fake. Visitors would feel cheated if it wasn't.

He passed a fortune teller's tent. He was not inclined to inflict his future on the occupant, or on himself, for that matter. The particulars of destiny could wait – until after McGuire's revelations, at least. Through the tent awning he glimpsed a table and a crystal ball and a woman in a turban and florid gypsy shawl as she rose and her beringed fingers closed the flap in a scramble.

The arcade was the expected riot of microchip enabled fruit machines he'd never understand how to play and car and bike race simulators with nothing about them to tempt him. The sound of bucketing cash in junk denominations erupted every few minutes. Most of the arcade's occupants were female and middle-aged, and they drifted along the rows of one-armed bandits expressionlessly, clutching plastic tubs of the coins that accessed their thrills.

There was a rear entrance, unless it was an exit. It went unannounced by the neon signage signalling 'drinks' and 'toilets' and 'change' and everything else. It was flanked by a laughing sailor in a glass case.

The sailor was antique, decommissioned, a legacy exhibit with the slot for an old-fashioned penny crudely soldered over. The style of his blues placed him in the early years of the twentieth century. His eyes were glass, his teeth bared in a grin of chipped enamel. His porcelain skin was raw, unless it was just weathered, Adam thought to himself, by all those years of salt and spray endured aboard some grey-funnelled ship of the line.

It would be a dreadnought, the vessel this rating served aboard, steaming through a North Sea swell, manned by crew as stiff-limbed as zombies. He studied the figure. He thought it sinister, a leering parody. Even still and silent, the sailor would frighten a child. It was an apparition summoned from an infant nightmare.

He walked outside. It was almost fully dark, the last of the sun a blood-coloured crescent on the horizon over to his right. He put his hands on the rail and looked down towards the sea. Its rhythm sounded wrong, its sound unfolding somehow backwards. And he blinked and stared.

The motion of the water wasn't right. The waves were rolling away from him, rising and cresting and then crashing outwards, running in reverse. Behind him, he heard the laughing sailor rise from his stool in his case with a creak and wheeze into chuckling life.

As Adam endured the feeling of being observed on Carlisle Station that morning, Jane Dobb sipped coffee from a flask at the edge of the main excavation in the centre of the Forest of Cree and watched Martin Prior walk the waterlogged ground a hundred yards distant, staring at it, scratching the stubble on his chin occasionally in a mannerism that had become familiar to her since the start of their fieldwork.

It signified concentration. Martin was thinking hard. He started to walk back to her and she blew on the surface of her drink to cool it, craving the caffeine. Her own concentration, after the turn taken by events the previous evening with Adam Parker, was proving difficult to sustain. She took out her mobile and thumbed Adam a hasty text as Martin splashed and slithered towards her. The mobile coverage here was patchy. She wanted to tell him that the previous evening had meant something to her.

'I know those tyre tracks,' Martin said, quietly, so that the rest of the team, already digging and sifting below them, wouldn't hear. 'They weren't here when we left yesterday evening. Grayling came back for some reason last night. He rolled up, parked over there for a bit, turned around and then exited the site the way he'd come.'

Jane nodded. Reading the ground was one of their incidental skills. A reasonably competent archaeology student couldn't help but become a fair tracker. The heavy rainfall made it easier. And the Defender's tyre tread was gnarled and distinctive. Her first thought was to wonder not what Grayling had been doing, but whether Adam had been in the Land Rover's passenger seat alongside him.

'Something's up,' Martin said. 'I think they've found something here. I think they've found something significant.'

'They?'

'The Prof and lover boy.'

Jane decided she would ignore this taunt. Martin knew she fancied Adam because she'd confided the fact. It hadn't occurred to her at the time, but it did now, that this might have been a tactless admission. On the other hand, he might just be hung-over. She had heard him come in the previous night as she drifted off to sleep, noisily drunk after a pub pool-fest fuelled by cheap lager.

She looked around. She peered over the edge of the deep excavation. Then, also speaking quietly, she said, 'There's nothing significant to find. No battles were fought here. No religious ceremonies were celebrated. The people who lived here did so at a subsistence level. Their lives were less a statement than an apology for existing at all.'

'Agreed,' Martin said.

'That's why Grayling chose the site, and you've seen the dreary evidence over the past fortnight for yourself. We are here to endure a test of our commitment. And to have it proven to us that archaeology is dirty and dull and not remotely glamorous or romantic.'

'Or even remotely interesting.'

'Exactly.'

'Nevertheless,' Martin said.

'Jesus, Martin, look around,' she said. She drained the last of her coffee. 'This was never even a route to anywhere. It isn't as though something could have been dropped accidentally and lost. Get real, for God's sake. No returning Crusade knights; no marauding robber barons and no outlaws, because there was never anything in this vicinity worth the trouble of stealing.'

He smiled and exhaled. His breath, in this proximity, smelled of the stale drink of the previous evening. It was one of the side effects of not smoking – and she had not smoked for over twelve hours now – your sense of smell quite rapidly improved. Objectively, Martin was very good looking, with his tousled hair and precise features. But he could be intellectually arrogant and that was an unattractive trait.

He began to walk away from the excavation and gestured for her to follow him. She did so, somewhat reluctantly. He was headed to where he had just said Grayling's Land Rover had parked on its mysterious visit of the previous night. 'You're making the mistake of confining yourself to a single time frame,' he said. 'And you're thinking in clichéd scenarios. How much do we actually know about the past?'

'Quite a lot,' she said.

He nodded. 'But only in purely forensic terms. We know what people ate and weighed and died of. We know about bone density and tooth decay and rates of venereal infection and how tall they were. We know the type of textiles they wore. We've got X-ray and spectral analysis and of course, we've got carbon dating. But we know nothing, really. From the Neolithic period to the end of the Dark Ages is pretty much guesswork and speculation.'

'There have been some significant finds,' Jane said.

Martin nodded. 'And all of them have raised more questions than answers. Take your father's theory about Stonehenge. All very elegant and persuasive, but we don't know. And I for one don't think we ever will.'

Jane frowned. In the quiet of the dripping forest, in that ancient and slightly desolate place, Martin's argument sounded convincing. But it also sounded weirdly defeatist. He was belittling what they did. He was saying that they were beaten before they began.

'I know what you're thinking,' he said. 'That I'm on the wrong course, right?'

'Pretty much.'

'I think Adam stumbled upon something that confounded the professor. I think Grayling told him to keep the fact of the discovery to himself.'

'And where do you think Adam is now?'

'Well, he isn't playing glorified postman, that's for sure. Gone off to get a second opinion, I should think, as to the veracity of the find.'

Jane said nothing. She had not yet had a reply to her text. Her phone was in the bag over her shoulder. She would have heard it.

'I think the past is stranger and more alien than we can imagine,'

Martin said. He looked at her. 'That's all, Jane. I think its mysteries
are likely terrifying and probably quite beyond our scope. I think
that Grayling was frightened by whatever Adam found. But the one
thing I'm bloody sure of is that Adam found something.' They had
stopped. 'Look at that,' he said, gesturing. From inside her bag, her
mobile signalled an incoming text. In front of her, there was a patch
of disturbed earth beyond and framed by the boughs of the two ash
trees flanking it. At its centre lay a litter of black feathers and the
pink bones of something freshly picked over. She walked between
the trees, on to the afflicted ground. Tufts of white, infant wool
were all that was left of a pelt.

'Carrion,' Jane said. 'That's all. Strange, though.'

'Curiouser and curiouser,' Martin said. 'There's something going
on here.'

'You got drunk last night and you're suffering for it this
morning and in a grouchy mood,' Jane said.

'Guilty on all counts,' Martin said. 'But Adam found something,
and I don't think it should have been there for him to find.'

'Let's get back,' Jane said. 'The others will have us down as
slackers if we don't start digging soon.' Martin looked at her and
smiled and nodded. They turned to go. Jane took a last look at the
remains on the ground before they did. She thought the arrangement
of black feathers and pale bones and the whisper of downy wool
there had a pagan, sacrificial aspect.

'Perhaps you should ask him – your picturesque friend – when
he returns.'

'He's your friend too. And it's bitchy to call him that.'

'Why? He is picturesque. Unless it's his mind you're attracted to.'

'Shut up.'

She was surprised at this reaction in Martin to the development
of the previous night. She had not even been sure of his sexual
inclination. He'd never declared a preference. He was enigmatic,
she had always thought deliberately so. She didn't even know how
he knew about what had happened.

Obviously he did. Someone must have seen them and told him
this morning. Student hostels were places short on privacy and long
on gossip. And it wasn't as if their group had a cache of important
finds to occupy their conversation. He was right, though. She should
ask Adam about his absence when he returned. Because Martin was
right, also, that there was something mysterious going on.

The problem was that Adam was not due back until tomorrow afternoon. Jane was not prepared to wait until then. She would ask Professor Grayling outright if anything remarkable had occurred. She would do so today.

She was curious too about the text she had just been sent. Careful to ensure that Martin could not overlook the display, she read the reply Adam had sent her from his seat aboard the train she now believed wasn't taking him to Cambridge at all.

How would she tackle Grayling? Head on, was how. She would ask him about the tracks the Land Rover had left. He could either admit or deny it. If he admitted it he would be obliged to explain. If he denied it he would confirm that he was hiding something.

She couldn't really imagine him doing that. It seemed totally out of character. He had never struck her as a cloak and dagger sort. Though he was handsome and in great shape for a man of his age and had that deadpan wit, he was an academic, not a spy. But she had to concede that his clandestine visit to the site with Adam riding shotgun seemed, itself, improbable. She was looking forward to hearing a truthful account of exactly why it had occurred. Except that by mid-afternoon, Professor Grayling had still not appeared at the site.

At mid-afternoon, while Jane and her course mates sifted and searched through the rich Scottish loam of the forest, Grayling was still in his hotel room. He was not involved in some administrative task and his mind was a long way removed from the Bronze Age and the present goings-on at the site. He was not thinking about archaeology at all.

He was thinking about twentieth-century history and in particular about the origin and consequences of the Great War. Like every archaeologist, he was fascinated by the remote past and knowledge-able about ancient history. But he was also a lot better versed in military history than most of his peers. This was partly a consequence of his personal experience.

Grayling had come to archaeology relatively late. He had not taken his degree until he was in his late twenties since he had spent the first part of his professional life in the army. He was a young officer serving in military intelligence and seconded to a Middle Eastern posting when archaeology first began to fascinate him.

Jane was wrong about him in one vital particular. He had been

a spy, of sorts. He knew a great deal about what she thought of as the world of cloak and dagger.

As Grayling continued to ponder on the cost and repercussions of the war, he thought about the way in which it reverberated through the following decades, triggering the other catastrophic events that made the century in which it was fought perhaps the bleakest in recent human history.

Estimates varied and statistics were never totally reliable, but the casualty figures Grayling had listed were not far wide of the mark. The Great War had left sixteen million dead and twenty-one million wounded, and many of those – the gassed and crippled and the amputees – were left permanently maimed.

Trench conditions, the overcrowding and absence of proper hygiene, had fostered the spread of the Spanish flu epidemic, and the soldiers had taken the virus home after the armistice aboard their troop ships. It had then killed another fifty million victims in its rapid spread around the globe.

The Great War had accelerated the unrest in Russia that led to the Bolshevik Revolution in 1917. Bolshevism had evolved into Stalinism. And Stalin had killed over thirty million Russians with his five-year plans and ethnic cleansing pogroms.

The peace brokered at Versailles in 1919 had been seen as vindictive by the defeated Germans and engendered the unrest that eventually enabled Hitler to come to power. National Socialism required war. It was an ideological necessity. It cleaned the soul and fired the will of the nation. Hitler got his war and the death toll in that six-year, mechanized conflict had been seventy-eight million.

At his hotel room desk, in front of his laptop computer screen, Grayling shook his head as he sipped the coffee that he had allowed to grow cold in its cup. He looked at his watch. It was a quarter to five. Adam Parker would surely have arrived in Brighton, but he would have to wait a while before his audience with Doctor McGuire.

Grayling would have been able to guess at the fencing and boxing without his pub interrogation. It had been part of his intelligence training. You looked for it in a potential adversary. You became sensitive to strength and balance and the capacity for swift and deadly movement.

Adam moved with a wary agility entirely at odds with the muddy, bookish discipline of archaeology, and his physical strength was obvious.

A week earlier one of the students had lost her footing on the lip of the deep excavation and after a moment of flailing for balance, she had toppled downwards, head first. Adam had risen from where he knelt and caught and righted her in what had looked like one deft movement.

It was genetic, this quality, Grayling decided. It could not be otherwise. It was about muscle and bone density rather than size. Burly was the last word he would have used to describe Adam's physique. But the strength was there. And the professor thought that the boy would likely require every ounce of it over the course of what was going to confront him.

By six o'clock, Jane had just about tolerated enough. Martin had taken advantage of Grayling's absence from the site and left at five. She rose and brushed dried mud from her knees. Almost everyone else had gone.

Martha Collier would drive the stragglers back in the minibus when they had cleaned and covered up, Big Martha who would have broken her neck the week before if Adam Parker hadn't been so alert when her ample shape had toppled head first into the excavation.

The tidying and securing of the site would take about twenty minutes. Jane decided that she would go and take another look at that strange spot a hundred yards away that she had examined with Martin that morning. There was no one there now, she saw, as she climbed the ladder to ground level and looked across the forest floor.

The sun had shone palely above them for most of the day, and though dusk was approaching now, the ground was firmer under her feet than it had been in the morning. There was no wind and the ferns thickening about her as she left the clearing and approached the trees could have been frozen, so still were they in the absence of any breeze.

The odour of tree bark sharpened in her nostrils and she noticed how many of the trees were mottled by moss and lichen and how many were swollen at the bases of their trunks by parasitic blotches of yellow fungi. She had not previously thought of the forest as a place of death. She was thinking it now.

With every step she took the silence and gloom seemed to deepen, as though she was provoking both effects herself, simply by drawing nearer to the place. She had the strong intuition that the air would lighten and the forest sounds amplify back into life if she started to walk backwards in retreat.

She paused in her progress. She had an even stronger intuition that someone was observing her. She turned her head. She could still clearly see the paraphernalia of the dig, the metal posts that moored the plastic sheeting and the wooden warning sign that marked the excavation.

She had thought that perhaps Martha Collier was rounding up stragglers for the minibus ride back and had spotted her and she had sensed Martha's scrutiny. But there was no one.

Jane started moving again. Her eyes focused on the spot between the two ash trees where the pagan litter of the morning had lain. The ground there was not flat, she observed. It formed a shallow, circular depression. It looked a little like a bomb or shell crater grown over and now barely noticeable.

She had seen such craters on battlefield sites years earlier on a school trip to Flanders. She did not know how she could have missed this feature in the morning with Martin. But Martin had missed it too. And this made her think with a cold suddenness that perhaps it had not been there then for them to see.

She was aware that her progress towards the spot had slowed. She felt that the silence had somehow thickened the air. It was as though she struggled through it, her feet trailing the ground heavily. She felt watched and weighed upon and almost overcome by a feeling of dread.

It required all her physical will to keep on approaching the place. The trees were in motion, she saw. Their leafless autumn branches were not moving, there was not even the whisper of a breeze to shift them. Their skins were moving, rippling under the moss and lichen in a manner impossible and revolting to witness.

A bark of laughter stopped her. It came from her left. She turned her head and looked. And she recognized Adam with a surge of relief that thinned quickly to fear and then to something close to horror.

The figure was that of a man. He was very tall. His hair was the exact chestnut shade of Adam's hair but much longer, falling from his bare head to halfway down his chest. His face wore Adam's features. But they were contorted into a leer of cruel amusement and the eyes fixed on hers, the familiar grey-green of Adam's eyes, gazed so coldly they provoked a feeling of dismay that caused her to shiver uncontrollably. It was the look of a predator assessing prey. There was no mistaking it. And she was its focus.

She closed her eyes. She could move nothing else; her limbs were petrified. She waited for the loping sound of his stride through the undergrowth, growing louder as the figure approached. She wondered if she could summon a scream. But when she opened her eyes again, the man had gone.

She forced herself to walk to the spot he had occupied a moment before. She needed some proof of him for the sake of her sanity, she thought. She did not want to think herself capable of dreaming up so disturbing a creature.

And it was there. He had left no footprints. But in his absence there was a slight scent, an oily miasma that had no place amid the bark and bracken of an ancient wood. She had not imagined him. That fact provided a sort of relief. But she was halfway back to the dig before the needle pricks of terror stopped tingling in her scalp.

Grayling turned his wrist and looked at his watch. It was almost six-thirty p.m. The watch had been a gift, a parting souvenir from a German special forces colonel after a NATO exercise in the old Cold War days. It was a Sinn and he still wore it on a leather *bund* military strap. It was a clue as to his old life, but he did not think it one that any of his clever and observant students would pick up on. They lived now in the age of Polish plumbers and Russian oligarchs. It was as though the Cold War had never occurred.

His thoughts were on Northern Europe, but far removed from the power games played out against the old Soviet Bloc. Now he was thinking about the end of the fourteenth century, about the spread of the Black Death and the more subtle psychological and behavioural shifts that had followed the plague itself.

In some ways, Grayling agreed with the sentiments about the past expressed by Martin Prior in his conversation with Jane Dobb much earlier in the day. He thought that the people and events of the distant past were largely unknowable and that whatever scholarly research was carried out, remote times were destined to remain precisely that.

But he had worked at some of the mass grave sites; the hasty trenches into which victims of the Black Death had been cast, the infant dead crammed into pockets of space between the cadavers of the fully grown. And in so doing he felt he had come to appreciate the scale and the relentlessness of the pestilence and of the appalling grief and hopelessness it provoked.

Scientists no longer agreed on the nature of the bacterium that caused bubonic plague, though it was generally thought to have originated in Central Asia. By 1346 it had spread to the Crimea. Trade encouraged infection because the bacterium was carried by the fleas infesting ships' rats. Between 1348 and 1350 it was believed to have killed sixty per cent of the population of Europe. It took 150 years for the world's population to recover from the Black Death. And it triggered crises in religious faith and social and political thinking that changed the world forever.

This catastrophe was not given the name by which the world now remembered it until Scandinavian chroniclers first used the term 'Black Death' in the sixteenth century. Before that it was the 'Great Pestilence' or the 'Great Mortality.'

'Black' was the adjective chosen to describe the deadly pandemic because of the dreadful mood of fear and pessimism it inflicted upon mankind. It fostered a fatalism that caused people to live recklessly, for the moment, incautious of the consequences of the things they did.

It seemed to contaminate the spirit and the soul. It led to the lynching and burning and extermination of foreigners, lepers and religious minorities. It did not just kill its victims; it debased the natures of those who survived.

Grayling pondered on cause and effect. He thought about the mood of decadence that had followed the Great War. Black magic had flourished among Europe's wealthy and blue-blooded elite. Fashionable society created a vogue for narcotic drugs. The Jazz Age prevailed in America, with its bootleg gangsters and brittle excess.

He wondered whether the mood in Cologne in the high summer of 1349, when the Jewish community there was exterminated, was any different from emotions when the Warsaw Ghetto occupants were rounded up by the Gestapo. Humanity had come through these cataclysmic events, but by how narrow a margin? And was it by luck or prayer or fortitude? He wondered.

He shut down his laptop and stood, stretching to lengthen the muscles and tendons that had grown stiff through the course of a sedentary day. At that moment there was a knock at his door.

'Come in.'

It was Jane Dobb. She was very pale. She was pale anyway, he thought, with a natural redhead's ivory complexion. But now her eyes looked drained of their usual vitality and her facial skin seemed almost translucent. She habitually used clips to constrain her gorgeous mane but they were not present now, and her hair flared in wild abundance about her head.

'I need to talk to you,' she said.

'I think you should do so sitting down.'

She nodded. Her eyes searched for somewhere to sit.

'Not here,' he said.

She smiled without mirth. 'You won't be compromised by me, Professor.'

'The thought hadn't even occurred to me, Jane. You need hot broth and a warm fire, and the Black Horse offers both not five minutes from here. I'm buying you your dinner. And I am all ears.'

'I want answers, Professor Grayling. Adam found something yesterday, didn't he? I want you to tell me what it was and where he's gone and what it signifies.'

'What a lot of questions,' Grayling said.

She managed a smile, a proper one. 'You always said that curiosity was an essential attribute in a good archaeologist.'

Grayling did not think the young woman in front of him at all short of attributes. Nor was the tense she had just used lost on him. Matters had taken a turn. Nothing would ever be the same again as it was before the find in the forest.

THREE

Adam was followed off the pier. He first noticed them as he picked up his rucksack from the souvenir stall student and handed over the fiver promised for looking after the bag.

He didn't turn to look at them directly because he didn't want to provoke trouble. But in the sly glances he was able to sneak, he thought that they looked like a couple of the smackheads who polluted English seaside resorts now that most people went abroad for their holidays, leaving lots of cheap accommodation for benefits agencies to rent.

They had definitely singled him out. One of them walked slightly behind and so partially concealed by the other. And he thought the smackhead to the rear was probably doing this to obscure the fact that his right hand was hidden behind his back.

That was an unusual posture for a stroll along a seaside pier, unless the hand was gripping the hilt of a knife hidden under a jacket hem. Adam thought it probably was. He'd seen a lot of street crime as a young lad, growing up in Bootle. He was familiar with its twitchy choreography. He felt slightly indignant that it was now afflicting a seaside resort that, in his mind at least, had always enjoyed a glamorous reputation.

He tackled them as they fanned to right and left in a flanking move, intent on taking him, shortly after he stepped off the pier, at the darkest spot between two streetlamps on a quiet stretch of promenade.

He swivelled on the sole of his left boot and sank a short left hook under the ribcage of the one to his right. Hearing the knife clatter on the flagstones, he reached and grabbed the second attacker by the hair on the back of his head and brought the head down to meet the driven piston of his knee. He heard the nose bone break wetly and dropped the bloke next to his pal on the pavement. Broken-nose was out cold. His mate was gasping, the floating rib shoved into his lung by the force of Adam's single punch hindering his breathing.

He looked around. No one had witnessed what had just taken

place. Traffic was sporadic and there were no pedestrians to fuss over what had occurred. The fight had been over in a few seconds. He crossed the road, as a precaution, to put distance between himself and the incident his would-be attackers would now represent if the boys in blue turned up.

His principle objective had been making them safe without using his fists on their faces. If you hit a druggie in the face you risked cutting your knuckles on their teeth. Contracting something like Hepatitis C or HIV wasn't worth the contents of his wallet. But they would have taken the rucksack, too, at knifepoint, and he could not have allowed that, what with his curiosity, and the rarity of the object, and having come all this way.

He supposed he could have handled the incident in a more diplomatic and less heavy-handed manner – but what was the point of having heavy hands if you didn't use them from time to time? Adam did not consider himself a bully, but he was the product of a fatherless upbringing, and that had been tough.

He'd read that people classically reacted to trouble with what was called the fight or flight response. He always stood his ground. That was his instinct, and the polish of his education hadn't rubbed away at his instinct in the slightest.

The stall vendor he'd had down as a student from somewhere in South Lancashire had definitely been in on it. He'd poked around in the rucksack, seen the artefact and concluded it was a valuable antique.

I should go back and give him a slap, Adam thought. *Retrieve my five-pound note.* But there were too many people at the end of the pier and anyway, if he went back to do that now, he would be late for his appointment with the old scholar he was here to see. Elderly people tended to set great store by good manners and it would be discourteous to be late.

He paused, there on the promenade, in front of Doctor McGuire's handsome Deco apartment block: he had reached his destination.

McGuire lived on the top floor. Adam stepped into a mirrored lift. The rucksack felt warmer than it should have done in the spot between his shoulder blades. It was almost as if the metal beast within now radiated a snuggly sort of heat.

He had a sudden suspicion that it had approved of what he had done outside, the way he had dealt with the danger, and was showing that now in a gesture of affection for him. He shuddered. It was not a very comfortable thought. He could see his reflection, multiplied into infinity in the polished, reflective glass of the four walls confining him.

He closed his eyes and thought of scented candles and Jane's velvety skin, the burnished cascade of her hair in the candlelight, Stevie Nicks plangent on her little radio. And the intimacy of that imagined moment seemed to him far away and improbable.

The doctor had a kind face. That was Adam's first impression. Only the grizzle of his bushy eyebrows hinted at his true age. His eyes were hazel and clear under a full head of unruly white hair and when he smiled his teeth were his own and healthy and straight.

There was no one else around. Taking in the bachelor clutter of the place, the piles of books and papers and the trophies from a lifetime of fieldwork heaped and dotted on shelves, Adam thought this the home of a man who had always lived the single life.

'Stuart speaks very highly of you, Adam,' McGuire said. 'May I take your jacket? Sit down, please. I shall prepare us both a drink.' He left the room and Adam sat in an armchair with the rucksack on his lap.

He was in what he supposed was the doctor's sitting room. It could have been a study, being full of books, but it was a very spacious room with veined marble walls and a stone floor, and there was a hostess trolley beside a table set for two people under the wide window dominating the exterior wall.

He further supposed the Stuart to whom McGuire referred must be Professor Grayling. He had not been aware of the professor's Christian name. The doctor spoke with a strong Scottish accent. Grayling too spoke with a Scots accent but his was much milder.

There were many remarkable objects in the room: framed photographs that Adam would have been studying, had he not been instructed to sit, and paintings on the walls that looked familiar to him from books. He thought them probably originals.

In a way the most remarkable artefact was that hostess trolley, rippling the air above it slightly with the electric heat of whatever food it kept warm. It was beige and satin steel and immaculate, and Adam thought the doctor must have been wheeling it out whenever he entertained company since its original purchase sometime in the 1970s.

McGuire returned. He held a silver tray bearing a schooner of sherry and a bottle of Becks with a beer glass next to it. The bottle was cold, already beaded with condensation. McGuire moved fluently and the tray was steady between his hands. Without knowing, Adam would have guessed his age at around sixty-five. He reckoned he must have taken very good care of himself.

Adam stood. He put the rucksack on his chair and took the proffered beer. Doctor McGuire waited while Adam poured it and replaced the empty bottle on the tray; he then put the tray down on an occasional table. Straightening up, he raised his sherry schooner in a salute, and Adam was aware of how rock steady the glass was between his fingers. He looked Adam in the eye. He had not yet looked at the rucksack at all. Yet he could not, surely, be indifferent to its contents.

'To what shall we raise our toast, young man?'

Adam thought for a moment. 'Shall we drink to mysteries solved?'

McGuire smiled. 'That is a noble aspiration. To mysteries solved,' he said.

They drank and then sat down, McGuire in an armchair opposite the one Adam had chosen. He put his drink down on the low table between them, sat back and looked at Adam over the steeple of his fingers. 'I confess I thought I'd made a terrible mistake for a moment when I first opened the door to you just now.'

'You thought I was an intruder? Do I look so thuggish?'

'On the contrary, Adam, you look very comely. It is an archaic word but it suits your appearance perfectly. You are pleasing to the eye.'

'What, then?'

'You had the smell of violence about you. You still have it, though it is dissipating now.'

Adam felt his cheeks reddening. He wondered if there was blood on his trousers or shoes from the bloke whose nose he had smashed on the promenade. Surely he would have noticed it in the mirrored lift that had brought him up from the block's vestibule? He looked at his hands and feet but could see no visible residue of the fight.

'I said the smell, Adam, not forensic evidence. Please describe your assailant.'

'There were two of them, junkies, I think. One of them had a knife.'

'Was there nothing unconventional about them? I am thinking of attire and perhaps also height.'

Adam shook his head. 'They were wearing smackhead clothes. Track tops, trainers. They were both about the same size as me. How can you smell violence?'

McGuire sipped his sherry. 'Over a long life, I have lived and worked in some hostile places. You develop a set of skills, senses, coping mechanisms. You seem unscathed.'

'I inflicted the violence, Doctor. I wasn't its victim. I beat them to it.'

McGuire smiled at him. The strengthening wail of a police siren came from the promenade outside. For the first time, he looked at the rucksack. 'You had better show me what you brought here to have me examine,' he said.

Grayling sat watching Jane spooning hot broth and wondered how they would appear to a third party, what conclusions a reasonably observant witness would make about the two of them, seated on opposite sides of their table close to the large saloon bar hearth in the Black Horse, both of them highlighted in the gloom by dabs of orange and umber light from the logs burning fiercely in the grate.

Vanity provoked the question, he supposed. The truth was that he wondered whether anyone could mistake them for a couple. He was vain enough to think they might. It wasn't lust for Jane provoking this wishful thinking. It was a sort of mourning for his lost and deeply lamented youth. He sometimes wondered where that youth had gone. The loss of his innocence had taken some of it. Too much responsibility taken on too young had deprived him of what had been left.

But they did not look a very likely couple, did they? Jane Dobb was nineteen and carelessly beautiful. He was toned and fit and carefully maintained. She was a feat of nature. He was well preserved. He grimaced and sipped his beer. Well preserved was not a happy phrase. He could smell Jane's perfume and recognized the scent and felt a sudden, savage pang of envy for the magnetic quality of attraction Adam Parker possessed; for his strength and youth and handsomeness.

'He was as fresh as is the month of May,' Grayling quoted, out loud.

Jane looked up from her now empty bowl. 'Chaucer,' she said.

'I'm impressed,' said Grayling.

'It's from *The Canterbury Tales*. It is the first line of Chaucer's description of the Squire. Were you thinking of Adam, when it came into your mind?'

'You're very perceptive, Jane. He smelled of your perfume, by the way, when I drove him to the station this morning. I do hope he isn't stealing it.'

'I remember the knight that squire served in Chaucer's story. He was old and knackered and living on past glories on borrowed time. Is that how you see yourself, Professor Grayling?'

Grayling did not answer the question. He shrugged and smiled.

'Where have you sent him?'

'Did he tell you? About the find, I mean?'

'Martin Prior pretty much worked it out this morning. I expect you swore Adam to secrecy. He's honourable and he respects you and I think he's the sort of person who would keep his word. He wouldn't steal perfume or anything else. And he doesn't tell lies.'

'I was joking about the perfume.'

'You were making a point.'

'You're right, of course. He did find something. I sent him to establish the significance of the find. He's gone to see a man who knows more than I ever will about pretty much every sphere of human knowledge. He's taken the artefact with him and he'll return tomorrow. I can't really tell you much more until he does. I must ask you to accept that, for now.'

'I do accept it. And I don't think you're remotely like Chaucer's knight. I can see no rust on your armour, Professor. Not yet.'

'Well, that's a relief. Would you tell me about your experience in the forest earlier, Jane? I'd very much like to know what happened to you there. Something shook you rather badly and I need to know what it was.'

'I suppose you do. He might still be there, after all,' she said. 'And even if he isn't, he might come back.'

She related her tale. Grayling listened, impressed by how much detail Jane had observed. She was bright and aware and a fluent speaker, and the experience had clearly terrified her.

As he listened, he realized that he would never be able to convince her that what she had seen had been cooked up by an over-active imagination in the twilit isolation of an atmospheric place. She was reciting from real life, however unlikely some of her story seemed in the warmth and matter-of-factness of the pub. It would never seem unreal to her. It had happened and she would never forget its strange and unnerving particulars.

'He really looked like Adam?'

'Like Adam's evil twin.'

'Except taller and with shoulder-length hair.' Grayling remembered vaguely that someone had told him Jane was a twin, unless he had come across that detail in a piece about one of her illustrious parents. He was fairly sure it was the case. But whether it was or not, it would be tactless to bring it up now.

'Adam has a scar on his face, Jane.'

'I know he does. He would be too perfect without his scar. It humanizes him.'

'Do you know how he came by it?'

'I asked him shortly after we met,' she said, 'at the beginning of the academic year.'

'I'll bet that went down well.'

'Because he's self-conscious about it, you mean?'

Grayling nodded.

'He didn't seem to mind. He said he was cut by an épée blade in a fencing competition. The blade broke and his opponent could not check his thrust. The broken point speared through the mesh grille of Adam's mask and sliced the skin open from his eye socket to his temple, leaving that pale, jagged line. I told him I thought it looked dashing, which is only the truth.'

'I can't remember – which side of his face does the scar afflict?'

'The left,' she said without hesitation. 'Adam has this mannerism. When he's unsure of himself, he raises his left hand and traces the scar with his thumb. An inch to the right, I sometimes think, and the blade would have gone through his eye socket and pierced his brain and killed him.'

Grayling said nothing. Jane blinked and sat back in her chair. She was staring at nothing, back in the forest, he thought, remembering.

'Oh, Jesus,' she said.

'What?'

'The scar was on the wrong side. The tall man in the forest with Adam's face had an identical scar. But it was on the right side of his face and not the left.'

'Like a mirror image,' Grayling said. 'Everything reflected and warped and reversed.'

'You know what's going on here, don't you, Professor?'

Grayling only looked at her. Then he smiled. He thought the smile probably a sad expression, if it represented truthfully the weight of the burden carried by his heart.

But Jane did not think the smile merely sad. Much later, recalling it, she described his smile as defeated.

'I can think of no rational explanation for what I saw,' she said. 'But I did see it. Was it a ghost, do you think, or some kind of demon?'

'I think it was flesh and blood, Jane, as real as you or me, nothing ghostly or supernatural about it at all.'

'The look on its face was demonic,' she said.

'We're packing up tomorrow,' he said. 'I don't want you to revisit the site. It won't take more than four or five of us to finish up and clear away. A fortnight of fieldwork is enough when the pickings are as scant as they've been at Cree. We need to get out of the woods.'

'So you think Adam's find a one-off?'

'A one-off, yes, I do. It's an anomalous find with no significant link to the locality. We could stay for another year and sift out only bones and pottery shards. In any event, I don't want you going back there.'

'Shouldn't we face down our demons?'

'New age platitudes don't apply to this particular set of circumstances. If they did, I could drive you back there now. Is that what you'd like me to do?'

She didn't reply. It had started to rain on the short walk to the pub, the rain falling heavy and cold, and she thought that it was probably still raining outside now. She thought of the tall figure she'd seen, standing in the dripping forest. He had worn boots and gauntlets and a dark green tunic with metal buttons that had glimmered dully like pewter. His breath would bloom and his hair would trail in wet coils and he would be entirely oblivious to the freezing deluge.

He'd been hunting, hadn't he, when she had seen him? He would have his prey by now, plucked and bloodied in the grip of one gloved fist. That was unless, in his hunger, he had consumed it already.

'Jane?'

She blinked and sighed. But still she didn't reply. Her eyes were drawn to the fire. She was remembering Chaucer's knight and the battles he had fought, a long, cruel litany of the most savage conflicts of the Middle Ages. She had the fanciful notion suddenly that the time would soon come when Grayling would unsaddle his war horse and unbuckle his broadsword for the last time. And it would be Adam to whom he would be passing them on.

Martin Prior was not used to being sidelined. He was witty, attractive and comfortably off, and believed he belonged at the centre of things. Life's spotlight shone on him and centre stage was his rightful place. But Jane Dodd was not answering her mobile phone. And Professor Grayling had sent Adam Parker off on some secret mission somewhere.

Worst of all, Jane and Adam had embarked upon a romance. And Jane's failure earlier in the day to rise to his taunts had done nothing to convince him it wasn't serious. She had looked different: flushed by her porcelain-pale standards, and bright-eyed and distracted. He suspected miserably it was the look of love.

His tactics with Jane had been determined by the fact that she was clever and independent and wouldn't go for chat-up lines. His plan had been to insinuate himself; to become the entertaining friend in whom she could confide and on whom she could rely. He had determined that the route to her heart was to become her trusted ally.

Jane wasn't going to sleep with someone unless she trusted them. She was cautious and had too much self-respect. But when it came to seduction, Martin was a very patient man, happy to play the long game if it meant landing a prize like her.

It was hard for him to believe now that he had not seen Adam Parker as a threat. He had inventoried Adam in his mind and Adam had come up short. He was provincial and poor and rough around the edges, with his flat vowels and terrible wardrobe.

He had always been humourless too in Jane's company, in awe of her, intimidated by her chic sophistication and her striking good looks. He didn't ski or sail or even drive a car. He had grown up on a council estate and didn't even know the whereabouts of his own father. He was gauche to the point of awkwardness, with his discount shoes and cheap wristwatch.

But these were superficial failings, weren't they? Since the revelations of the morning, whispered to him by that fizzy-haired dumpling Martha Collier over breakfast, Martin had tried to imagine how Adam would look through Jane's eyes.

And the picture, of course, was totally different. The Adam she saw was modest and courteous and impressively self-taught. He was someone fulfilling not just aspirations, but a childhood dream. He was beautifully put together, powerful and athletic. Martin had been forced to concede that the average girl would find Adam very easy on the eye. Jane was hardly average, but she had eyes in her head and when they looked at Adam, they liked what they saw.

The find just added insult to injury. It had been a fluke, hadn't it? There had been no logical reason to dig in the spot at the end of Grayling's tyre tracks, the site marked earlier in the day by that curious litter of feathers and lambswool and bones. Nothing, no clue, had existed to separate that place from any other outside the area of the main excavation. Adam had literally stumbled upon whatever he'd discovered there.

Martin couldn't understand it, really. All his life he had been not only privileged, but blessed by Lady Luck. In his hands, even in his orbit, things had always had a happy habit of turning to gold. But now fate, or providence, in the solid shape of Adam Parker, had dealt him a double blow.

There had to be something he could do about it. He thought that he could sow the seeds of doubt in Jane's mind. He'd done it before, with other girls, faced by the awkward obstacle of a boyfriend. He was subtle and crafty and he believed that everything was fair in love and war.

That was a medium-term project, though. And it didn't address the bigger, immediate problem of how to detract from Adam's find. Unless Jane was wrong, of course – unless there was a cache of stuff to uncover and Adam had only chanced upon the one item that led to it.

It was worth a punt, he thought, trying Jane's mobile number again and coming up with only the recorded message telling him her phone was still switched off. It was worth a trip to the site just to check privately that there was not more buried treasure to be found.

How bad would he feel if they dug thoroughly on Adam's return from wherever he'd gone and found a whole hoard of priceless items?

It was worth enduring a bit of rain and mud to check out that possibility. He owed it to himself to make absolutely sure the ground there had surrendered all its secrets. It was not like he was missing out on a hot date with a beautiful girl, he thought bitterly, wondering where Jane could have got to. And he didn't feel in the mood to swill cheap lager while playing pool against strangers in the Bell. He really had nothing to lose.

He laced on his waterproof boots, pulled on a sweater and grabbed his poncho from where it hung on the back of the door. He looked at his watch. It was seven-fifteen. He would have to walk to the site and that would take him half an hour. It wasn't a hazardous route. There was never any traffic on the road.

What he was about to do was strictly against the rules, but he thought his chances of being caught were remote. If he found anything, he would just hide it well enough to make damn sure he was the one who located it again before anyone else did in the morning.

The logical thing to do of course was to wait for the morning himself. He had a pair of night vision goggles in his backpack but it was always more practical, not to say safer, to dig in the daylight. He couldn't wait, though. He needed to expend some energy, to do something diverting and positive, frustrated as he was about being unable to contact Jane.

And there was something else, a feeling growing increasingly urgent inside him as he put his flashlight and trowel and brushes and a roll of Ziploc bags into his pack. There was his intuition. It told him there was something at the site, waiting to be found, waiting for him to be the one to discover it. It was almost beckoning him aloud. And like all gamblers, Martin Prior trusted his hunches.

McGuire had plucked the artefact from Adam's hands and examined it with a wistful smile on his face, as a person might if reunited with a lost and cherished souvenir. Its fierce ugliness did not seem to offend him in the slightest. He squinted at the tusked, snarling jaws and fingered the metallic muscle bunched behind the creature's opposing heads.

He seemed to weigh the figure in his palm. And then he said, 'We'll eat first and talk later. There's much to discuss. We'll have more stamina for our conversation when our stomachs are full. I'll provide you with answers to some of your questions, Adam, though they may not be expected or terribly welcome answers.'

They ate their dinner pretty much in silence. It was a relaxed silence and Adam was hungry after the travel and the exposure in the early evening to a couple of hours of Brighton's sea air. He'd served their coffee before his host began to speak seriously.

'The object you brought me was fashioned from silver at a smithy in Babylon, about five thousand years before the birth of Christ.'

'It feels harder than silver, denser, more durable,' Adam said.

'Indeed. Their silversmiths were very skilled. And they discovered a process in the casting and cooling that tempered the precious metal. This formula of theirs has been lost.'

'People were not that advanced, Doctor McGuire, with respect, sir. Not seven thousand years ago. They couldn't have been. They possessed neither the tools nor the necessary knowledge of chemistry. The technology wasn't invented – the bellows to generate the required heat.'

'The world is a great deal older than you think,' said McGuire.

And so are you, Adam thought. But he kept this intuition to himself. 'Why are the two heads attacking one another?'

'Decoratively and symbolically, the artefact is both a metaphor and a statement. Practically, it is an invitation. If you were of a gloomy turn of mind, you might call it a summoning.'

'It had no place in the ground where I found it, did it, Doctor?'

'None, Adam, but as Stuart Grayling has already intimated, *it* found *you*.'

They had not drawn the curtains. Through the wide window, the night sea glittered in the moonlight beyond the promenade and pier. Outside that pane of glass, the universe seemed indifferent. Inside this spacious room, Adam had the sense that everything paused on the brink of permanent change. He was grateful for the food in his belly. Without it he knew that he would have felt, at that moment, hollow and sick.

'Have you ever felt uneasy looking in a mirror, Adam?'

'Always, since I was a child. It's been with me for as long as I can remember. Sometimes I have the sensation of being watched and think that if I look hard enough the watcher will get careless and I will see some snatch of his reflection at the edge of the frame and my suspicion will be proven and my fear founded.'

'Interesting, go on.'

'Sometimes I'm just disturbed by my own reflection, as if it might move independently of me, wink or grin wildly while I stare back with a poker face. It's a shameful, phobic thing. I'm embarrassed about it.'

'It isn't a phobia. It is an instinct. It's nothing to be embarrassed about.'

'Speak plainly, Doctor. I'm not clever enough for riddles.'

'Imagine a world that is the dark twin of ours. This is a malevolent and hopeless place, a landscape of despair and wilful cruelty. It has no idealism, no notion of progress, none of the selflessness that can distinguish the nobler examples of humanity.

'It has but one ambition. And that is supremacy over us. It seeks to supersede and replace us and to erase everything we have accomplished. It has striven since the dawn of history to achieve this and once or twice almost succeeded. Now it is about to try again.'

'I don't wish to be unkind, Doctor, but I have no appetite for fantasy.' Adam was remembering, though, the sea at the end of Brighton pier, the momentum of the water underneath him, occurring in reverse.

'You won't be able to dismiss it as fantasy for long, lad. You will not be allowed that luxury.'

'You really believe in this place?'

'I've been there.'

'It sounds like Hell.'

'That is what some cultures and faiths have called it. And some have called it Hades or the Underworld. It has been variously known as Tartarus, Uffern, Mictlan, Arula and a host of other aliases. Every creed and mythology has a name for it.'

'Then why is it not generally known about?'

'Sometimes the myth is more easily endured than the reality that fosters it. If mankind knew of the struggle, mankind would despair and the battle would be lost. The knowledge would be self-defeating, so the secret is maintained.'

'But you know. And so does Professor Grayling. Others must, too.'

McGuire nodded. 'A very few, through the centuries, have known. And those have been mostly archaeologists and architects, zoologists, mathematicians and so on. Nicholas Hawksmoor knew. It was where Shakespeare encountered his Caliban. Darwin knew, of course.'

Adam had heard of Hawksmoor. He was the Restoration architect about whom Jane Dobb's father had written a book. 'Historians must know. One of them would have said something.'

McGuire raised an eyebrow. 'But none of them has. For the very good reason I have already given you. This world is the shadow to our light, Adam. And you will not enjoy your scepticism concerning its existence for very much longer.'

'You are asking me to enter a waking nightmare, Doctor McGuire.'

'Have you never wondered at the source of our most potent myths; at how and where Frankenstein's monster and the vampire were inspired?'

'Are you telling me they're real?'

'Medical research breeds miracles. Dabbling with magic, by contrast, breeds monsters. Trust me on this. I've seen them.'

'And vampires?'

'The vampire is a metaphor for a parasitic creature that strayed deliberately from its evolutionary path. There is a tribe, a nation of them there. I have encountered them too.'

'What did you mean, when you said I hadn't a choice?'

'You have been called. The artefact you found is the summons.'

'Because I did not find it at all; because it found me.'

'Good. You're learning.'

'I'm sorry, Doctor McGuire,' Adam said. 'I just don't believe a single word of this.'

'No. Stuart Grayling is a fair judge of character. And he said that you would not.'

McGuire rose somewhat stiffly from the table. Adam wondered again at his true age. He took a key from his pocket and nodded at the door in the wall to the right of where he stood. 'Go through there and you will discover a corridor. Open the door at the end of it, on the left. Lock it immediately behind you. Under no circumstances attempt to touch the thing you see in there.'

The interior doors in McGuire's flat were all of a type, wooden and decorated with carved Deco motifs. The one confronting Adam at the end of the corridor was different: plain, heavier, banded in iron. It opened on darkness and a cold, feral stink. Adam entered, aware of the close confinement of narrow walls, and he heard the shuffle of something a few feet away, a sound so sudden and furtive it caused his fingers to tremble groping for the light switch.

The bulb was pearly, with a feeble wattage, and the light it cast was scant. Some bird of prey, the size of a vulture, was chained by a ring above the talons of one claw to a wooden rest. Its head, perfectly still now the light was on, was covered by a coarsely stitched leather hood.

Adam scrabbled the key into the keyhole to his rear and locked the door as he had been told to. The great bird tilted its head very slightly under the hood at the sound. It was about five or six feet away from him and he wanted to get no closer to it than he was already.

He stared at it, his eyes adjusting to the lack of real illumination and the way the bulb in the ceiling above leached all colour out of the objects in that dismal space. It was not feathered, he saw. He had assumed its plumage was a uniform grey – but the grey was not feathers, just a reptilian skin of rough goose bumps over its body and stretched between the struts of its folded wings.

It made a noise, then. *It must be aware of my presence and this scrutiny*, Adam thought. The noise was somewhere between a rattle and a purr. Its call was loud in the confines of that cell and as bleak as a threat. Then the creature bowed its head. The movement was supple and loathsome. And the claw that was not chained rose and gripped the hood and eased it from its head. Its beak was a baleful yellow, curved cruelly downward. It looked like a scimitar shaped from ancient bone. Its eyes were watchful and dead. Then it said something and the something it said sounded like human speech. Adam unlocked the door behind him and fled.

A fog had descended when Martin reached the site. It slithered along the ground, fingering depressions, embracing trees in grey blindness. He took his night vision goggles from his pack and put them on. But they did no good. Their lenses were infrared and worked by shaping the heat radiated by an object. The evening was cold and the fog had apparently chilled everything it enveloped so that no objects emerged when he stumbled about the forest until he collided with them.

He needed to locate only one familiar object in the landscape to be able to orient himself using his compass. The night did not faze him and neither did the weather.

His father had been determined that his moneyed upbringing would not leave him soft. Thus he had been packed off to Gordonstoun rather than to Eaton for his expensive education, where he had learned white water canoeing and how to dig a snow hole along with his Greek verbs and his Latin prep. He had been further toughened by teenage expeditions to Patagonia and the Antarctic.

He could climb and ride and abseil. He was more familiar than most people of his age with the remote and inhospitable regions of the world and he had a hard-earned expertise in how to survive in them.

This knowledge did not make him arrogant in the wilderness. He knew how quickly things could deteriorate in challenging conditions. He was deliberate and methodical and wary. And he was always very alert, which was why he was now having difficulty concentrating on his compass reading in the mist. He knew the conditions made it practically impossible. But he had the strong sensation that he was being watched.

He quartered the ground and searched for ten minutes before finding one of the metal poles that marked the deep excavation. In that time, Martin thought the temperature dropped significantly. The fog was frozen in places into visible crystals. His own breath emerged in a cloud so white it seemed solid in the freezing air.

The ground crunched invisibly with stiffened autumnal leaves under his booted feet. He had on a woollen sweater and a pea coat under his poncho. He wished he had worn his winter parka. Then he found the rolled sheeting that covered them when they dug in the rain. He remembered its position relative to the spot where he suspected Adam had made the find. He took a compass bearing and made for the spot, unable to believe just how silent, beyond the sound of his own footsteps, the night forest had become under its mantle of grey.

He had strayed off track. He must have done. There was something in front of him he would not have encountered had his route to the location of Adam's find been true. It was a slab of stone. In the murk, Martin thought it looked like the sort of rough slab that might mark the tomb of a prominent man in medieval times. He crouched and removed a glove to finger its surface, which was pitted and worn and icy to the touch.

His fingers hit something. And Martin gasped. It was not a tomb at all. It was a set of ascending steps. He could just make out the second of them now that his reaching hand had found it. And when he really looked, he could see a third and a fourth. They were deeper than they were wide. He could not see their ascent when he looked up; the thickness of the fog prevented it. But he had the sense that the steps rose to a towering height.

A thrill ran through him. He had to discover where the steps led. They looked to him to be as old as time. They were logically impossible but would not be denied in their stony ascent to wherever they went. He had to take them.

FOUR

A dam strode back into McGuire's sitting room, struggling to regularize his breathing and bring order to his reeling mind. The object he had found in the ground in the Forest of Cree lay where the doctor had left it, uncovered on the table between the two armchairs.

He allowed it a glance on his way towards the window. He needed the view of what lay outside. The pier was out there, of course. And the pier had proven to be a much stranger experience than he had anticipated. The sea beneath it had betrayed his expectations too. But he needed the twinkle of the night sky and the drift along the seafront of car headlamps to look at. His assaulted senses craved normality.

McGuire was standing in the far corner, facing away from him when he re-entered the room. He was holding the receiver of an old-fashioned telephone to his ear. The coiled cable linking the receiver to the cradle shivered with what Adam thought might be a tremor in the old man's hand. His grip was not so steady now as it had been earlier on the stem of his sherry glass. There was something confidential in his stance and attitude. He was listening and nodding. Eventually he looked around and across at Adam and said something into the phone and then put it down. Its bell jingled as the connection broke.

'Well?'

'It's real, isn't it?'

'Oh, yes. It's real all right.'

'Why would anyone keep so grotesque a pet?'

'It comes from a place alien to the notion of pets, Adam. The beasts there are put to work. At least, the ones that can be domesticated are. The rest are best described as natural hazards it is wise to avoid entirely.'

Adam laughed. 'You mean monsters, dragons and sea serpents and the like?'

'You have seen what you have just seen. I am surprised it amuses you.'

Adam remembered something Grayling had said to him in the

tent at the site, after his find, during their first conversation concerning the artefact. He nodded in the direction of the object, engaged in its continual duel against itself on the table top. 'That thing exists there, doesn't it, Doctor McGuire? That creature lives and breathes.'

McGuire smiled and nodded. He now looked much more like the frail and elderly figure Adam had expected to find on his journey to Brighton. Thinking about the shadow world had aged him. Or thinking about the vile creature he kept behind a fortified door had done so. Or maybe, Adam thought, the subject matter of the telephone call had done this. That was the new consideration. The rest he had expected and planned. Some fresh bad news had been inflicted upon him. Adam wondered who the caller could have been. He thought that he probably knew.

'Why do you keep that thing along the corridor?'

McGuire attempted a smile but gave up on it, the effort just now evidently too much. 'It prevents my natural optimism from deluding me about the threat we face,' he said. 'In language you would be familiar with, its presence here keeps me grounded.'

Adam took a last, reluctant look through the window at the sanity outside and then walked back to the two armchairs and the table between them bearing the object he had discovered. McGuire joined him as they sat for a while in silent appraisal of something created in Babylon seven millennia ago.

'Are you a student of history, Adam?'

'I have to be, to an extent. Every archaeology student does.'

McGuire shook his head. 'No. I mean modern history. What do you know, for example, about the Great War? Could you answer some straightforward questions about the course of the war? When would you say it originated? When did the conflict conclude?'

Adam had taken history A-level and his revision was recent enough for him to remember plenty of detail about the Great War. He'd found it too interesting to forget, really, the helter-skelter ride towards catastrophe aboard which all the great nations had scrambled for a seat. 'Most people would trace the origin of the war to the assassination of the Archduke Franz Ferdinand of Austria in Sarajevo in the late June of 1914.'

'Just so,' McGuire said. 'Can you remember the name and fate of the assassin?'

'Gavrilo Princip,' Adam said. 'He was a nineteen-year-old Serbian and a member of the secret society that planned the killing of the archduke and his wife. They were called the Black Hand. He died in a prison cell in 1918 before the conclusion of the war his actions either caused or accelerated, depending upon your point of view.'

'I think my point of view will be very different from yours,' the doctor said.

Because you were there, Adam thought. It was an insane thing to think. But it had come upon him with the force of intuition. 'You mean about the origin of the war?'

But McGuire did not answer him. Instead, he asked, 'When would you say the conflict concluded?'

Adam blew out a breath of air. He felt thirsty and shaken by the confrontation in the room along the corridor a few minutes earlier. He thought that what he would like right now was a drink, not a trawl through the stuff he had studied in sixth form.

As though reading his mind, McGuire stood and said, 'We could both use some liquid refreshment, I think. Ponder on your answer while I fetch your beer from the kitchen.'

'I don't need to ponder on my answer,' Adam said, looking up at him. 'The Germans and their allies surrendered in the autumn of 1918.'

McGuire smiled. He seemed to have recovered himself. 'I take a rather broader view than that,' he said. 'I'll get you a cold beer from the refrigerator and pour myself a larger whisky than can possibly be good for me. Then I will tell you when I think the Great War really concluded.'

Neither man made any further comment until Adam's beer was drunk down to the suds at the bottom of his glass.

'Well?' Adam asked.

'You could conceivably argue that the Great War concluded only with the Velvet Revolution of 1989, when the Berlin Wall came down. The links are compelling ones. And they travel all the way from the path of Princip's bullet to the finish of the Cold War.'

'You're saying the war went on for almost a century,' said Adam.

'Yes, and at a colossal cost.'

'It could have been much worse, the cost.'

'Could it?'

'Of course it could. You know that better than I do. You were alive to remember it.'

Adam was thinking about the Cuban Missile Crisis, about fourteen days in October, 1962 when Russia and America stood on the brink of nuclear war. They did so with the will to obliterate one another, because their rival arsenals housed only offensive bombs, all-out attack the only means of defence available to their rival technologies.

Had Russian Premier Nikita Khrushchev pressed the button, had American President John F. Kennedy blinked, the world would then have destroyed itself.

He glanced at the object on the table top. Familiarity did not make it any more comfortable to look at. The rucksack still lay on the floor at the side of his chair. He reached for it and placed the artefact inside and zipped it up.

'That was Professor Grayling on the phone earlier, wasn't it?'

McGuire did not answer him.

'What's happened?'

The doctor's hazel eyes met his with their innocent focus. 'There has been an escalation. Matters are accelerating. You must not go back to Scotland, Adam. It is too dangerous. It would be foolhardy.'

'Bollocks,' Adam said. 'I'm sorry, Doctor, for the language, I mean. But I have no intention of not going back. You don't run away from a mystery. You try to solve it.'

'Stuart is closing up the site. The Cree project is at an end. There is nothing to go back to Scotland for. The rest of the party will be returning to Cambridge tomorrow or the day after at the latest. I'm going to tell you as much as I can tonight about the part you are expected to play in all this, about what you have been summoned to try to accomplish. You can believe or disbelieve as you wish. You can take on the duty I will insist is yours, or you can reject it out of turn. All I ask is that you hear me out and sleep on your decision.'

He had been there, Adam thought again, and this time the intuition hit him with the strength of certainty. He had been there on that hot and restless day in Sarajevo on 28 June, 1914. There had been five would-be Black Hand assassins. Princip had all but given up and had gone off to seek out some lunch when the royal coach trundled through the street junction he was attempting to cross by fluke alone and he took out his revolver and fired the two fatal shots. There had been five and McGuire had gambled on the wrong assassin and the gamble had failed. The odds had beaten him. Probability had beaten him. Had there been more to it? Had chance enjoyed some diabolical help?

'I'll hear you out,' Adam said. He got to his feet. There had been no invitation to do so. But he was not a prisoner here. He felt restless. He stretched muscles cramped by the confinement of a day spent largely aboard trains. He had enjoyed no real exercise, and he habitually exercised strenuously for at least an hour every day.

He looked at some of the stuff on the shelves on the walls surrounding him – the bric-a-brac and souvenirs and solid fragments of a long and learned life. A cane lying on one shelf caught his attention. It was about three and a half feet long and sturdy. It was burnished to a nicotine brown by age and the silver pommel topping it had been allowed to tarnish. This neglect seemed out of character. McGuire was a fastidious man, the owner of a spotless hostess trolley. His back to his host, facing the wall, Adam smiled to himself and reached for the cane. It was surprisingly heavy.

Because it conceals a blade, he thought. *That fine Toledo steel is pitted by time now but still keen along its edge. He was armed with this there, at Sarajevo. He would have used it, too, would have skewered the boy assassin without a single troubling thought. Why not? He had used it often enough before. And that had been the whole point of his presence.*

Adam was there, on the teeming summer streets of the Balkan city, the rich aromas of coffee and cigar smoke and pedestrian sweat rising in the hot, stagnant air, the dusty trundle of coach wheels and the clip of escorting cavalry hooves and the pressing crowds gathered for the sight of royal pomp parading in vivid procession through their streets.

And the doctor, with the murderous weapon that Adam now held sheathed between his hands, sweating through his pale linen suit and desperate, young then and lithe and strong and ruthless but, on this occasion, thwarted. It was impossible, of course. The Sarajevo assassination had occurred almost a century ago.

'You are a very perceptive boy,' McGuire said, from somewhere behind him. 'Put the swordstick back where it reposes. It long ago earned its retirement from the fray. Come and sit down, Adam. It is late now for an old man and I am tired and I have much to tell you.'

Jane Dobb did revisit the site in the forest the following morning. This was nothing to do with facing down her demons or attempting to get closure or any other New Age novelty.

A rap from Martha Collier's meaty fist on Martin Prior's door at the hostel at seven a.m. had raised only the groan of someone who sounded terminally hung-over. They needed her to help, a pair of hands she was happy to volunteer in Martin's absence from the effort to neatly and conclusively wrap up the dig.

Grayling gave her a somewhat severe look when he saw her jump down from the rear of the minibus. But he raised no explicit objection to her being there. Too many people around for a public row about an experience he had urged her to keep private, she supposed. He merely stared at her for a moment and frowned, then looked around as Jane thought the point-man of an infantry company might do on hostile ground in search of a holed-up sniper.

It rained. Of course it did. It was their last day and on their last day it had always been destined to rain. They were finished up after two muddy hours and Jane indulged the bleak enjoyment of a cigarette in the downpour as their sheltering tarp was folded and lashed by the burlier students to the roof rack of Grayling's Land Rover.

She felt sad. And the sadness was provoked by more than just the failure of her smoking resolution and the end of their Scottish adventure, melancholy as the end of something so closely shared among so few, like this, so often was.

She did not think that she would see Adam Parker again. That was the whole of it. Oh, she would see him, of course. She would do so in the factual sense. But she would not see him again in the circumstances they had enjoyed here.

It was a shame, she thought, exhaling smoke, grinding out the butt of her Marlboro under the heel of her boot before scrupulously retrieving it and putting it into a Ziploc bag to join the rest of the site detritus they would dutifully take away with them.

She did not feel nervous or watched. She supposed that was something. But it was absence that filled her senses, absence with a name, and its name was Adam Parker. She did not feel relieved that her cruel observer had gone from the forest. She thought that it was to be expected. She had the certain intuition that he would not welcome a crowd of curious students and their tutor, watching him. Solitariness and stealth were the cold essentials of his character. So he was not there now. She felt sure of it.

Grayling was suddenly behind her. She knew his aftershave. 'You lied to me,' she said. She sniffed. Her nose was cold and runny and the loss in her felt a bit like grief. 'Adam isn't coming back today.'

'No,' Grayling said. 'He isn't.'

She turned to face the professor. 'You said that matters would be explained on his return. But now he isn't returning. Where does that leave your explanation?'

He raised an eyebrow and looked around again. He did so discreetly, but still scrutinized the full 360 degrees of their desolate vista. She had not previously thought him a man who had ever been concerned with cloak and dagger aspects of the world. Now she did.

'I need to speak to your father, Jane,' he said. 'I need to seek his counsel before talking truthfully to you about events.'

She sniffed again and rubbed at the tip of her nose with the back of her hand. The burned tobacco from her cigarette tasted foul in her throat. That, at least, she supposed, was a positive thing. 'I'm not close to my father. I'm not close to either of my parents.'

'It's the protocol.'

Ignoring his last comment, she explained, 'We grew up feeling sort of peripheral, Dora and me, a bit like accessories. My folks didn't have a lot of time for mundane obligations like childcare.'

'Dora is your twin?'

Jane nodded. 'Identical, as makes no difference.'

'Are you close to her?'

'Do you ask out of your duty of pastoral care?'

'I ask because I'm intrigued.'

'We don't get on at all. I haven't even spoken to her since the beginning of term. We don't phone or email one another. We're strangers, really. We don't even text.'

'So your upbringing wasn't as idyllic as people must generally suppose.'

'Why would people suppose anything?'

'You grew up in public, Jane.'

'I didn't have a choice in that. I wasn't aware then there was any other way of doing it.'

Grayling looked down at the wet ground and then his head rose and he fixed her with his eyes. They were a pale blue contradiction, cold but filled with a kindly concern at the same time. 'How does it feel, coming back to this place?'

'Normal,' she said. 'What happened yesterday was abnormal. The person I saw was not of this place or even, I think, properly of this world.'

'You mean you imagined him?'

'I don't mean that at all. What I mean is that he seemed like a trespasser. But even that isn't strong enough.' She shivered. 'He seemed more a violation. There was something so unnatural and threatening about him. He should have seemed natural, with those antique clothes and that old-fashioned hairstyle, thoroughly at home in an ancient place. But he didn't. He seemed instead like an insult to the world.'

'You should get into the van,' Grayling said. 'You should go before Martha becomes impatient and starts to pound on her bloody horn.'

Jane turned and started to walk away from him.

'Wait,' he said. 'They're going to have to go back and exhume Martin before their drive back to Cambridge. If you would prefer, you can ride back there in the Land Rover, with me.'

'That's considerate of you,' she said.

'It isn't anything of the sort. I'm merely thinking of the reduction a passenger will represent in the size of my carbon footprint.'

'Great,' she said. 'I'll get my rucksack from the van. Does the Land Rover have a radio? I can't remember. It's a long journey without music.'

'No radio,' Grayling said. 'But I am blessed with a very fine singing voice, should music be required.'

He was teasing her about the radio. Of course he was. He needed one for the traffic bulletins. At the wheel of the Land Rover, she thought there was some hint of the military about his bearing and demeanor she had never really noticed before.

'What did Adam find?'

'Something pricelessly rare and impossible to explain in any terms I have taught you to understand. He found something so old we know almost nothing about the civilization responsible for its creation.'

'Was it plundered, then?'

Grayling smiled tightly. Sleet was slashing in frozen sheets across the windscreen. There were things about Scotland Jane did not think she would miss. 'No. It was not something the Vikings or the Celts stole. The Vikings were great travellers, but even on their marauding voyages they did not reach the place where this item was originally created. You must wait until after I have spoken to your father, Jane. Then I expect to be in a position to tell you more.'

'What if he forbids you to tell me?'

Grayling glanced at her. 'I do not think he will.'

'Have you ever met my dad?'

'Yes.'

'I thought so.'

'This is not a conspiracy. It is certainly no conspiracy of silence. It is merely protocol, as I have already explained.'

'If my dad forbids you to tell me more I will simply ask Adam.'

'Well,' Grayling said. 'I can't prevent you from doing that. But as you said yourself last night, Adam is in the habit of keeping his word.'

And you have sworn him to silence on the matter of the find, Jane thought. But she did not bother to say so. She knew it was the fact just then on both their minds. Instead, she reached for the radio's controls. She got Coldplay performing 'Yellow'. She would have preferred something a bit more upbeat. But it was better than nothing. To her surprise, Grayling sang along. To her further surprise, he really did have an excellent singing voice.

The Land Rover ate miles in its stolid progress south. Jane thought of her father's Jaguar and her mother's Porsche and how seldom over recent years she had been ferried willingly in either vehicle. Her parents had their lives, she supposed.

Eventually, she dropped off and dozed. And she dreamed of an elderly sailor in mottled blues, singing sea shanties in a language alien to her. His movements were sly and spasmodic and strange, and their strangeness provoked her back into consciousness, eventually. She awoke with the look in his unblinking glass eyes disapproving, in her dream memory.

'A nightmare?'

'Did I cry out?'

'You moaned and mumbled a bit.'

'It was all very random,' Jane said. 'I was aboard an old warship, steaming through the North Sea crewed by sailors who moved like dolls. No earthly logic to it.'

'Nothing earthly at all, by the sound of it,' Grayling said.

Jane looked at the speedometer and out at the passing landscape. Grayling had switched the radio off. She realized that they were unlikely to arrive in Cambridge before dark. She wanted to speak to Adam but could not very well do it now. And he had not yet called her. He rented digs in the town but she did not know the address. Maybe Martin Prior had it.

'There's a bag on the seat behind you,' said Grayling. 'There's a flask of coffee and sandwiches.'

'I can't eat your lunch,' Jane said. She was hungry, though. Her impromptu visit to the site had not allowed time for breakfast.

'I'm provisioned for two,' Grayling said. 'I was hoping that you would agree to travel back with me.'

'Why?'

'I'm curious about you. I'd like you to tell me about yourself.'

'My favourite subject,' she said, reaching behind her for the lunch bag.

'Except that it isn't. Most young people can't stop talking about themselves, but you are quite reticent. It's an unusual trait.'

Jane bit into a sandwich. The bread was coarse and thickly buttered and the filling was strong Scottish cheese and fresh cucumber. It tasted delicious. It occurred to her that she had, that morning, smoked her last cigarette. She chewed and swallowed. 'I don't know, Professor,' she said. 'Adam Parker is pretty reticent.'

'He is,' Grayling said, 'which makes it doubly unusual. Provide a bored driver with a distraction, Jane.' He nodded at the radio. 'I can't get a decent signal in this weather on that. Tell me about yourself.'

And so she did.

His long and strange evening of revelation with McGuire had compelled Adam to think about his father. The memory of his dad was not strong. At least, it wasn't at first. It was enfeebled by time and deliberate effort, he realized now, reminiscing after a night's sleep and most of a day, remembering with something like surprise just how brutally hurtful the breach had been for him.

The truth he was now obliged to acknowledge was that, actually, he had adored his dad. And his dad had left him completely and without apparent regret. There had been no hesitation and no compunction. And he had only been eleven years old when he suffered this unsustainable loss.

He had been honest, but not wholly honest with Grayling in their brief discussion of the matter on the day after his find. His mum did pretend his dad was dead. But he did that too. It was his as well as her way of dealing with an absence that had hurt him when it happened the way he imagined it might hurt to be torn fully conscious limb from protesting limb.

He stopped walking and looked at nothing and breathed in the chill November air. He was remembering his dad's smell. His father had smelled of oil and sweat and the salt of the sea and hand-rolled tobacco. He had smelled of a sort of manliness Adam had smelled on no one since. But he had not hugged a mature man since his father's departure, so perhaps that was the reason for this.

He had not invited or been offered the same physical closeness. For better or for worse, you only got one dad. His father had smelled sure and familiar and safe. But in the end he had been none of those things, had he? He had possessed none of those qualities. His scent had been a seductive lie, like everything else about him, like the strong, cradling embraces that had felt like love. Adam clenched his fists and blinked back tears now, knowing he still missed the comfort of those embraces terribly.

His dad had been a seaman. He had worn a sailor's tattoos in fading ink on the brawny forearms concealed by the sleeves of his reefer jacket. He wore jeans and boots and a ribbed wool hat pulled down low over his hair. He had gazed for a long moment outside their front door at his son, looking back up at him. The expression on his face had been new and unreadable. Then he had hoisted his duffle bag up on to one broad shoulder and turned and was gone in the rapid, loping stride that was so familiar and that Adam had never seen again.

He had been obliged to run, as a child, just to keep up with his dad. He remembered the callus that had always felt like a coin in his palm when they held hands and Adam's enclosed fingertips found it. It had felt like a ten-pence piece.

Adam's eyes felt raw. He sniffed. There had been a lot packed into those brief periods when his father had been home from the sea. He would leave for the ship clean-shaven and with his black hair shorn and return tousled and bearded, and they would do everything there was for a man and his boy to do together. There had been a lot of his dad, Adam realized, every time in those days and weeks of precious shore leave, and then there had been nothing at all.

He must remember to ask his father why, for that had been McGuire's instruction to him. He was to seek out and talk to his father about the strange object he had uncovered from the Scottish forest loam. The reason for doing this had not been explained. McGuire had insisted that it was his father's place to tell him.

McGuire had given him an address. He would, dutifully, ask his dad about the object. Then he would ask him how he had found it in his heart to go with such finality.

A twig snapped on the ground to his rear and he wheeled around and Jane Dobb was there, her hair a glorious halo in the gloaming, the green glitter of her eyes almost feral in the last of the light, her lips slightly parted, all of her unreal, so gorgeous and surprising was the sight of her.

'You've been crying,' she said. 'Oh, Adam.' And she closed the distance between them and reached for him. As she held him he heaved a sob he could not prevent, there on the bank of the river in the unexpected tenderness of her embrace.

'Are you real?' he said. 'You look like a dream.'

She found his mouth with hers and kissed him. And he tasted her and knew that she was real.

'Grayling brought me back,' she said. 'I hoped I might find you here.' She smiled. 'I'm not stalking you, I promise. I've seen you walking here.'

'I've never seen you.'

'From the river,' she said. 'I scull with the rowing club. You dawdle and daydream. You wouldn't have noticed.'

'I didn't.'

'But I did.'

'Thank God.'

'What's wrong?'

'Everything,' he said, 'but nothing, Jane, now you're here.'

He could not hold back with her. There was a way of dealing with relationships in the early stages. It involved coolness and detachment and a light sprinkling of irony. Adam Parker knew that he could never do this with Jane Dobb. He could not play a role with her. She took him truthfully or not at all.

He thought that he would love her, if he didn't love her already. He thought in truth that he did love her already. It did not matter if she knew. She would know. He could not conceal feelings so strong and anyway, what was the point of doing so?

'Why did you travel back with Grayling?'

'To satisfy his curiosity, I think. He wanted to know about me. He asked me questions about you, too, to which I didn't know any of the answers. Not that I would have told him if I had.'

'But you told him about yourself?'

'I did.'

'Did he tell you about what's going on? About what's happened?'

'He said he had to consult my father first. The protocol, apparently, whatever that means.'

Adam nodded. He felt more grateful for Jane's presence there than he could have expressed. He delighted in her company, but it was more than that. She had distracted him from the bleak sorrow of his grief.

'Will you tell me what's going on?' she said.

'I'm going away,' Adam said. 'I've got to go to Rotterdam. Grayling has to talk to your father. I have to talk to mine.'

'I assumed he was dead.'

'No, just buried. He's buried aboard a barge in Rotterdam, apparently.'

'I know a nice restaurant. Not quiet, nowhere is in Cambridge that's worth going to, really. But there's privacy, you don't see our crowd there. We'll find a secluded corner.' She smiled. 'The table for two they always have in old-fashioned films. Are you hungry?'

'I am for you,' he said, truthfully. 'I'm sorry.'

'Don't be,' she said. 'Don't be sorry. I expect I'm every bit as hungry for you.'

Martin Prior sat in the study of his flat and considered the revelations of the previous evening. The experience had left him exhausted and exalted at the same time. He was glad that he had been able to isolate himself on the minibus between the white buds of his iPod earphones. He would not have been capable of the small-talk with which people felt obliged to fill tedious journeys.

He felt grateful for his father's generosity in providing him with a private and well-appointed place in which to live. He often felt grateful to his father, despite having known nothing but parental largesse all his life. He was observant enough to know that he was privileged. He felt he deserved it, but that didn't prevent him from being appreciative.

Right now he felt that he needed his privacy, his seclusion, as he never had before. He had a lot to think about. The implications of what he had seen were profound and staggering. The responsibility he had been offered, should he consent to take it on, was more enormous than anything he had experienced in his relatively short life.

He looked again at the artefact he had been given. He had adjusted his desk lamp so that it sat bathed in a pool of yellow light. He stroked it with a finger, aware of the sheer alien strangeness of the thing and the exquisite workmanship it embodied. They had said it was taken from life, that the creature it depicted was real.

He felt as though he had been there weeks, rather than just for most of a single night. That was the power of revelation, though. That was the impact of profound truths of which he had been unaware. He had returned to the hostel sometime after five a.m. and no one there had been any the wiser as to his absence from it. Even though he'd been exhausted, he had not slept.

Instead, he had taken out the artefact he was examining now and cradled it, crooning a song he had heard his father play, an old favourite of the old man's own university days, some prog rock anthem performed by Genesis or Yes or Pink Floyd.

Martin was very glad of the seclusion his flat afforded. He could do the research he needed to do here without curious eyes looking at the computer screen over his shoulder or riffling through his written notes. His privacy was guaranteed. But he would be cautious, nevertheless. He would hide the artefact for a start. He would tuck that fabulous item of treasure away.

Truth be told, he was pretty impressed with himself. He had been chosen to accomplish something significant. It was a rare accolade and it was also vital. He had needed this, he realized, this magnitude of responsibility. He had craved it.

His life had been without genuine challenge. This was no doubt the cause of his womanizing. He had been eager for victory but deprived of a meaningful cause and had done what attractive men resort to doing when they are empty of purpose. He had been narcissistic and directionless, going through the motions of sexual conquest in the absence of anything more fulfilling. No wonder he had felt so hollow for so long. He did not feel hollow now.

This fresh and honest self-appraisal did not mean giving up on Jane Dobb. It meant just the opposite. She was beautiful and brilliant and he thought more than ever worth competing for. His approach and purpose would be different now, though, in pursuing Jane.

It was no longer a question of resorting to dubious means to eventually bed her. There would be no subterfuge, no seduction by stealth and no careful demolition of the character of Adam Parker.

She was not simply someone at the head of a horny list he'd compiled. She was instead the only name on the list. And she would be treated with the consideration she deserved. He would woo her. He did not think she would find him, with his new accomplishments, easy to resist. It would happen over time, of course. But as the herald had been at pains to emphasize, Martin could be a very patient man.

After crooning that song as he caressed the object given him, at the hostel early that morning, Martin had tried to find it on the internet so that he could download it on to his iPod and listen to it on the long journey back. He found it, searching for a snatch of the lyric.

To his surprise, it was not by Genesis or by any other of what he thought of as the usual prog rock suspects. It was a song by a band called King Crimson. He thought that his father must have played it, though, for it to seem so familiar to him. He could not imagine where else he could have heard it. Its title was, 'The Court of the Crimson King', and he could not rid his head of its mournful verses and solemn melody.

FIVE

F ull darkness had by now descended. Their corner table was candlelit. The walls were covered in a sort of velvet plush and embellished with plaster details painted gold. Adam looked up from his menu at Jane. Candlelight complimented her. She suited any light, but it gave her skin a smoothly sculpted look, and its flickering shadows made a ruby cascade of her hair.

She became aware of his scrutiny and looked back, raising an eyebrow in an expression of ironic counter-appraisal, and he was hit by the full force of her; not just by her good looks but by the glamour she possessed. Jane's glamour was a very potent quality in those slightly hokey surroundings, away from the mud and the grey air of the dig. It seemed not so much an attribute, as a force.

'You're going to have to get a trim pretty soon,' she said. 'Either that, or get measured up for your armour. It's your choice, Adam.' She smiled and raised her glass in a silent toast and sipped. They were sharing a bottle of Chianti.

'It feels as though choice is becoming a bit of a luxury,' he said.

'Well. You have the luxury, here, of being able at least to choose your food.'

They ordered. Then Jane told Adam about the frightening apparition in the forest.

'And the professor closed the dig on the strength of this?'

She shook her head. 'He said we were done anyway. Cree was basically an endurance test and I think he felt we'd all endured enough.'

'What did Martin say about what you saw?'

'I haven't told him. I haven't seen him since the experience. I don't know if I will tell him, to be honest. I can't imagine his reaction would be much of a comfort.'

'You must be aware of that theory,' he said, 'the one claiming that nobody knows anyone else really well.'

'Of course I am. I'm an optimist, so prefer not to subscribe to it. You don't believe it either. You're too sentimental.'

'But I do believe people are capable of surprising us. Martin might be sympathetic.'

'Well, it's a life of surprises.'

'You've said that before.'

'I think there is more to Grayling than meets the eye,' she said. 'Do you know anything about his background?'

Adam shook his head. 'I didn't even know his Christian name until last night. He's Professor Grayling to us. He's S.M. Grayling on the spines of his books. He's very eminent, both in the field and in the lecture hall. And last night I discovered that he's Stuart to his friends. Though I suspect he doesn't have many of those. And I'd say that's through choice.'

'I think he's probably gay,' Jane said.

Adam laughed. 'That word seems ridiculous, applied to him. He's far too serious.'

'Then I think he's probably queer.'

'Does it matter?'

'I reckon he's been something important in the military,' Jane said. 'He's occupied some clandestine role. He's disciplined and courageous and can endure a lot.'

Adam thought about what Jane had just said. It was all plausible. It could be a flight of fancy or it could be shrewd judgment, but after his experience of the previous evening, he could not dismiss it out of turn. He pictured McGuire's swordstick, the lethal ornament gathering dust on its neglected shelf and McGuire's verdict on the weapon: *it long ago earned its retirement from the fray.*

Jane tilted back her head and laughed. He saw the rise of her pale neck, lovely between the ropes of burnished hair falling to her shoulders, and the generous sound of her laughter filled their corner space until she stifled it with a hand, blushing. 'I'll tell you something you don't know about Professor Grayling,' she said. 'He sings Coldplay songs on karaoke nights.'

'I think you quite fancy him,' Adam said. 'And now he's gone off to see your father.'

'He hasn't yet gone, but he is going. They're meeting tomorrow in Canterbury.'

'Is that where your family live?'

'Not to my knowledge,' Jane said. 'But my parents are pretty nomadic people. Their domestic roots have never reached very deep, and I haven't spoken to either of them for weeks. They were in the

Surrey Hills. It wouldn't be beyond them to have moved to east Kent.'

'Without telling you?' Adam did not know whether she was joking or not. 'Tell me about your father,' he said.

Their food finally arrived and they began to eat. Adam was surprised at how hungry he was. Jane seemed hungry too. She spoke between mouthfuls. Her words emerged as fluent as a recitation, which it was, he realized, because she was no doubt repeating to him what she had told Grayling on the road aboard the Land Rover earlier in the day.

Sir Rupert Dobb had earned his notoriety and wealth as an architect. He was also a gifted mathematician and an instinctively brilliant engineer. He had patented innovations as disparate as high fidelity speaker drivers and a self-sharpening drill-bit while still an undergraduate. Ideas came very easily to him. But this had never had the effect of making him bored or jaded or complacent.

History fascinated him. So did comparative religions, folklore, philosophy, theosophy and magic. He was an authority on numerology who could play jazz piano with a panache professional musicians respected. His buildings, whatever else they were, were temples to the ecological and environmental principles considered so important over recent years.

'He sounds fascinating,' Adam said, 'much larger than life.'

'He's charismatic and generous and entertaining.'

'But?'

'He isn't a very nice man underneath it all. Every child carries the burden of parental baggage, with varying degrees of resentment about what it weighs. I know that. And I don't think I mind bearing the weight of my father's reputation.

'But when he looks at me, I never see anything more than obligation. I don't think he loves me and I don't think he ever has. I don't think he's any more capable of the emotion than he is of flapping his arms and taking flight as a consequence.'

'Or walking on water?' Adam said. He smiled.

'Oh, I'm fairly sure he can do that,' Jane said. She smiled back. 'Read the profiles carried over the years in the quality press, if you doubt it.'

Sir Rupert was almost sixty when his daughters were born. Jane's theory was that fatherhood was such a glaring omission on his long catalogue of accomplishments that he'd felt compelled to become one. He had wanted a child for the wrong reasons. He had probably wanted a son and heir. He had not wanted a daughter and had certainly not wanted a matching pair of them.

Adam did not really know what to say. Jane's experience was so far removed from his that he found her predicament difficult to imagine, let alone to sympathize with. Her father had been a willing constant in her life. Even if you ignored the genetic gold she had inherited from him, Adam felt that she had good reason to be grateful.

Love cut both ways, didn't it? It was possible that from her father's perspective, he was the one spurned, coldly distanced by his daughter's unfeeling disdain. Adam's limited experience of Jane was that she was anything but cold. But without seeing her together with Sir Rupert, he found the situation she described quite difficult to believe.

'There's something else,' she said, biting her lower lip and looking pensive, which he had never seen before. 'He is hiding something. He's been hiding it for a long time. He nurses a secret, something corrosive, though he might not think so.

'He's always eaten healthily and always exercised, long before it was the fashion. He was a champion middle-distance runner at college, another of his accomplishments, and he kept the running up. I think that the health problems he suffered before Dora and I were born are a consequence of discovering and hiding his secret. I think it has put a strain on him that's almost been too much for him to bear.'

'It could be congenital, the heart problem.'

'There's no history of heart disease in his family, and he isn't and never has been overweight. And people as talented as he is aren't afflicted by the work related stress suffered by the lesser mortals who work for them.'

'But he was old when you were born. He's lived a long and eventful life. If there is a secret, it could be anything. That said, you could always ask him.'

'I could never ask him.'

'Then you'll never know.'

'I asked my mum,' Jane said. 'My mum still gets high. She only does it very occasionally, but old hippie habits die hard and life at Dad's beck and call probably gives her good reason for the odd moment of druggy escape.

'I was seventeen. Dad was jetting back from some project in

Central America. Mum had half an hour earlier smoked a huge joint in our conservatory. She was listening to Van the Man. My mum can be tricky. You have to be alert to the clues. Van Morrison is as serene as her personal soundtrack gets. She was blissed-out. It seemed a good moment. I sparked up conversation and then asked her outright.'

'What did she say?'

'That she had her suspicions. She had harboured them since about five or six years before we were born. Dad was researching one of his amateur projects on some alchemist he suspected had made an important discovery in what we now think of as biochemistry just before the outbreak of the Black Death.'

'Except that your dad was anything but amateur,' Adam said.

'Mum said he found out something. That was her supposition, anyway. He found out something that stopped him looking for anything further. He deleted the files on whatever primitive home computer he was using then, and he burned his written notes on a garden bonfire. With the research abandoned, nothing on the subject was ever completed or published. And he wouldn't talk about it, either.'

'That does sound odd.'

'Mum said he destroyed the source material of his research, Adam. Priceless antique books and formulae scrawled in the Dark Ages on vellum went on to that panicky bonfire.'

'That could have been the dope talking.'

'It was so uncharacteristic, Mum said. Dad lives for arcane knowledge. The sources were sacred texts.'

'OK. I'll buy it. Your dad hides a fearful secret and maintaining the secrecy is damaging to him. It doesn't mean he doesn't love you. Do you want a dessert?'

'I was reminded of Mum's story yesterday morning, at the site. We were speculating on what you might have found and Martin was theorizing about history, saying it was stranger than we suppose. What if my dad found out something really terrifying?'

'Do you or do you not want a dessert?'

'No,' she said. 'I'm the only woman in the Western world who doesn't like puddings. I want you to take me home.'

He thought her flat incredible. He made no comment about it, but his feelings must have shown. She took his jacket and dispensed with her own coat and hung them somewhere. She switched on lights that illuminated the room at waist level and triggered low music at the same time. She fetched him a beer along with something in a tall glass for herself and they sat on a sofa together, facing a wood-burning stove which she fired into life with a remote console lifted from the low table in front of them.

'I know what you're thinking. But I paid for this place myself.'

She kicked off her shoes. He felt the tug of desire as they clunked against the hardwood floor and she sighed with something between pleasure and relief and sat back against the plush.

'You must be one of the Lotto winners who ticked the "no publicity" box,' he said. 'I would have remembered your tabloid picture, the pretty face grinning smugly behind the raised glass of champagne.'

She laughed at that. And when she stopped laughing, Adam kissed her. It was a long kiss and when it ended she held him and he felt her hot breath on his neck and knew that her eyes were closed, and that the strength of his embrace was a comfort after the fearful encounter she had undergone the day before in the forest at Cree.

Gradually her hold on him softened. She pulled back her head and looked at him in the firelight. The flames were tiny orange sparks reflected and glittering in the green of her eyes. Her parted lips wore a succulent, ruby hue. Her hands shifted, though her grip on him remained. She held him tenderly, for him now, out of want and not merely the need for whatever refuge his arms might provide her with.

They kissed again. He could smell the rising heat of arousal on her skin beneath the perfume she wore. The perfume was civilized. Beneath it rose the urgent pungency of flesh. A moan of pleasure purred in her throat. In the taste and touch and scent of her, as her body writhed, beneath him now, it was all he could do to remember to breathe.

Its great Gothic cathedral defined Canterbury. It was a place of worship almost a thousand years old. The Black Prince lay under the still splendour of his stone effigy in the crypt. Saint Thomas à Becket had been murdered by knights wielding broadswords before one of the side altars. Some places celebrated their past; others were defined by it, and to Grayling's mind, Canterbury was one of those. It held the position in his mind occupied elsewhere in Britain by Lewes and Bath and Stratford, and by Edinburgh, where the ghosts of the resurrection men still panted in dark thoroughfares pushing their stolen cadavers on carts through the night.

Sir Rupert came into view. He was standing at the centre of a construction site atop a small hill of sand. Jane Dobb was a tall girl and her height had been inherited from her father. His position at the peak of the hill made supplicants of the men surrounding him. His stature made them seem obsequious. He was holding a blueprint in one hand and as he talked he stabbed at it with a forefinger. The men encircling him were nodding without comment. It was ever thus for him, Grayling thought. This was a man who had spent his professional life surrounded by inferiors who were paid to agree.

He was different from them in another significant respect. To a man, they wore regulation yellow construction helmets. He was bare-headed. His large, shaven dome wore the tan of another continent. *Probably he has special dispensation to flout health and safety regulations*, Grayling thought. The idea of a falling brick singling out Sir Rupert Dobb seemed unlikely. What brick would dare?

He saw Grayling and stopped, seemingly in mid-sentence. Handing the blueprint to one of the hard hats, he grinned and slithered down his hill of sand. He reached Grayling and they shook hands.

'How did you get in here?'

'I walked in through the gate.'

'I'll have to beef up site security. They're supposed to stop and question anyone who looks suspicious.'

'You just can't get the staff, these days, Rupert,' said Grayling.

Sir Rupert put a hand on his shoulder and squeezed. 'It's been too long, Stuart.'

'You're a busy man.'

Sir Rupert looked around. 'We make willing slaves of ourselves,' he said. 'It's human nature. How is that clever daughter of mine doing?'

'Outstandingly well, she shines even amid the general brightness.'

'Then I hope you're not here to dull the flame. Would you care for coffee or for something stronger?'

'Coffee would be fine.'

'We'll walk to my hotel and take it in the lounge there.'

They walked the short and picturesque route to the riverside inn at which Sir Rupert was a guest. It was a mild day and the old buildings of the city were bathed in gentle afternoon light. It picked out blackened beams and ancient patches of sagging brickwork and Grayling wondered what glass and steel monstrosity would rise from the ground on the site they had just vacated in brutal contrast.

There had been an intimacy about Sir Rupert's greeting that was unusual considering they had only met on one previous occasion. But that meeting had been unforgettable in its intensity. The man had come to him the way someone guilty of committing some terrible sin might do in seeking absolution from a priest.

Their encounter had been confidential, another feature of the confessional. And Grayling had kept it so, mentioning the subject matter of it to no one in the intervening years. It had been before the birth of the twins. Grayling thought that physically, the time elapsed since then had been kinder to him than to the billionaire knight of the realm whose secret discovery he had, for a quarter of a century, been party to.

His own secret was that he had known what Sir Rupert had told him already. His great challenge in the moment had been to try to look as surprised as he should have been by the revelation. Secrecy burdened some people more than others, he thought. Jane's architect father lacked his talent and perhaps also his appetite for conceal-ment. Then there were the implications of what he had discovered. He rode roughshod in his professional life over his inferiors, as the cliché would have it. But staring into the abyss had given him a bad case of vertigo and he was a man still haunted by that black and depthless view.

He had sought out Grayling having read his book about the Black Death burials in York. It was a fluke, really. He could equally have gone to a historian specializing in the period. He had been compelled to unburden himself. He did not want any public association with what he had learned. What he really wanted was to forget about it, but that was impossible. He had been fortunate in his choice of confidant, in the professor's view. He got a more sympathetic hearing than he would have elsewhere, along with the assurance he required.

Grayling had received him in the seclusion of his office at the college. He had been pale and distracted and he had looked like a man who had not slept well for several nights. He had opened with a question. 'Have you ever heard of a place known only as *the land we do not dare name?*'

'No,' Grayling had lied. 'The phraseology sounds Arabic. And the metaphysical implication sounds Arabic, too.'

'Have you heard of an alchemist called Hieronymus Slee?'

And Grayling told his second lie. 'No,' he said.

'He was active in the fourteenth century in Germany and the Low Countries, and later in Russia.'

'He sounds as though he was running.'

'He was. And he was running from a formidable foe. I discovered a deposition mentioning him written by a medieval knight named Robert de Morey. Sir Robert was a warlord and sometimes mercenary but of genuinely noble birth and good education. He was literate and schooled.'

'Where is this going, Mr Dobb?' The architect was then a decade away from being granted his own title.

'There was a reason de Morey was charged with the pursuit and execution of Slee. His crime was the creation and nurturing and spread of the plague bacillus. Slee engineered the start of the Black Death. He created the bacteria in a laboratory. The pestilence was deliberate.'

Grayling smiled, grateful for the savoir-faire his years in military intelligence had endowed him with. His experience of espionage had made him an excellent poker player. 'That's impossible.'

Rupert Dobb held out his hands in an expression imploring patience and perhaps also faith. 'I know,' he said. 'It presupposes medical knowledge of the spread of contagious infection of which the world was quite ignorant in the Middle Ages.'

'It does more than that, Mr Dobb. It anticipates germ warfare by several centuries, and I do not believe in the possibility of time travel, tempting though that daydream is.'

'I am not a fantasist, Professor.'

'I am sure.'

'I have the deposition in my briefcase. You should read it. Robert de Morey pursued this alchemist relentlessly. He actually went to the land they did not dare name, followed him there with a troop of hand-picked men.'

'And they found him?'

'Only de Morey returned. He did so after two years, having found Slee there and finally butchered him.'

'So he travelled back accompanied by no witnesses, meaning no one to contradict his account. Does that not strike you as convenient?'

'I've had the document I found carbon dated. It is genuine.'

'So are many accounts of the Grail Quest. It does not mean that King Arthur ever lived or that Camelot was a real location or that the Grail was ever there in the first place. Chroniclers tended to deal in the truth in the times we are discussing, but de Morey's story could well have been written as a deliberate fiction. The novel form had not been invented then, but the saga had. With television still several centuries away, they enjoyed their stories.'

Dobb sighed. 'Except for that medical insight of which he would not have been capable. What if Slee was from a place where people had discovered the real cause of bacterial infection? This land de Morey writes of sounds like another world. What if Slee really did come from there and really did deliberately concoct the plague bacillus? We've never been able to identify the exact nature of the infection.'

'We have never been able successfully to identify the viral profile of the Spanish Influenza. What does that prove?'

'It doesn't prove anything,' Dobb said. 'But it raises an interesting possibility. Perhaps we cannot identify these infections because they are not of our world. They are effective against us, devastatingly so. But they did not originate here. They were manufactured, but are not of our making. They are the work of an enemy foreign to us.'

Grayling pondered on what he had been told. He thought about the York graves, the consequence of mass destruction, death on a mechanized scale with the plague victims packed like items of factory spoil in the earth.

He wanted to get the de Morey deposition out of his visitor's possession. It was not a proof, but it would be compelling evidence and would certainly prompt press interest and further academic research. Some avenues were best left unexplored and some historic truths much safer avoided. 'A crime needs a motive,' he said. 'What possible motive could Hieronymus Slee have had to inflict murder and suffering of such appalling magnitude?'

'You know more about the Black Death than I do, about its consequences and repercussions. There comes a tipping point. In the middle of the fourteenth century, humanity almost reached it. That was the motive. Our destruction was the intention.'

'You can't discuss this openly, you know. You will be dismissed as a crank and ridiculed. It will greatly damage your career.'

There was a silence then. It was longer and more uncomfortable than Grayling would have liked. He wanted his visitor to think pragmatically. But he knew that Dobb was an egotistical man and suspected a strong streak of stubbornness. He was not used to being told he was wrong and he was a stranger to compromise. Against all that, though, he wasn't a fool.

'Speaking to you about it has helped,' Dobb said, eventually. 'I had to confide in someone qualified to discuss what I found. I believe you will keep the secret. It is not something I would wish to talk about or even think about again. If you decide to act on the information, that's your choice. If you choose to disregard what I have told you, you can probably do so with your conscience clear. You get your evidence of what happened in the past, after all, by unearthing relics from the ground.'

He unlatched the briefcase he had brought with him and took out a thick envelope. 'I'd like you to take this,' he said.

Grayling took the deposition from him. He tried not to let the relief he felt at doing so show in his expression. 'Where did you find it?'

'It lay between the pages of a medieval atlas on a neglected shelf in a library at an old seminary at the foot of the French Alps.'

'Not catalogued, then.'

Dobb smiled. 'It was in the appropriate place, I think. It describes a domain missing from the maps drawn elsewhere in that volume.'

Now, twenty-five years on, older, stiffer and each more eminent, the two men sat in opposing armchairs at the fireside under the low oak beams of Sir Rupert's comfortable hotel lounge. Tourism in Canterbury was strictly seasonal and the city was blissfully free of business conference bookings. So they had the lounge to themselves. They could speak confidentially with freedom. As they started to do so, Grayling realized with surprise that their shared secret of a quarter of a century had made friends of them. And friendship demanded frankness, did it not?

'You are here to give me a warning,' Sir Rupert said.

'You have a lot to lose.'

'We all do. One man's everything is much the same as another's. There's no stronger instinct than self-preservation.'

'Yet some people overcome that.'

'People like you,' Sir Rupert said. He reached for the poker and lifted logs in the fireplace, rearranging them, increasing at once the fierceness of the flames and the radiant heat expelled from the grate. It was not cold in the room; on the contrary, the day was unseasonably mild. But he simply could not help himself. He was a cause and effect sort of person. More, he was the sort of person who liked personally to cause the effect.

'How much do you know?' Grayling asked. 'How much more do you know now, than you did then?'

Sir Rupert stared into the fire. 'My wife, Jane's mother, is one of those people on a constant search for enlightenment, Stuart. The search has deteriorated over time from the study of Van Morrison lyrics, to the reading of self-help books. The oxymoron of the self-help guru has never occurred to her. My wife does not do irony. No one in the fashion world does.'

'A luxury they can't afford, I suppose.' Grayling wished he was drinking something stiffer than coffee from a white china cup.

'But her quest, its clichéd and limited parameters, set me on mine. The distinction was that I didn't want affirmation of what I already believed. I wanted what I believed confounded and disproven.'

'You didn't find what you were looking for.'

'I did not. I discovered instead that I was right about de Morey's account. The deposition was real and his words truthful. And you bloody well knew it. And you are here about my daughter, your pupil, because there is a dynastic element to this struggle, isn't there? That was in the de Morey too, though I didn't appreciate its significance all those years ago.'

'You weren't a father then.'

'He was. The scholar warrior de Morey was. And he schooled his only son, Simon, for the fight.'

'It's destiny, Rupert,' Grayling said gently. 'It is inescapable. I am here to tell you that it cannot be avoided.'

'How many people know? Globally, I mean?'

'I doubt more than a hundred.'

'How many attempts to destroy us have there been?

'It's been going on since the dawn of recorded time. The first event written about was the Flood.'

'Christ.'

'Christ is not involved.'

'Nor am I, Stuart. How has my daughter become embroiled?'

'She is close and I believe growing closer to someone chosen to fight on our behalf. This is a very formidable young man, a man if you like in the mould of de Morey, though he does not know it yet. She saw someone from the land we do not dare name. The confrontation was deliberately engineered by him. That was her challenge, her invitation to join the fray. And I can tell you from experience that there is no rejecting it.'

The fire burned. On the wall above the mantle, a clock with a pendulum in a walnut case ticked implacably. Sir Rupert Dobb put his hand over his eyes and the hand shook visibly. 'Do what you can to protect my daughter,' he said. 'I love her very much.'

Grayling had travelled by train to Canterbury. He walked back towards the railway station. It was no great distance and of course he knew the city. It should have been a relaxed stroll through the twilight descending upon one of the most beautiful urban settlements in a still largely beautiful country.

But it was not. As he walked the route, Grayling felt not just watched and followed, but lethally threatened. The hairs on the back of his neck bristled with impending danger. He knew the feeling, remembered it, and not with any sort of fondness or nostalgia.

He had felt like this before the accord in the Province on the bandit streets of Ulster in the mid-eighties. He had occupied the sights of sniper rifles held by men who were murderous shots. He had escaped death on two certain occasions only by good fortune. The experiences had sharpened his instinct for self-preservation.

He accelerated, weaving through a cluster of students on the pavement and dodging down a narrow alleyway to his right. It led to a street roughly parallel to the one he had been walking down. He hurried back along it in the direction from which he had come and then took another right, bringing him out a block back on his original route.

He saw his pursuer straight away. A man a head taller than the other pedestrians idling along the street was standing fifty feet distant, facing away from him and still. He wore his hair to an extravagant length and even in the limited light of Canterbury's old streetlamps, he looked powerfully built. Studied, though, he was not standing completely still. He was breathing deeply, sniffing the air, Grayling knew, for the scent of the prey that had slipped from his sight.

It was dark when Adam arrived in Rotterdam. He did so aboard a ferry. He had two hundred Euros in his wallet, money described as necessary expenses and given him the morning of the previous day as he left the Brighton home of Dr McGuire. McGuire had bought the ferry tickets in advance. He would not be punished for his absence from his lectures and seminars, McGuire explained. Grayling was head of department and decided what disciplinary penalties should be imposed. Adam had been granted leave of absence on compassionate grounds. There was a family matter to deal with, a domestic issue to reconcile. It would take as long as it took, McGuire assured him. The college was very sympathetic in such circumstances. There was no hurry.

He had not slept with Jane Dobb the previous night. He had wanted to, and up to a point of course he had tried to do so, because he was only human and she was gorgeous. She was enthusiastic too, but on her terms.

He had not earned her yet, that was the thing. She had not said so in so many words. She had verbalized her feelings though, as they untangled themselves from her sofa, gathering items of clothing to put back on and both struggling to get their breath back and compose themselves.

'I'm not ready to sleep with you yet. My feelings for you run too deep.' She frowned. 'Does that sound like a contradiction?'

'No. It's very flattering,' he said. Then he sat and waited for the erection swelling his underwear to subside so that he could stand up and gather his clothes and dress with something approaching dignity. It took a fairly long time. While he waited, he asked Jane how she had raised the money to buy such a luxurious place in which to live.

She had helped her mother design a clothing range. It had been her idea. She had been looking at some Lycra pieces in the show-room and thinking about how sweaty Lycra was and she started to think about breathable fabrics, the waterproof membranes used in performance clothing. It was a shame, she thought, that they were always used in the dorky designs worn typically by train-spotters and geography teachers.

'And archaeology students on rainy Scottish digs,' Adam said.

'Quite,' said Jane.

She saw no reason why functional weatherproof clothes should not be stylish. So she came up with the range and gave the collection a name, Roam, which was sexier than hike or ramble and given the cut and detail of the garments, might have greater than average anorak appeal. And it went down very successfully in such storm-challenged locations as Notting Hill and the Fulham Road and became essential wear at the wheels of their Range Rovers among the footballers' wives of Cheshire.

'Martin was wearing a Roam jacket in the enrolment queue on the first day of term,' Jane said. 'It was how we got talking.'

'What's happened to Martin? He seems to have disappeared from the face of the earth.'

'He's made himself scarce since I told him about you,' she said. 'It's a surprise, because I thought he was gay.'

'You think everyone is gay.'

'Not you, I don't.'

'I'm just in serious denial.' At last, he had been able to get up and put his trousers back on.

'Ha bloody ha.'

'It's uncharacteristic,' Adam said. 'He's a garrulous sort of bloke. He's forever emailing and texting and suggesting a drink. And I won't be seeing him now because I've got to go away.'

Jane was brushing her hair. 'I wish you didn't have to go.'

He looked at her. His caressing fingers were the reason she had to smooth out the tresses he had tangled as they kissed and touched. He still could not quite believe he was with her. He had listened to what she had said and understood it but could still not quite fathom why she had chosen him.

She was staring at his naked torso. 'I'm shallow,' she said, as though having read his mind. 'You're beautiful.'

Rotterdam was not beautiful. It was bleary in a succession of harbour lights that managed to be garish without illuminating much. Rainbow puddles were slick on the oily ground. A misty and insistent rain leached out of low cloud. The horns of ships were mournful in a distance invisible through the darkness.

And it took Adam longer than it should have to find the address McGuire had given him, a dockside bar with a corrugated roof and steel flanks that looked like it had come ashore on a container vessel. The metal walls were rust splotched. Windows were spyholes crudely cut by a welder's torch. A neon sign announced it as *Delilah's*. The neon fizzed, flashing above a fortified wooden door.

Everything about this ugly destination suggested trouble to Adam. He could not imagine McGuire coming here, sipping a schooner of sherry with his pinkie raised, even armed with his swordstick. It was a dive. It was the kind of bar in which bored losers fought one another for entertainment. It was not the sort of place that would welcome strangers.

He took a breath and pushed open the door.

Three heavily tattooed men sat in a thuggish cluster around a single table. None of them was Adam's father. Cigarette smoke hung in a pall under the metal ceiling. Perhaps the harbour precincts were beyond the jurisdiction of whatever body enforced the law concerning smoking in public places. Adam thought it more likely that the bar he was in was outside any sort of law beyond its own.

He was aware that each of the inked trio was looking at him. He did not feel particularly threatened by this. He had done nothing more offensive in entering the bar than lighten the general tedium. That said, it was very early days. And he thought getting out likely to be an entirely more challenging proposition than getting in.

His focus was fixed on the woman behind the bar. Like her three customers, she was smoking. Like them, she was tattooed. She wore a white strapless dress and some bird of paradise had been etched skilfully into the flesh of her upper arm.

But there the resemblance to her punters ended. The woman behind the bar was pale-skinned with hair that framed her face and draped her shoulders in shiny black coils. Her eyelids were heavy with kohl. Her mouth was full under dark lipstick. Her expression was very difficult to read. That might have been the make-up, Adam thought. Her grey eyes were either cold or appraising, depending on your outlook.

When she plucked her cigarette from where it rested in an ashtray, the painted nails of her hand were almost talon-like in length. Adam could not have begun to guess at her age. He thought her one of the most strikingly attractive women he had ever seen.

'What's your pleasure?' She smiled.

She had guessed correctly at his nationality. And the deliberate ambiguity of the question wasn't lost on him. One of the regulars grunted something guttural and offensive. Adam ignored it. It wasn't the odds, and in some circumstances he wasn't averse to a tear-up. People who provoked a beating to his mind deserved to get one. But it wasn't what he was here for. He carefully skirted the occupied table and returned the woman's smile. He ordered a beer.

She spoke as she started to draw it from the tap, her voice no more than a murmur. 'You look like him.'

'Like who?'

'Like the man you're here to find. You look like your father.' Her eyes widened, fixed on him. It was a difficult look to hold and return, almost aggressively frank. 'Tough and shy at the same time, like he said you'd be. It's a charming contradiction in a young man. I'm Delilah.'

'Clearly you know my father.'

'As well as anyone can,' she said. She had an accent. It was as seductive as everything else about her. Adam did not think it local to Rotterdam. She did not sound Dutch. He could not place it, it was too subtle.

'It sounds like he knew I was coming.'

'No one escapes their destiny.'

Adam sipped his beer. Delilah smoked. Her nails wore vermilion polish and they sparkled. He said, 'I don't understand that remark.'

'Your father is dying, Adam. He does not have more than a few weeks. He owes you an explanation for what happened between you and he has been hoping to live long enough to provide it.'

'There was no need to wait. He could have given me what he owed me on the day of his departure.'

She smiled. The smile was sympathetic but the expression in her eyes was complex. 'If he could have done that, then he would have. Hear him out, before you judge him.'

'I've judged him already and found him wanting.'

'Please hear him out.'

'I'll listen to what he has to say. It's what I'm here for. Where do I find him?'

'I'll take you to him.'

'What about your customers?'

'Regulars, drinking on a tab. They're not the brightest, but they've the wit to serve themselves for half an hour. I'm not expecting anyone else. We don't do coach parties.'

The bird on her arm was etched in vivid greens and yellows and the one eye portrayed in its cruel profile glimmered brightly. The flesh around it was smooth and firm and almost luminous in the gloomy light. As she unhooked her coat from behind her he was struck by the feeling that someone so exquisite looking could only be a prisoner in so miserable a place. He wondered again where her accent came from.

She had put on a black leather coat cinched at the waist by a belt tied rather than buckled and when they left the bar she linked her arm in his. Her breath was smoky and a loose strand of her hair slipped on to his shoulder, and he was aware of her hip touching his as she huddled against the night and the rain at his side.

He felt the strong erotic thrill of her and wondered at the nature of her relationship with his father. She had said she knew him as well as anyone alive. But his father was dying, she had said. And to Adam, Delilah did not seem especially lovelorn at that moment.

SIX

Martin had taken the ascending steps in the forest, increasingly confused about the sensation he felt in doing so. His feet were climbing. There was no question about that. But he felt in his ears and brain and on his prickling skin as though he travelled downwards. The fog did not lift. If anything, it intensified, blank and blind. He should have felt endangered, he thought, unable to see anything to right or left, to gauge altitude or direction or to sense the closeness of his eventual destination.

His mind kept filling with vivid pictures that distracted him. His progress was steady enough, but his thoughts were everywhere. A nautical image kept intruding. He was on the bridge of an old warship, a dreadnought hauling its vast and bristling tonnage through a North Sea swell, a following wind shrieking through the webbing over the gun turrets and pushing the smoke belching from the vessel's funnels before them in a filthy trail. The crew members were clumsy and doll-like, marionettes with their strings cut, faces bland as porcelain, gazes glassy and dead.

He saw a seaside pier, fat women waddling in polyester between one-armed bandits spewing copper coins, the tide beneath slopping against the stanchions pink as candyfloss in the light of a descending sun.

A turban-wearing women waved a finger like a warning at him through the awning of a fortune teller's tent. A lad about his own age grinned, fingering a lock-knife behind the counter of a canvas stall lurid with cheap souvenirs. A Wurlitzer pumped out music to accompany all this, but when he listened to the melody it made for an anachronistic soundtrack, Martin thought. Of all things it was the old Coldplay anthem, 'Yellow'.

There was nothing wrong with his balance physically. His progress was sure. But he did not any longer own the direction of his mind. There he travelled now to streets full of jostling people somewhere hot, shouting in a language he didn't understand, surrounding an old-fashioned open carriage replete with gold flourishes and upholstery spattered in gore. Its unharnessed team reared among the uniformed men trying to calm the horses, snorting and kicking in wide-eyed terror.

He had reached a door. He almost walked into it. He had been travelling for a long time. He must be very high up, he thought, though he felt a long way down, the way he felt if he swam deep, snorkelling on holiday.

He looked at his watch. The fog wreathed so thickly around the outside of the door that he could only read the face because it was a Rolex Sea Dweller and, as a divers' watch, brightly luminous. It was just after midnight. The watch had been an eighteenth birthday present from his dad. The information it provided was superfluous to his journey. He did not remember what time it had been when he embarked upon this strange adventure.

The door was made of oak planks so smoothly joined that he could not have got a fingernail between them. It was studded with nails fashioned from iron, with large triangular heads. It had the character about it of expensive handiwork from the Tudor or even Plantagenet period. The style could not have been more traditional. But the wood was unblemished by weather or time. It had to have been recently crafted.

The door yawed inward on smooth hinges. The chamber within was lit. He walked through, closed the door behind him and looked around. He was in a room so vast he wondered that the fog did not obscure its reach. But he had left the fog outside.

There was a long wooden table with candles burning in pewter holders set at intervals. Most of the interior light, though, came from a fire in the wall furthest from him, over to his left. It occupied a massive fireplace and the logs in it looked like cut sections of mature trees, spitting and flaring as they furiously burned.

A man stared into the flames, illuminated by them, leaning against the wall beside the fire with his back to where Martin stood. He was of a piece with the room, dressed in clothes that could not really have passed without comment or attention in the modern world. He was of a piece with this place. Martin knew that about him, even before he turned to acknowledge his visitor with a short bow and a welcoming smile.

'You were right, Martin.'

'Is this a dream?'

'You were right about history. It is much stranger than people suppose. You were shrewd enough to suspect that's been the case.

But there is a conspiracy and you have been its victim and its perpetrators have used you cynically.'

'Where am I?'

'You are in my home. You are my guest. Forgive me, my name is Sebastian Dray. I am an emissary and guide and hope very much you and I can be friends.'

'Where am I? What year is this?'

'Please,' Dray said. He approached and placed an arm around Martin's shoulder. 'Let us refresh ourselves with a glass of wine and perhaps a morsel of food. There is someone I want you to meet. He is on his way. He should be here before very long. Matters will be much clearer when you have spoken to Jakob Slee.'

Martin was suddenly ravenous. He thought it must be the arduous climb through the fog. He could smell meat roasting sweetly somewhere, imagined it turning slowly on a spit, succulent juices dribbling from its covering of crisply browning fat. The aroma of freshly baking bread drifted warmly from the same source.

'Is Mr Slee eating with us?'

For some reason, this assumption seemed to amuse Dray. He stopped and chuckled and then steered Martin to a curtained arch at the far end of the room away from the fire. 'He will have taken care of his nutritional needs already. We will eat in the kitchen. There is no need for the formality of a banqueting table. I want to get to know you, Martin. I want to know what measure of man is my clever and perceptive guest.'

'Is Professor Grayling in on this conspiracy?'

'There. You prove my point about you in a sentence. We call it the Great Lie. Grayling perpetuates it with vigour and cunning. It is an insult to the integrity of every honest and ambitious student.'

Martin was comfortable with being called clever and ambitious. He felt his claims to honesty perhaps less secure. But they had by now reached the kitchen beyond the curtained arch. And he was not about to labour the point with himself.

A feast was being laid out by a red-faced serving girl. The wine was already uncorked and its bouquet rose from a cluster of dusty bottles, rich and full-blooded. This was an exotic adventure. It might all be an elaborate dream. Or it might be proof of everything he had suspected about the strange and alien nature of the past. Either way, there was no reason why he should not enjoy it.

'I'll pour and we'll raise a toast,' Dray said. He proffered a deep and heavy crystal glass. He seemed as cheerful to Martin as someone recently released from a jail spell spent in solitary confinement. He sparkled. He positively gleamed. He was a handsome man, dark-eyed and tall with longish hair, strong facial bones and a light-footed agility. Grace, Martin thought, was the quality he possessed. 'To mysteries solved,' he said. Did he wink at that? Martin thought that he did. Certainly, and for the second time, Sebastian Dray allowed himself a chuckle.

The mood became more sombre and serious towards the conclusion of their dinner. Martin had drunk fairly sparingly throughout. This was not deliberate self-denial. He had been too busy chatting to consume very much of the wine.

'Jakob Slee awaits us in the library,' Dray said, as the cheeseboard was taken away and the brandy poured. The fingers of his right hand drummed a tattoo on the table top when he said the name and Martin had an intuition that Dray, for all his bonhomie, was slightly nervous of the man they were shortly to meet.

'I didn't hear him arrive.'

'It's a large house,' Dray said. 'The library is in the east wing. And it is not his habit to blunder and crash. A less noisome individual than he would be difficult to imagine. Come,' he stood. 'And bring the brandy bottle if you wish. You have been miserly with yourself in your cups tonight. Eat, drink and be merry, Martin.'

'For tomorrow we die?'

'No, my young friend, we do not. Death is in my plans for neither of us. Come.'

There were doors in each of the four kitchen walls. He had not noticed that until now. Martin grasped the brandy bottle by the neck and followed Dray through the door he now knew faced east. It opened on a lengthy corridor. There were pictures at intervals along the corridor, portraits of men and women he did not recognize. None of the faces looked kind. Some of the men were as handsome as his host and some of the women really quite beautiful, but there was a calculation about their expressions, a certain unappealing quality of watchful coldness.

The corridor did not possess any windows. This gave it the closed-in atmosphere, Martin thought, of a catacomb. The illumination strengthened this impression, candles pooling scant yellow light at intervals between the scowling likenesses. He realized that he was nervous about meeting Jakob Slee, almost to the point of being afraid. Without his noticing, his knuckles whitened as his grip tightened on the bottle held in his hand.

Slee was seated at a reading table, but stood when they entered the library and smiled in Martin's direction, rolling up the chart he must have been studying as he did so. He slipped a knotted circle of twine around the chart and performed that gesture, somewhere between a bow and a nod, with which Martin had earlier been acknowledged by Dray.

Slee was dressed in a black ankle-length garment that looked like a priest's cassock. But there was no clerical collar encircling his throat. He was tall and very slender, and so fine-featured Martin thought him almost as pretty as a girl. His hands were small and girlish too and he wore a silver ring on every finger. Only his thumbs were without adornment.

There were three chairs around the table and it was there that they sat. Slee looked at Martin, who put down his brandy bottle and the two glasses he had brought. He frowned, thinking he should have brought three.

'Feel free to serve Sebastian and yourself,' Slee said. 'I've already taken my evening's refreshment. I expect you would like to know where you are.'

There was a slight accent to his speech. It was melodious, hypnotic, a sound so seductive you wanted to hear more of it immediately. 'When, would be a more likely question than where,' Martin said. 'I've seen nothing I'd call modern since my arrival here. If it wasn't for the contractions in your speech, I could believe I've been transported back centuries.'

As if to stress the point, he looked around at the library walls. Lamps were suspended from them. The light they cast was perfectly adequate, but they were not powered by electricity. They possessed wicks and burned oil or paraffin, giving off a slight odour, and above each had spread a faint round soot stain on the plaster ceiling.

'It is discourteous, to criticize someone's home when you are their guest,' Slee said. His tone was mild, but the rebuke was a sharp one.

'I apologize.'

Dray filled both their glasses almost to the brim. He pushed Martin's towards him. 'You meant no deliberate offence,' he said. 'I possess a fastidious nature and this house is very old. I prefer it to be of a piece. Modernity for its own sake has never appealed to me. I am not a man much impressed by novelty.'

Martin cleared his throat and helped himself to a large gulp of brandy. 'I do not wish to be rude,' he said. 'But certain things strike me as unusual.'

Dray chuckled. Slee stared. 'Go on,' he said.

'Neither of you wear a wristwatch.'

'There is more than one way of knowing the hour,' Slee said. 'Look at your watch.'

Martin looked. He had to lift his sleeve to do so.

'It is twenty-seven minutes past two in the morning,' Slee said. 'You are four seconds slow, Martin. Not unacceptably tardy. But then the instrument on your wrist was expensive, so you have the right to expect accuracy from it.'

Slee had not seen the face of his watch, he was certain. Nor was there a clock to consult on any of the library walls. And the cassock was sewn with no pockets in which to conceal any sort of timepiece. 'That's an impressive trick,' Martin said. His throat felt dry. He drank more brandy and Dray refilled his glass.

Slee shrugged and looked at Dray and then back at Martin. 'It is no trick at all. You would be able to do it yourself had history been different, had men like your Professor Grayling not tinkered and dabbled and meddled with destiny.'

'On the subject of time,' Dray said, 'the moment has arrived for serious talk. You can help us, Martin. And we can certainly be of service to you.'

Slee lifted a hand to the buttoned collar of his cassock and his fingers disappeared and then emerged again, gripping the links of a thin chain worn around his neck.

He lifted it over his head and held it dangling above the table from one hand. Depending from it was a blood-coloured stone set in a circle of pitted gold. His elbow on the table, his grip on the chain was relaxed. The stone swung back and forth and twirled languidly. 'Tell me what you most want,' he said in that mellifluous, mesmeric voice. Facets of light jittered in the twirling stone in a way that claimed the eye and absorbed the attention. 'What do you most desire? We can deliver it for you if you choose to be our friend.'

'I want to be successful. I want to achieve great things and I want those achievements to be properly recognized and rewarded. I want respect and admiration.'

'You certainly have the potential to gain all of those things,' Dray said.

'I want a girl. That probably seems a shallow ambition in the judgment of serious men. But there it is. What I really want is for her to want me.'

'You want Jane Dobb,' Dray said. 'No man with blood in his veins could blame you for that. And you shall have her.'

Grayling turned back and walked through the West Gate and took the Whitstable road. He was more than capable of travelling the four miles to the little seaside town on foot. There were trains travelling regularly through Whitstable for London, where he would change for the journey to Cambridge. The route to Whistable was hilly and it was now fully dark. But it was an altogether less hazardous choice than a confrontation with the man they had sent after him.

That confrontation would inevitably come. They did not give up. His opponent was young and obviously strong and would have no compunction at all. He would possess the merciless energy and doggedness of a born hunter and it would be combined with a mercenary's martial skill.

He would not have magic in his armoury; they would not risk that. It would be too conspicuous an asset. But he would be formidable, and it was only sensible to choose the ground and the time for the fight. Grayling was himself skilled at combat. And he did not know anyone remotely as fit as he was for his age. But he was a middle-aged man and had not fancied grappling desperately in the street at dusk with someone youthful enough to be his son.

It could have been much worse. They could have sent Proctor Maul. McGuire had once seen Maul and had described him since to Grayling. The sighting had been many years ago but the moment vivid enough to remain very clear in McGuire's memory. This time they had not sent their most fearsome and sadistic assassin. If they had, he would probably be dead instead of speculating on the identity of his pursuer. He was not Maul and neither was he the Adam Parker doppelgänger who had so terrified Jane Dobb in the forest. The Adam lookalike was a puzzle. But the moment for solving puzzles would come later. Now was the time simply for eluding danger.

The road ascended towards the hamlet of Blean. It was a clear night and he could make out constellations in the stars above him. The air smelled of smoke from the coal fire of a cottage he could not see. Hedges grew wild and high to either side of the road, only breached by the trunks of occasional trees. Birds sang in their high branches. The earlier autumn sun had warmed the land throughout the day and Grayling could smell that too, cooling now, the grasses and loam sweeter and less sharp on the senses in this gentler climate of the south-east of England than they had been in the Scottish lowlands, 500 miles to the north.

He had not considered a new assault on the world a likely event in his own lifetime. McGuire maintained that the last effort to undermine humanity had finally failed only with the fall of the Berlin Wall. The struggle had endured for the better part of a century and now, less than a quarter century after its failure, they were orchestrating another attack. They must have known how close they had come, he thought. The taste of victory had almost been theirs. It had given them the appetite for another attempt. There was no mistaking the portents. Adam's clarion call at Cree was a signal no one on earth a party to this ancient, secret conflict could ignore.

His attacker emerged in a flailing blur from the hedge at the side of the road and aimed a dagger blow at Grayling's heart that sent him hurtling, gasping, on to his back on the ground. His hands reached for anything while his grinning enemy closed to take a trophy from his victim. He stooped over Grayling's body with the weapon held loosely in his right fist, convinced, quite reasonably, that he was dealing with a man already dead.

Grayling's right hand had gripped a section of fallen tree branch. He prayed briefly that it was as thick and heavy as it felt. Light with rot, and he was dead, he knew. He gripped and swung at the temple of his attacker, who was straddling him now, and he felt through his arm and shoulder the explosive impact of the blow.

The man's head juddered and he fell as Grayling rolled to his right beneath him, out of the way. He dropped the knife with a thud as he fell. Grayling reached for it and then squatted and put two fingers together on the artery in his neck. There was no pulse. He was dead. That was a relief, Grayling thought, because though he would have used the knife, killing in cold blood was not something he relished.

He flattened himself on the ground as a set of headlights briefly unfurled the road in front of them in a bleached path to the right. He waited for the engine noise to fade into the distance, then rose and quickly dragged the body under the roadside hedge, where he covered it with fallen leaves, thankful it was autumn and the conceal-ment was available.

He did not concern himself with thoughts about forensic evidence and criminal enquiries to follow the discovery of the corpse. There would be no corpse to recover. McGuire had told him that they disappeared in the hours after their deaths, and there was a long time till the morning and the possibility of someone stumbling upon it.

He had to be sure, though. He listened for approaching road traffic, but the night was silent. The killing had stilled the songs of the birds in the trees. He went back to his victim and, using the small torch at the tip of his cellular phone to see by, prised open his jaw. The tongue had been crudely severed at the root. They did it to guarantee their silence if they were captured. It was said that Proctor Maul had carried out this procedure on himself with pincers heated in the forge.

Already, the corpse had started to stink. The decomposition churning through its innards rose foully from its mouth. It was a gruesome piece of sorcery, but Grayling was grateful for it. Better a rank stain on the earth in the morning than a murder hunt.

He turned back for Canterbury. It was the pragmatic thing to do. He was still much less than halfway to Whitstable and there would be no tiresome changing of tickets if he caught the train from his planned departure point. His chest was already starting to bruise from the impact of the knife blow and it felt very tender there. His heartbeat alone was enough to provoke the spot into pain. He was aware that two decisions, one made out of courtesy and the other from generosity, had combined to save his life.

He had worn a tailored suit and college tie and newly polished shoes for his meeting with Sir Rupert Dobb. It was a question of respect and due formality, a nod towards Sir Rupert's status in the world and the gravity of the subject they were to discuss.

He had been early for their meeting. That too had been out of respect, a precaution against delay on the journey there. And this was where the act of generosity had come into play. He had whiled the time away window shopping, and as he was studying an antique shop display, he had spotted a silver cigarette case with a ticket claiming that it had belonged to Lawrence of Arabia.

Angus McGuire, who had in those far-off days gone under an entirely different guise, had known T.E. Lawrence in the war, and he would occasionally reminisce fondly about him with his few confidants. Grayling had bought the cigarette case as a gift for his venerable mentor and comrade in the secret struggle. He had slipped it into the breast pocket of his suit, then he had pretty much forgotten about it as the eventful day began to take absorbing shape. It had stopped dead a knife blow that would otherwise certainly have killed him.

The thought made him frown. The dagger had been a substantial weapon and the blow had been a very heavy one. Silver was a soft metal, and so surely the cigarette case should have punctured and the blade been driven home?

He slipped a hand inside his coat and took out the case. It was slightly crumpled and there was a nick almost at its centre. He examined the damage closely. It was not silver at all but steel, probably electro-plated and certainly without the provenance claimed for it. He had been had.

He discarded the case as soon as he came to a bin, on Canterbury's outskirts. On balance, he did not begrudge the money it had cost him. His thoughts were more on the conversation that he would be obliged to have with Jane Dobb, once he got back to Cambridge.

He took out his mobile phone and called McGuire. The only bonus in dealing with someone of the doctor's great age and relative frailty was that he was almost always at home.

'Hello?'

'It's me.'

'Hello, Stuart.'

'Things are escalating at some speed, Angus.'

'They certainly are. There is a young chap skulking around outside.'

'Is he one of theirs?'

'If he is he's better than usually disguised and less physically prepossessing than one would expect. I don't think he's one of theirs. He's wearing designer jeans and a trendy anorak.'

'Be careful, Angus.'

'I'm always careful,' said McGuire.

Adam's first thought was that his father had shrunk. He was seated in an armchair and his clothing had the drape on him of garments belonging to someone bigger. They gaped at neck and wrist and flapped at his thin ankles. James Parker had never been fat in the past; he had possessed the same strong, sinewy build his son had inherited. But now he looked diminished and wasted. Death had marked him and Adam could not mask his own distress at what had befallen his dad.

His father tried to stand to greet him. He struggled to lever himself to his feet with the use of a cane; his grip on the cane was feeble and there wasn't the strength in his legs properly to rise. Adam closed the distance between them in a stride and helped him up. Then they held one another and Adam closed his eyes with the memory of love and the reality of loss shuddering through him.

He had not anticipated such grief. It was not an emotion he had the strength to contain. He felt the bristle of his father's beard against his cheek and caught the remembered smell of him, and he wept. He could not help himself. He could feel his father sobbing, through the too-big sweater he wore, holding on to his son with all of the grip he still had.

'There,' he heard Delilah say, somewhere behind him. 'Not before time, I would imagine.' Her tone sounded sardonic and relieved at the same moment. 'You two have much to discuss,' she said. 'And I have a bar to run.' He heard her turn and ascend the ladder that had delivered them to the living quarters of the moored barge his father lived aboard.

They sat in opposing chairs in the narrow cabin. The walls were lined by neat rows of closed portholes. They were anchored beside a wooden jetty on a tidal creek. Adam had thought it a sadly isolated spot, approaching it with Delilah. He did not think that daylight would greatly prettify much the surrounding scene. The boat itself, his father's home, was immaculately neat and clean. It was comfortable and well provisioned and warm. But the desolation outside suggested exile more than it did willing escape.

'McGuire sent me.'

'He wasn't McGuire when I met him. He did not call himself that to me. But I think I know the man you mean.'

'How old were you then?'

'About four years older than you were the last time I saw you. I was crewing aboard a mixed cargo and passenger vessel. He was one of the passengers. Is he a slight, smallish man, the owner of a boyish face and a pair of hazel eyes?'

'That's him.'

'He was travelling in the guise of a geologist. We were fogbound and obliged to anchor off the Scandinavian coast at a spot littered with small islands. Navigation was impossible in the fog. We would have beached, or we would have holed the hull on rocks.

'He approached me on the evening of the third day. He was wearing an oilskin and he had a compass in his hand and a heavy stick under his arm. A pair of binoculars was hanging on a leather strap around his neck. They were distinctive, the binoculars. They were the kind issued to German U-boat captains during the Great War. I asked him about them and he said he had taken them as a souvenir. I thought he was joking, of course. That was the moment when I first began to wonder in my own mind as to his true age.

'He told me he needed an oarsman and that he had cleared what we were going to do with the captain. There was an island with a cave he wished to explore because it contained rare mineral deposits. He asked if I would take him there in one of the lifeboats and said that we'd be back for certain by the following day.'

'What did you say?'

'It was all I could do not to laugh in his face. In that fog I knew that he would never find his island. There are hundreds of them there, some of them not much bigger than the boat I'd be rowing. It would require a miracle of seamanship.

'That's what I thought. But that's not what I said, because I was fifteen and the captain gave the orders and my job was to obey them. And truth be told, I was bored. Any sailor becomes bored on a vessel unable to voyage to where it's bound.'

'Did he say anything else?'

'The whole endeavour struck me as bogus right from the outset. He didn't even have the pretence of a rock hammer or a sample case to store in the locker. We provisioned some rations and drinking water and the boat was lowered from its davits over the side.'

Everything about the expedition felt wrong to young Jimmy Parker, once they got properly clear of the ship. The texture of the water felt wrong against the blades of his oars. He could not have explained it precisely, but there seemed a weird counter-rhythm in the run of the sea to his strokes.

The fog developed a yellow taint and a low, luminous sparkle. And though he said nothing about it to his passenger and the man's face remained blandly expressionless, Jimmy kept hearing snatches of music. He heard a flute, tremulous and lonely. He heard the faint pluck of mandolin strings. And unpleasantly, he heard something harsh ground out on a barrel organ out there somewhere on the briny wastes.

The self-styled geologist went by the name of Ericson. Perhaps he was deaf to the melodies Jimmy kept hearing. Periodically he would glance at his compass and correct their course by a point or two; his concentration seemed unwavering. Eventually, he could not have said after how long, Jimmy felt the spine of the boat judder on a sandy shore and the two of them were out, hauling the craft higher up the beach where it could be safely left.

Except that Jimmy was told not to leave it. Together, under Ericson's instructions, they groped at the tideline for driftwood. Then Ericson used one of the bigger pieces to hammer two others as supports into the sand. They flipped the boat and balanced its starboard gunwale by two rowlocks on the edges of their improvised stilts. Thus the boat was transformed into a serviceable shelter.

'You've done this before,' Jimmy said.

Ericson merely said, 'You stay with the boat. You keep the bulk of the rations. You stay out of sight.'

'There is no seeing, Mr Ericson, sir. Not in this fog there isn't.'

'If it rains you'll be dry and there are blankets stored in the boat's locker. You'll be warm enough.' He had changed, had Ericson. He was no longer the diffident scholar who seemed uncomfortably out of place when he wasn't studying books by lamplight in his cabin. This was a man transformed.

'Good luck, sir.'

'What?'

'Finding your cave, I mean.'

'Yes. Quite.' Ericson bent and picked his heavy stick up from the beach where he had left it to work on the shelter. He tucked it under his elbow and the mist enveloped him.

Jimmy thought he was dreaming. Then he knew what had woken him and feared he was being approached by a large animal, moving with the lithe grace of a predator. But he was tricked by the fact that the woman capering towards him was on all-fours, and what he had thought was a mane was only her wild and abundant hair.

He had never been with a woman, was a virgin with so little experience even of kissing that he associated the thrill of that coy and recent pleasure with Christmas and sprigs of mistletoe. She teased and aroused and wordlessly straddled him. And then she rolled him on top of her. And when he came, with the bucking frenzy of youth, he did so with her thighs clamped tight around his waist and her back arched and straining on the sand under him.

'She was as wanton a woman as a boy could have dreamed of, Adam. And I was flattered, God help me. And it never occurred to me that I was the victim of a trap.'

'You were there. You were in the shadow world. And you fathered a child there.'

'God help me I did.'

'When did you tell Ericson?'

'I never told Ericson. He was McGuire by the time I told him. And I only told him because he confronted me. Something must have happened in the intervening years that made him suspect. I told him when you were eleven years old.'

'And he told you that you had to leave.'

James Parker nodded. 'Because my shadow world son would find me and kill you. An earth father enables him to come here more or less at will. He would not tolerate a half-brother. He would not tolerate the competition or the taint. I had to hide from him and by doing so, hide you.'

'Except that there's more to it,' Adam said. 'There is more to it, isn't there, Dad?'

His father coughed, then gestured at the whisky bottle on the Dutch cabinet. Adam rose and poured them both a generous drink. His father sipped and swallowed and doing so provoked another bout of coughing. There was something loose sounding in his chest. It was the thing killing him, Adam knew with gloomy certainty. He thought of the man who had frightened Jane in the forest, an enemy bound to him by shared blood. He looked forward now to punishing him for the forced absence of his father from his life.

'There's a dynastic element to it all,' his father said. 'There's some biological imperative. The man you call McGuire took me there deliberately.'

'So my half-brother could be born and come here and kill people?'

'No. The conception of Rabanus Bloor was not a part of his plans. That was some scheme of theirs, unless it was just opportunism. He took me there so that you would one day be born, able to join the fray. Look at you, Adam. There's more of destiny to how you've turned out than chance. I'll bet you're quite something in a fight.'

'Bloor. Is that Delilah's surname?'

Adam's father stared at him. And then he wheezed laughter so hard that Adam thought he might choke on his whisky. 'What did McGuire tell you? Did he tell you anything?'

'He told me that the shadow world is sometimes referred to as, the land we dare not name. But it does have a name. Everywhere real is distinguished by a name. It is called Endrimor.'

'It's unlucky to give voice to that word.'

'You're a sailor, Dad, so you would say that, just as you wouldn't whistle aboard a ship.'

''Course I bloody wouldn't.'

'Or name the Scottish play.'

'Which is only common sense.'

'Or put your left shoe on before your right.'

'And openly court disaster?'

'I can't believe how good it is to see you, Dad.'

'Likewise, son.' He blinked. 'There is more joy in my heart tonight than I'd dared think possible.'

They were silent for a moment, each contemplating his own thoughts. It was Adam who broke the reverie they shared.

'McGuire said it's feudal, deliberately so, a place of great refinement in some ways, and sophistication. But it's also endlessly cruel. He said it's a bleak world sustained only by the will to usurp ours.'

'Delilah was born there,' his father said quietly. 'She lives here in exile. She knew we were fleeing the same thing the moment I laid eyes on her. Not many can pass. They give themselves away. But she can. She has educated herself.

'She says there's a Luddite aspect to their ideology that makes them abhor technologies beyond the primitive. They do not much differentiate between science and sorcery. And she says it is more fascistic there than feudal in terms of their hierarchy. Not that fine distinctions really matter very much. It's angels on the heads of pins stuff. According to McGuire they seek our destruction. That's the only really relevant point, Adam, about the shadow world; that, and the fact that it exists at all.'

'What would you say is the relevant point about McGuire?'

'That he's on the side of right.'

'He was in Serbia in 1914 on a desperate mission that failed. He was young, but still a grown man then. He's not aged naturally. He's worked some magic.'

'Or been its victim?'

'Either way,' Adam said, 'there'll surely be a price to pay. Every story I've ever read about sorcery insists you defy nature at your peril.' He sipped his whisky. 'I can barely believe I'm having this conversation.'

'Because of the subject matter?'

'That too, Dad. But more because I'm having it with you.'

'Age is not the same there,' his father said. 'Nothing is.'

'Jesus. You went back.'

'I'm a seafaring man, have been all my life. I'm a traveller. I had to go back. But it's a tale for another time. I'm tired. You've worn me out.'

'You never sent any money.'

'McGuire was very insistent on that. You needed to be brought up tough.'

'It was harsh. My mother has suffered.'

'It was necessary, Adam. We've all suffered. You'll get everything of mine when I'm gone. I've saved faithfully on your behalf. You'll get your legacy. You would be very wrong to think it has been easy on me.'

Adam nodded. But money was not what he wanted from his father now. It was too late. It was too late also for what he did want from him. Delilah had measured his remaining time in weeks.

'I'm going to kill Rabanus Bloor.'

'It's easy to talk about killing a man, Adam. It is a much harder thing to do.'

'Have you met him?'

'I'm tired.'

'Have you?'

'Yes. He is not a son of whom a father could be proud. I expect you do have it in you to kill. And if you do not kill him, you will die at his hands.'

Adam did not say anything more. It grew quiet and very still in the cabin, and he knew eventually that his dad had fallen asleep. He went over and plumped a cushion for him and placed it gently under his head. Then he found a blanket and covered him. The only source of heat was a small oil stove, and he left that lit on a low and steady flame to keep his father warm. There was not much flesh left on his bones to repel the cold approach of the coming winter, but he would not live to endure it.

His dad had been little more than a boy himself when he had

fathered Rabanus Bloor. So his half-brother was much older than Adam was, probably in his mid-forties. Yet Jane had said they resembled one another as strongly as twins. People did age differently in the shadow world, where they spurned scientific advancement, and probably still settled disputes in star chambers or at the point of a sword in single combat. There were spells there, and curses, and sorcerers who were not the silly charlatans and fantasists of earth. They conjured real and potent magic. They harnessed ancient power that earthly civilizations had chosen to forget about in the ascent towards enlightenment.

If he had ever thought his existence bland and boring, he did not think so any longer. There was such a thing as alien life. It had been proven to him. It was here. It had not arrived aboard space-ships from galaxies light years away. It had been here all the time, no further than a blink away.

It was hostile, but he had always imagined it would be. Whether you studied history or anthropology or zoology, the lesson was always the same. No species tolerated open competition. You fought and you won or you were vanquished. That was the immutable law of nature.

His father's sleep was blessedly deep. The meeting with his son had been a happy one, a reconciliation in the end. But it had still worn him out. It had taken its emotional toll. It had on Adam, too. He would go back to Delilah's, he decided. It wasn't far; he remembered the way.

There were no doubt more salubrious venues for a few beers in Rotterdam, but in Delilah's he was guaranteed to be greeted by at least one relatively friendly face. He had liked her immediately. Partly, he supposed, the attraction lay simply in how sexy she was, but it was more than that.

He walked outside. There was a glimmer of moonlight on the water of the creek. A derelict dockside crane cast a sprawling spider web of shadow over the quayside. A rat scuttled close to his feet. It was an ugly place, this, but at least he did not feel followed. For the moment, the danger had receded. For now, at least, Adam Parker felt that he was safe.

SEVEN

Sebastian Dray did not enjoy the spectacle of public execution. He could not see the taking of life as sport. He had no appetite for wagering on how long the condemned prisoner could elude death. Perhaps he was too fastidious by nature for it.

The Vorp was a bird that enjoyed killing slowly. Some philosophers held that man was the only animal deliberately capable of cruelty. The lesser species killed out of necessity. Any torture they apparently inflicted on their prey was just man's fanciful misinterpretation of what was actually taking place.

But Dray had seen too many executions to think the Vorp anything but a truly sadistic creature. He was always disconcerted by its relative enormity. He did not like the carrion stench when you found yourself downwind of it. It was ugly to watch in repose, in flight and in the kill.

He was obliged to attend the executions. It was not politic to be thought weak, either in mental resolve or in the stomach, but in his heart he had long wearied of occasions such as the one he was attending today. The truth was that he had come over recent years to loathe them.

Today's victim had been broken on the wheel during the questioning carried out by the prosecution in the court. The prisoner had been crippled. Jakob Slee had repaired the damage.

There had been nothing benevolent about the healing. It merely guaranteed the prisoner's legs were sound for the chase. How far they would travel would depend upon the hunger and alertness of the Vorp. Terror could propel a human at prodigious speed, but the great carnivorous bird could not be outrun.

Only once had Dray seen one outfought and that, he remembered now, had been real competition.

That Vorp, a much admired and feared female specimen, had turned on its handler in a deadly attack. It had been marked reluctantly for extermination. The Crimson King himself had taken an interest in the fate of the creature. He had asked if anyone was willing to fight the avian predator to the death.

Proctor Maul had answered the challenge. Not verbally, of course.

Like all the assassins marked for the cross, he was rendered dumb. But it had been made known that he would take on the Vorp, armed only with the short sword condemned criminals carried as they fled from its murderous pursuit.

Maul had not fled; he had stood his ground. The fight had been terrible. But it had been fascinating too, Dray thought, to see a man match a monster for bloodlust and ferocity.

It had not been an equal contest, but the betting had been even, despite the natural physical advantages enjoyed by the Vorp. Dray had wagered that day and his stake had been on Maul. He had won handsomely and so, he remembered, had Slee. It was rumoured that the king too had favoured the human protagonist. Certainly he had led the applause in the aftermath of the fight.

Dray shivered as he made his way to the killing ground on the drear outskirts of the hovels. It was cold and a bitter winter seemed a likely prospect. Smoke rose from the hovels. It darkened the low morning sky and was acrid in the nostrils.

In summer the hovels were busy with human industry as their inhabitants scavenged and scrapped, the urchin children of the poor playing amid the garbage piles and piss runnels. There was the consolation of sunlight and warmth.

There would be nothing there now but endurance until the spring. It was a wonder there was not more unrest, Dray thought. It was a wonder and it wasn't. Rebellion required energy and ideology and leadership. There was precious little of any of those hazards in the vast slum warren under its pall of smoke. There would be even less after the execution that people were gathering to witness.

The crowd was smaller than usual for an execution, he thought. The most recent cull had left the population of the hovels comparatively thin. He suspected also that there might be some general sympathy abroad for the victim and that the sparse crowd might be a reflection of that.

He was obliged to pass close by the Vorp in order to get to his seat. Since it was caged he could only guess at the wingspan of this particular specimen. But its beak was about five feet long, horny and white, splintered at its edges by conflict with its own kind during its training. Its lidless eyes were the size of dinner plates and blank with instinctive menace. Its breath emerged in white plumes at ponderous intervals from twin slits above the beak. It was breathing slowly, conserving energy.

The chill of the morning repressed the stink of the giant bird and, as he slithered over patches of frozen mud on the start of the run, Dray was grateful for that. But he thought it would be difficult for a runner to gain purchase on such treacherous ground, especially barefooted. The chase would likely be brief.

He took his seat in the stand and nodded to Slee. He was senior enough in the hierarchy to be only three rows down from where the stand topped out and the king occupied his solitary throne. He found the proximity of their ruler considerably more uncomfortable than the sensation of passing close to the Vorp.

The hovel dwellers behind the rope barrier on the far side of the run roused themselves into cheers and whistles and odd cries of insult and encouragement. It was the signal that they were bringing her out.

Naked, she did not shiver. She held her head high. Her bearing was regal and there was no affectation in this. She was nobly born. Her hair was still a luxuriant wonder, despite the filth with which it had become caked during her incarceration. She was still beautiful. And Slee had done his work of restoration well. She walked without the hint of a limp out on to the course.

Proctor Maul emerged from among a cluster of officials at the start to present her with the sword with which she would attempt her hopeless fight and at the unexpected sight of him, Dray thought that she flinched slightly. He heard a deep chuckle to his rear and as the hairs rose and prickled on the back of his neck at the sound, he knew that Maul's attendance and the ceremonial duty he had just performed, was the king's ironic jest.

Maul grinned and indulged a bow so extravagant before the condemned woman that his head descended to the level of her knees. Doing so, of course, exposed his neck and beyond the rope the crowd gasped as one at this act of bravado and provocation.

A single swift blow with the sword in her hand and she could surely decapitate the man who had hunted her down. That was the crowd's thinking. But compared to the liquid swiftness of Proctor Maul, his preternatural speed of reaction, others moved as though their limbs struggled through treacle. And the countess of Sarth knew it.

The sword trailed from her limp hand, its point grazing the ground. She might still struggle for her life, but the cause for which she would die was dead in her heart already. Dray thought again that the morning's entertainment would be brief. Maul rose and retreated, and at a distance Dray could not be sure but thought that as he did so he winked at her.

She was on her own. The crime of which she stood convicted was explained to the throng. The verdict was repeated. The punishment was described. And the countess began to run as the Vorp's handlers wrestled with the stiff bolts on the cage containing her drear living instrument of execution.

Dray wondered how his young visitor of a couple of nights ago would react to this particular spectacle. In the prelude to the real hypnotism, Slee had all but mesmerized the boy with a series of small but authentic miracles at their table in the library, achieved to show him how civilized and superior they were in Endrimor to the world from which he had been lured.

He had given the boy a sort of tour before his departure. Martin had been suitably impressed. But he had not shown him the hovels or the pit of spoil from the most recent cull. He had told him about the Great Lie. He had spared him problematic details concerning the Miasmic Sea and the Kingdom of Parasites and other domestic issues.

He had said nothing about the justice system on Endrimor that was about to see a woman from whom a confession had been extracted under torture consumed by an avian monster bred for the purpose. Martin had departed in thrall to them, but he had not witnessed this sordid killing in the frozen mud of the morning.

The Vorp flapped free of its cage with a clang of juddering metal. It opened its beak wide and expelled a shriek that would have shattered glass. In the silence that followed Dray distinctly heard the fleeing woman cry out in despair. The sword clattered from her grip on to a puddle of ice. He was obliged to watch. He could not look away. If he did, someone looking at him might conclude he lacked an appetite for justice. The king had eyes everywhere and men of rank were obliged to possess a hunger for righteous punishment.

Once airborne, the great bird was upon her in two or three strokes of its vast wings. With horrible precision, it swooped and bit at the base of her spine as the countess ran, closing the very tip of its open beak with an audible snap.

She fell, face forward on to the track. The Vorp settled beside her and raised a talon to begin the flaying. Dray prayed that the spinal severing had paralysed her completely, had cut the nerves cleanly and put her beyond the reach of physical pain. But as the first strip of flesh was torn from her shoulder, she screamed and he knew that this entreaty had gone unanswered. On the cold air of the morning, even at this distance, he could smell the coppery welling of fresh blood.

Adam travelled back to Cambridge from Rotterdam after two days.

'You're different,' Jane said, when she met him at the station on his return, as he had made her promise before his departure that she would.

He kissed and hugged her. Then he let her go and tried to smile. 'Sadder?' he said. 'Wiser?'

She still had her arms around him. She was looking at him and the look was appraising and shrewd. It should have made him feel self-conscious, but it didn't.

'There's more substance to you,' she said. 'Not that you were exactly lacking in substance before, but you seem to have grown, somehow. You look very strong and resolute, Adam.' She smiled, then, perhaps aware of the solemnity of her language. 'It's a good look,' she said. 'You should stick with it.'

'I need a haircut,' he said. He felt very grateful for her company. He had felt bad on the ferry, desolate on the train. He had discovered that he still loved his father very deeply.

'No,' Jane said. 'You absolutely do not need a haircut. You are growing your hair. I've decided. It's official.'

'Have you spoken to Grayling?'

'I called him this morning, after speaking to you last night. I told him you were coming back. He wants to see us both this afternoon. He wants us to read something my father unearthed a long time ago.'

'So your dad *was* keeping a secret.'

'It would seem so. He said the details contained in this document will come as a great shock to me, less of one to you. It was written in Middle English. But Grayling has transcribed it into something a bit more idiomatic and reader friendly.'

'And he's done that just for us?'

'No. I asked him exactly that question. He said he always thought he would be compelled to reveal the story some day, but he did not think he would ever be obliged to do so to some of his own students.'

They walked the distance from the station to the college. Adam assumed that they were on their way to learn a lesson Grayling had prepared for them about the secret magnitude of events. They walked through a light rain. Jane wore a fawn raincoat that made her face look very pale and the hair loosely framing it rich and lustrous.

She stopped walking. 'I've lied to you, Adam,' she said. 'I had dinner with the professor last night, at his invitation. I didn't tell him about your phone call this morning; I didn't have to. He was there when I took it at the table in the restaurant last night.'

Adam did not know what to say. He let go of her hand and stood on the street in the strengthening rain as cars swished by and water dribbled down the shoulders of Jane's raincoat on to the slope of her breasts. He swallowed. 'Why did you lie?'

'I find him attractive. He's about as attractive an older man as I have ever met and I think that the attraction is mutual. It isn't that, though. I accepted his invitation because I wanted to hear what he had to tell me about his meeting in Canterbury with my father and to learn about my father's part in this mystery. I lied because I thought you might be angry, that's all. I don't want to lose you before I've even properly got you. Do you mind?'

'I mind the lying.'

'You don't mind the dinner?'

'I only mind the dinner if you stayed for breakfast.'

'I didn't.'

Adam frowned. Then he laughed. 'You should see the company I've been keeping over the last two evenings.'

'Picturesque?'

'Very.'

'But chaste?'

'My virtue remained unsullied. Anyway, she wasn't interested.'

'I'm glad to hear it.'

'Please don't lie to me again, Jane. Please don't.'

'I won't, ever, I promise.'

'We should be walking. We'll get soaked, standing here.'

She reached for his hand. 'He was a soldier, the professor. He served in military intelligence before his career in archaeology and teaching began.'

'I've always thought him a bit fit for an academic.'

'Old habits, I suppose.'

'What did he tell you? I mean, apart from impressing you with his adventures in espionage serving queen and country in a fetching uniform.'

'You sound just like Martin.'

'He's my evil twin.'

'No he isn't.' She shivered. 'I've seen your evil twin and it isn't Martin.'

'Did Grayling tell you much?'

'He hinted at something pretty cataclysmic. But he said the material we're going to read this afternoon should be looked at first. Apparently it supports some of the other claims he wants to discuss. He told me very gently but quite firmly that I can't just walk away from all this now. I've been compromised in some way by that confrontation in the forest at Cree. I'm involved. He said he had been obliged to tell my father that.'

'How did your father react?'

'By the sound of it, he was apparently very shaken and upset. I think we're in quite a lot of trouble. There's something else, too. I think something happened to the professor in Canterbury. I think he was physically injured. When I arrived at the restaurant, he was already sitting there. He rose to greet me and grimaced. Then he kept touching his chest tenderly through dinner.'

'That's just Jane Dobb syndrome.'

'What?'

'A hammer blow to the heart.'

'Very funny, but I'm serious. I'd have suspected coronary trouble if he wasn't in such good shape. I think he's been wounded and I can't help suspecting it was deliberate.'

'We should ask him. Once we're in on whatever it was your father discovered, we should just ask him outright. If it's anything to do with what began at Cree, I'm pretty sure he'll be prepared to tell us.'

There were two thin folders on Grayling's desk. He was habitually neat and his office Spartan, so Adam could not help noticing a tube of Arnica cream on the desk. He was standing, staring out of the window when they came in. When he turned to them his expression was very serious and he was clearly deep in thought. It took him a moment to realize how wet the walk had left Jane and to offer to take her damp raincoat from her and hang it up to air and dry.

He gestured at the folders. 'This material can't leave this office.

Nor can the contents be freely discussed. You will appreciate why when you've read what is written there. Your father discovered the original, Jane. He found it in the library of a medieval seminary in the French Alps and brought it to me twenty-five years ago.

'Its claims are sensational, by any standards. But I can assure you that the source is utterly genuine. When you have read this, you will appreciate that history is very different from how you assumed it was. And you will have some notion of the nature and scale of the threat we face and some idea about its origin.'

They stood silently in front of him. Adam had never seen the professor look so stern or sound so ominous in tone. He glanced to his right and saw Jane bite her lower lip, staring at the floor. In this mood, Grayling could reduce you to the status of a naughty child. Except that children were never trusted with the sort of secrets they were about to be invited to share.

'The man who wrote what you are about to read was a knight. He was a clever and literate man whose name was de Morey, and people were obliged to call him Sir Robert. But it goes a long way beyond titular status. What you need to know is precisely what, in medieval times, being a knight involved.'

'He would have been schooled in combat.'

'He would, Jane. That schooling would have started when he was seven years old, and from the outset, the weapons would have been edged and the lessons immensely skilled and almost unimaginably brutal. By the age of twenty he would have been a fighting machine, capable of wielding a broadsword through hours of battle astride a warhorse.'

'Formidable, then,' Adam said.

'Terrifying,' Grayling said, 'and also relentless. De Morey adhered to the chivalric code. He was fluent in English and French, the language of the court, and Latin, in which this account was originally written. Apparently he danced and enjoyed poetry. For all I know, he was a dab hand at embroidery too. But he was a killing machine by training and inclination, unquestioningly obedient to his God and his king. Charged with a mission in the name of either, the only thing that would stop him would be death.'

'And he was hard to kill.' Adam was reminded that Grayling had been a soldier himself. Duty was something of which he had a professional understanding.

'Oh, yes. As you're shortly to discover, Robert de Morey was very hard indeed to kill. Sir Rupert, Jane's father, thought that he was a mercenary, though I've found no evidence to support the claim. He was at the call of the Crown. But he was a ruthless warlord who fought decisively in a number of crucial engagements. He fought in France under the Black Prince, his king's son and heir to the throne, at Crécy and Poitier. His name inspired terror. Sight of his coat of arms in the field would breed panic among the enemy. He was the nearest thing the Middle Ages had to a guided missile.'

'And somebody pressed the big red button,' Adam guessed.

'King Edward the Third,' Grayling said, 'an amenable monarch by Plantagenet standards and a ruler who was rightly popular. But he was very hard pressed by the time he called upon de Morey to pursue this peculiar quest.

'This is a contemporary account, and the Black Prince is a name given to Edward of Woodstock after his death. During his life, he was Earl of Chester and then Duke of Cornwall and finally, of course, he was Prince of Wales. But they were friends in youth and de Morey called him Woodstock. I must stress that every word you are about to read is authentic.'

It was the second time he had made that point and Adam knew that Grayling was not a man generally given to repeating himself. Now he gestured for Adam and Jane to sit in the easy chairs facing his desk and handed them a folder each. 'I'll make some coffee while you make a start,' he said. He looked at his wristwatch. Then before he left for the kitchen along the corridor, he unplugged his office phone. Adam opened his folder and focused on the first page, half expecting to hear the jingle of the professor's keys as he locked them in.

The events concerning myself and faithfully recounted here began when I answered a summons from the king received late one evening thirty years ago. I am an old man now, left stiff and ailing from the many wounds endured in battles fought during a long and sometimes turbulent lifetime.

I was young in body when the summons came, and strong. Though I confess my heart was heavy and my spirit listless with grief, having recently lost my wife and daughter to the Great Pestilence. My son was spared and that was a solace to me. I tried to take comfort in the certain knowledge that those

I had lost were now with God. But I missed them. Their absence was a cleaving blow to me. I had nowhere near recovered when the call to duty came.

I was not to present myself at court, the king's courier informed me. In this the command he conveyed was unusual. Unusual it was too, in the further particulars. I was to meet the king instead at the abbey at Bayham, about two days' ride from my own estate. I was to tell no one of my business or destination. I was to travel armed. I was to take no escort. No one was permitted to accompany me, not even my squire. I was to saddle my horse and leave at once. A mission of the greatest import and urgency awaited me.

I delayed only to have my sword sharpened on a whetting stone before ordering my horse prepared and provisioning hastily in the kitchens with my own hands. I made fond farewell to Simon, my son, unsure of when I would likely see him again. I rode away from my castle thankful for the trustworthiness and piety of the household left me after the loss of lives cruelly ended by the recent pestilence.

My journey was unremarkable, though it was saddening to see how depleted lay the country in the aftermath of the plague. I could not count the number of hasty roadside graves I was obliged to pass on the route. The hooves of my horse echoed through empty villages and clopped through untilled fields. There are not the hands to plough. There are not the mouths to feed in order to require the cultivation of crops.

The whole of our land lies grievously wounded. Ashes and scorch marks still scar the land in great circles. They are a reminder that there was no remedy to the pestilence; not prayer, posies, garlands, potions, spells, flagellation, lotions or charms. Fire could not purge it. Only when it had satisfied its own appetite for death did the plague finally desist. We have truly lived through a terrible age and an awful catastrophe.

I arrived at my destination at about noontime of the second day. I recognized men of the king's own bodyguard patrolling about, fully armed, and his personal company of archers was there also, armed with their longbows and with the arrows in their quivers freshly flighted, bright with new feathers in the spring sunlight. I was shown into the presence of the king with sombre deference, and to my great astonishment the archbishop was there too, summoned from Canterbury for our grave and secret conference.

The two greatest men in our kingdom shared a small and modest chamber at the abbey with a third. This man was of Germanic appearance and dress. He did not look to me like a man of gentle birth, but he showed little deference to either of his exalted fellows.

There was a guard at the door but the door itself was of such a stout nature, with such a perfect fit in its narrow arch, that standing outside it he would not have heard a word of our hushed exchange. The light in the chamber was dismal. There was but the one narrow north-facing window, and despite the strength of the sun in the clear sky outside, it was chill in there and candles had been lit of necessity to illuminate the scene.

We conversed in Latin. The commoner was an apothecary from Hanover. The king asked me if I was aware of a notion or theory he described by a word alien to all my past learning. He called this principle *contagion*. I confessed that the idea of contagion was entirely new to me.

'Think of the heat of battle,' the Hanoverian said quietly. 'Think of its tumult and clamour and the way it can inspire fear and fury in equal measure, and the way those feelings are able to spread and find communication without the necessity for a single spoken word.'

And I had it, for I had seen it so often. I well remember the bloodlust at Poitier, the mutilations indulged by our infantry when the battle had lulled and victory was already ours. Bloodlust spread that afternoon through the minds of men with a swiftness that made them seem spellbound.

I have seen it too with fear. Sometimes men cannot govern the terror communicated between them when they are faced by the thunder of cavalry assault. There comes the point when their stand, resolute until that very moment, turns into shared and headlong flight.

'I think I understand contagion,' I said.

'The Great Pestilence was a contagious disease,' the Hanoverian said. 'Men communicating physically with men ensured its spread. Travel and proximity enabled it to flourish.'

I nodded acquiescence. The notion was not quite such a novelty, after all. I had heard of the monastic communities which had isolated themselves against contact with a single stranger for the duration of the plague. And before it ever came upon us, we were all familiar with the doleful warning peal of the leper's bell. What the Hanover apothecary had done was oblige me to consider not the fact of contagion but the speed of it. The speed of the contagion had been the shocking aspect to it.

'How is the contagion achieved? Is it in our sweat? Does it taint our breath?'

'That is not the point, Sir Robert,' the archbishop said.

'Then what is?'

'The source,' said the king.

I confess I had never seen him so solemn in aspect. It was as though the very sun had set in that noble face.

'The pestilence was created deliberately,' the apothecary said. 'I myself discovered the proof of this. The devil that did the work was careless or merely vain enough to leave the evidence behind. Perhaps he thought it would kill anyone who discovered it. But it leaves some people unscathed, Sir Robert. It did not kill me.'

I thought of battlefields and my place on them and the fact that I had always been indifferent in my own self to the contagion of fear. Then I thought of my lovely wife Helena and my beloved daughter Catherine and the breathless swiftness with which they were snatched from life.

But I could not believe the apothecary's claim. I have seen much deliberate cruelty in armed conflict. The evil he was suggesting had been deliberately conjured, though, was beyond my capacity to understand. I could not conceive of a man who would employ the necessary skill and education to accomplish such a violation of nature. It would require such coldness and calculation. It was a sin beyond comprehension, if only because it would condemn he who committed it to certain damnation.

The king smiled at me. He had read my mind. He put his hand on my shoulder. 'You are a noble spirit, Robert. No man faithful to me is braver or more constant. It pains me to expose you to such a cynical and horrid truth. But it is the truth. I will have wine fetched, and bread and meat, and we will tell you the secret with which great men in our world are sometimes forced to struggle.'

Thus did I learn of the existence of the land we do not dare name. Thus did I lean of Endrimor, the mirror world, the realm of blighted magick and antipathy to all we hold dear.

The Hanover apothecary, whose name was Helmut Brandt and who was much more than a mere apothecary despite his unprepossessing dress and churlish manner, showed me on a map the seven gateways of entry. And the archbishop himself told me about the sorcery employed to enable Endrimor's agents to come to do their calamitous dabbling with the destiny of earthly kingdoms.

Hieronymus Slee was either alchemist or physician, depending, Brandt said, on the tavern rumour to which you lent most weight. It was not a matter of great concern. What he certainly was, was the devil who had inflicted the Great Pestilence upon the world. He had created and nurtured the infection on Endrimor and delivered it to Russia, from where it had spread. Brandt's part in his subsequent pursuit was a matter that remained unexplained to me. French and Germanic agents too had hunted Slee but he had eluded them and returned to the mirror-world. The detail of the chase was unimportant. Significant only was the fact of his escape.

'Do they seek our extermination? Is it their ambition to expunge us from the earth?'

The Archbishop answered me. 'They seek to replace us, to usurp us and rob us of our rightful destiny. That is what we think. They seek to reach a tipping point where our spirit is defeated and we descend into chaos; faithless, barbaric and without hope.'

I think my masters chose wisely, when they chose me for the pursuit of Slee to his homeland. I say that not out of consideration for my own martial skills. Nor do I say it because my gateway was close enough to England, a short sea voyage to the desolate coast of Norway.

I say it because the quest offered me an opportunity to exact personal vengeance, absolved of the sin that doing so would usually inflict upon a man's soul. The Archbishop was quite clear on that. A man guilty of Slee's calamitous offence would find no favour with God. There could be no forgiveness.

Endrimor had declared war upon the world and all its peoples. He had put himself beyond salvation. I would find him and kill him in a state of grace. He would meet his death deservedly.

I duly met the men chosen to accompany me on the quest. All of them were familiar to me, veterans of the war against the French, a ferocious company in truth, twelve common soldiers of uncommon skill and spirit. They were gathered in a tent to the rear of the abbey and I was struck again by the grave secrecy surrounding our endeavour.

There were two men missing from the company whom I would have welcomed at my side and I requested them. They were John Ball of Ormskirk and Daniel Rimmer of York, and I confessed to the king that I would be glad of two such steadfast fighters among our party if they could be summoned to meet me in the port of Hull for the voyage.

The king looked at the ground. When he spoke his voice was hushed and his tone marked by humility. 'We sent for both,' he said. 'But both are dead, victims of the pestilence. It has taken its toll on our beloved kingdom, Robert. Of the twenty men we summoned only these twelve remained alive to answer the call. We have assembled the best company these grievous times allow.'

'Majesty, you have honoured me with a party of great strength and enterprise,' I said. I knelt before him and he offered me his hand and I kissed the ring that bears his seal of office. Then I rose and addressed the men. All of them knew me. They would follow me. I had their respect and through our various campaigns together had long justified their faith.

I spent the night in vigil in the lady chapel of the abbey church alone. I spoke to my wife and daughter and prayed to the Almighty for the safe-keeping of my son. I knelt before the altar till dawn and then buckled on my armour and sortied fiercely for better than an hour among the company.

The swordsmanship of common men so often lacks the quality of finesse, but these are the best in the land, skilled and cunning and veteran fighters. The matches were spirited, their mood ebullient, no quarter given so that at the finish all were bruised and some bloody and my own shield cracked and put beyond practical use.

A stream runs through the abbey grounds and the water was clear and cold. We bathed in it to ease the heat and abrasions of combat while our discarded arms glittered in sunlight on the deep green grass and the patrolling men of the king's bodyguard smiled and signalled their appreciation at the spectacle put on for them by our practice. After a hearty breakfast we mounted for the ride to Hull and the start of our strange and clandestine mission of retribution.

We rode hard north-east to Hull through the empty land. Four days it took us to reach our destination. During that time I learned that each of my cut-throats was a devout believer and that each of them had sworn before the archbishop with his right hand resting on the Holy Book that he would never disclose the particulars of our incursion into the mirror world.

A mounted escort awaited us at Hull. We were obliged to tarry on the outskirts of the port while we waited for darkness to descend. Then we clattered forth unseen with the smell of the sea growing stronger in the scouring easterly wind. There was under this wind a strong swell. The waves wore white edgings like fine lace filigrees in the starlight. I was glad the night was clear. The crew was made up of Hanover sailors and they knew the waters through which we would voyage from their constant trade with the Norse Men. But horses are nervous of storms and the swell alone would make them uneasy and skittish in their hold.

We cast off. My spirits were as buoyant as was our sturdy craft. It came to me again how black had been my humour over recent months since the pestilent deaths of my wife and daughter. And it occurred to me once more that Slee's scheme had come very close to achieving the victory over hope that it had been intended to.

As the lights of Hull dwindled at our stern I thought of the final thing the king had said to me when we supped with the alchemist and the archbishop in the gloomy confinement of that cell at the abbey. I had asked should I not bring Slee back to face a court of retribution and the torture which his foul actions had so certainly deserved. But the king would have none of it. He said that to achieve my confrontation with Slee I would need to inveigle my way into the inner court of their king.

'Endrimor is but a single kingdom of a world,' he said. 'They need to have it proven that they are vulnerable in their very heart. Seek him out and butcher him where the palace courtiers cannot but stumble upon his corpse. Kill him painfully.

Make his death an ordeal. Spread his spilled entrails about their marbled halls. Demonstrate to that accursed place that not one of its people is safe from our wrath.'

Sometimes the king could pass for a scholar, so mild can be his manner and so thoughtful the aspect he chooses to show when he displays his public face. He is wise and he is pious. But he committed us to the long war against the French, and he fathered Woodstock, the warrior prince, the scourge of Europe. And at that moment the bloodline made itself as plain to me as the salt in the sea when a wave breaks over the bow and slaps a man cold in the face. I was confident I would carry out my king's command.

My daughter died in my arms. Her mother followed, the pustules stinking on her, the breath of life choked from her by the pestilence, naught but an hour afterwards. Words do not exist in any language to describe the desolation that followed. Only the ordeal of waiting at my sick son's bedside while he strengthened and recovered, kept me from descending into madness. My son required a father in possession of his senses.

I could think of no duty it would give me greater delight to accomplish than that with which I was charged in regard to Hieronymus Slee. I felt at that moment, as the sails above me billowed and the lines grew taut, as the lights twinkled and shrank on the shore behind me and the horses neighed and whinnied under the deck beneath my feet, like a man perished and then enabled by some miracle of providence to be reborn. And I was duly grateful for the miracle.

Grayling observed that Jane completed her reading a couple of minutes before Adam did his. Adam was no slouch, but Jane was a quick study, a very bright girl, as he had truthfully told her father. Yet it was Adam who spoke first, once he had absorbed the last few lines.

'It was a suicide mission,' he said.

Grayling cleared his throat. 'No, it wasn't. It is revisionism of the crudest kind to interpret it that way. The Crusades of the century prior to this one were expeditions far more deserving of that description. They believed in God and predestination and they knew very little about the physical world. They undertook these quests sanguine about their own fates. They were not self-destructive, Adam. They were not intent upon martyrdom. They were brave and ingenious and steeled by fortitude.'

'It might not even have seemed all that remarkable to de Morey,' Jane said. 'They thought the earth was flat and that the sun revolved around the earth. They believed in witchcraft and phantoms and sirens and dragons. But they were telling him the truth, weren't they, his king and the archbishop?'

'They were,' Grayling said. 'Your father came to me a quarter century ago and I denied it. I scoffed at the notion, told him that his thesis concerning germ warfare in the fourteenth century would make him a laughing stock if publicly revealed. But it is all true.'

'And Endrimor exists.'

'You were confronted in the forest at Slee by one of its inhabitants.'

'My half-brother,' Adam said. 'He was my half-brother, Rabanus Bloor. You didn't know that, did you, Professor?'

'I would have worked it out. I'm not stupid.'

'But McGuire has not told you everything.'

'Sometimes we don't know which dots to join,' Grayling said. 'It is not always obvious.'

'I'd like to read the rest of this account,' Jane said.

'I've rationed you deliberately. It is a lot to take in, to accept. Are you sure that you want to read it now?'

'I'd like a few minutes first. Why have we not beaten them?'

Grayling hesitated before answering. He smiled, bravely but without real conviction. 'They are implacable. Their hatred of everything we represent is quite profound. They are very primitive and backward in some ways, but in other, significant ways, they are extremely powerful.

'Where we embraced science and rationality, they embraced magic. And their magic is potent. They can use it to breach our world by coming here more or less at will. We are obliged to use the gateways, and they knew about the gateways and guarded them vigilantly, then we lost their locations. Secrecy is self-nourishing. Over the centuries we forgot where all but one of the gateways were.'

'So the gateways are real? They're not metaphors?'

'All of this is real, Jane. Was the fellow you saw in the forest a metaphor?'

Jane shivered.

'I'm sorry.'

'Don't be. I'm being stupid.'

'Your father found the de Morey account in an atlas compiled in the Middle Ages. Its presence there was a clue. He did not see it, but the atlas itself gave the location of the gateways. They were coded, and I broke the code. It was a breakthrough. I think there are fewer people aware of the mirror or shadow world on earth today than there were in de Morey's time. I think fewer know the truth about the conflict than ever before.'

Adam said, 'You went back for the atlas?'

'I was at the foot of the French Alps on the trail of that book less than twenty-four hours after my scornful dismissal of what Jane's father had discovered.'

Jane nodded. 'What now, professor?'

'I think a short break and then the rest of de Morey's account. After that, I would suggest a trip to Brighton might be a pragmatic excursion for all three of us.'

'De Morey calls that Brandt character an apothecary. Then right at the end, on the brink of his departure for the mirror world, he refers to him as an alchemist. Was that just your scholarly mistake, professor?'

'No, Adam, it was not. I do not very often make scholarly mistakes, let alone errors as sloppy as that one would have been. The translation is entirely accurate. Do you really think a mere apothecary would have had the ear of the king of England and the principle representative in England of the Holy Church of Rome?'

'I'm not an historian.'

'No, you are not.'

'Nor am I a warrior in the mould of Robert de Morey.'

'Not yet.'

'Never in a million years.'

Grayling was silent for a moment, stroking stroked his beard. The rain lashed against the pane of his office window behind him. 'We all of us come out fired from the kiln,' he said. 'We each emerge with the strength or weakness of the clay that formed us. All I can say, Adam Parker, is that I wish more than anything I'd been moulded from the clay that made you.'

EIGHT

McGuire never forgot a face. It was a terrible cliché, but a truthful boast in his case. This alert predisposition to recognize even the vaguely familiar had saved his life on more occasions than he cared to number.

He had spent the first part of a very lengthy adulthood inflicting deliberate and premeditated death on opponents themselves skilled in the cold art of assassination. He did not think his enemies would have forgotten him. He knew that it was entirely beyond them to forgive. He remained careful, having discovered to his dismay that even after many years of relentless physical decline, he valued what was left of him. Having lived longer than any normal man had a right to, he still found he had no urgent wish at all to die.

The stylishly attired young man staring at him from the pier entrance on the promenade was the same person he had seen skulking down below outside his flat a few evenings earlier. He had mentioned him to Grayling in their brief telephone conversation when Grayling had been in Canterbury. Though Grayling had said nothing specific about it, clearly he had been involved in some trouble there.

That was the escalation to which he had referred. He had come through it all right, or he would not have been alive to make the call. His attacker would have come from Endrimor. The youth staring at him now was not from Endrimor, McGuire was pretty certain of that, but he remembered him and thought him almost certainly a part of Grayling's escalation.

The lad was handsome in a neatly featured sort of way. His hair looked expensively cut and his clothes exclusively priced. It was a bright day, early afternoon, and the sun sat at a low angle in a cloudless sky tinted the sullen blue of autumn. He was wearing sunglasses and they looked expensive, too. They should have obscured his expression, but they did not. He looked self-satisfied and secretly amused, a smug pucker around his mouth.

McGuire crossed the road and approached him warily, but not fearfully. What he felt most was curiosity. He carried the precaution of his lethal cane, using it to help propel him over the road. He had an assured grip on its tarnished silver pommel. His survival in hostile circumstances had been no fluke. The weight of the cane at the end of his arm brought him a warm glow of nostalgic pleasure. He had meant what he said to Adam Parker about it having earned its retirement from the fray, but he knew shadow world business when it stared him in the face.

'Good afternoon, Doctor McGuire. Shall we stroll along the pier together? I have a message for you.'

'From whom does it come?'

'It comes from the emissary, Doctor, from the diplomat Sebastian Dray.'

'Ah.' McGuire started to walk along the pier and Martin Prior fell into step beside him. This was a sobering development. He knew Dray from reputation and the reputation was impressive, but diplomacy was not a word in the Endrimor lexicon.

They believed in nothing but their long campaign of undermining and the subjugation it was intended to achieve. Any gesture of mediation from Endrimor had to be a trap. There was nothing to negotiate from the perspective of their opponents in this ancient war, unless it was the terms of earth's surrender. But McGuire would of course listen to what the vain and silly boy beside him had been sent to say.

'Shall we go for coffee at one of those places at the end of the pier, Doctor?'

'You might do me the courtesy of taking those sunglasses off. I like to see the eyes of those with whom I converse.'

Martin did so. In the gleam of the low sun his eyes had an ardent glitter. He did not speak until their coffee was in front of them. Neither of them did. He smiled at McGuire over his cup.

'You seem extremely pleased with yourself.'

'I've been doing some historical research. Have you ever heard of a naval warship called *Incomparable*?'

'That depends. What period are we talking about?'

'The Great War, a period you have good reason to remember all too vividly.'

'If you're going to talk nonsense, I'm going to leave,' McGuire said. He had rested his cane against the arm of his chair. Now he put his hand on the pommel and rose to go.

'Please sit down,' Martin said. 'Allow me to rephrase that.

What do you know about a Great War Royal Naval vessel called *Incomparable*?'

'It was a battle cruiser,' McGuire said. He sat back down. 'They were a class of ship thought up by Admiral John Fisher after his drive and ambition had delivered the dreadnought class into service. They were even more heavily armed than the dreadnoughts and they were faster. But the extra speed was delivered at a price. Three of them went to the bottom of the sea during a single afternoon at Jutland. The loss of life was catastrophic. They had a fatal design flaw. *Incomparable* would have shared that flaw and so she was never built.'

'But if she had been, what would have distinguished her?'

McGuire sipped his coffee. 'She would have been colossal,' he said. 'Twenty-inch guns, thirty-five knots at full speed, fifteen hundred souls crewing her. She would have dwarfed a dreadnought and her fire power and speed would have been superior to anything else afloat. But she would have been lightly armoured amidships, vulnerable where her magazine would have lain under only seven inches of plate steel. It would have been a fatal flaw and so, the harsh lesson of Jutland learned, *Incomparable* was never more than a blueprint.'

Martin smiled and cocked his head to one side. His mouth wore that amused pucker again. 'There are some people who believe that a lie repeated often enough becomes the truth. I've never thought so, myself. I err towards facts and figures, recorded details. I prefer the solid assurance of tangible documentation.

'Of course, if *Incomparable* had been built, the best proof would be the physical evidence. I've done some wreck diving, but that's one wreck I'll never dive. Nor was she ever broken up for scrap. And she has not become a floating museum.'

'That's because she was never constructed. Who are you? What's your name? What's the nature of this message you claim to bring from Dray?'

Martin ignored these questions. 'I've looked at the employment rosters for the naval dockyard in Portsmouth for the whole period over which these mechanized leviathans were laid down, Doctor McGuire. I've scrutinized the wage bills and calculated the manpower requirement and overtime payments, and studied the orders for sectioned steel tonnage and ordnance, and engine turbines and coal, and even rivets. Unless something the size of a large battle cruiser was clandestinely built, there are an awful lot of inefficiencies to account for. The discrepancies are enormous.'

'Your conclusion is absurd. Waste is part of war production. There are always inefficiencies.'

'Of course, the ship was enormous,' Martin said, 'as would have been the casualties aboard her. We must not forget about them.' He grinned, then abruptly got up and left.

He had done his work and done it well, McGuire thought, feeling shaken and demoralized. But he had done it in the service of a master tactician. Dray understood psychology. He could deploy weapons of the mind in the most debilitating way. McGuire rose and gripped his cane. The swordstick seemed to weigh twice what it had when he had set out half an hour earlier, sprightly and alert. He left the coffee shop and made for the painted railings looking out westward over the sea. There, reluctantly, he reminisced.

The last gasp of gunboat diplomacy, Lloyd George had called it. Lloyd George had been no diarist and no writer either. He was an orator and everything he committed to paper was written only in the way it would have played out before a fickle public listening to him as he vented forth from a podium. That was the only criterion by which he measured his words. But McGuire thought that on this occasion, the prime minister had been absolutely right in his withering appraisal of what they had done and in so doing, failed to accomplish and lost.

It had been Churchill's idea. McGuire's personal opinion of Winston Churchill tended towards the positive. Churchill had grown into a considerable and even indispensible leader in war in time for the struggle against Nazism. His Great War apprenticeship, by unhappy contrast, had been characterized by a kind of juvenile impulsiveness. It had proven very costly in the Dardanelles, in the heavy losses of the Gallipoli campaign, and his reputation among the Anzac forces had never recovered from that. But as First Lord of the Admiralty, he had also insisted upon the *Incomparable* deployment. Had history recorded that, Churchill's career really would have been meteoric, bright and brief and fatally extinguished in the void.

In ancient times the people of earth who were aware of the great conflict with the shadow world had charted the seven gateways of entry. Over the centuries, the location of six of these had been lost, but the legend of the eighth gateway had endured down the years. This was because, at least in principle, of the possibilities it invited.

It was located at sea. It was far larger than the rest. Time and tide and atmospheric conditions determined its accessibility. Of course, they had to be correctly aligned. Accessing the eighth gateway was more complex a procedure than plotting its position on a chart. The strategy was, nevertheless, worth persisting with. Because it was at sea, it was difficult to guard. If it could be found and breached, a flotilla could be sent.

In the time before the birth of Christ, legend insisted that the Romans had searched for the eighth gateway, with heavy cavalry, catapults and other engines of siege and hand-picked legions packed aboard galleys, ready to wreak havoc upon the enemy. The conquistadores had searched for it too under their bloodthirsty and plunder obsessed Spanish captain, Cortez. But no one had been successful in finding it.

And then in 1916 a unit of Greek partisans had discovered a Turkish mariner, washed up on a Cretan beach and barely alive. In his delirium this survivor spoke of lightning and a maelstrom, and the subsequent raw intelligence eventually reached a bright Whitehall civil servant seconded to the Assyrian Section.

Confidentially, the dots were joined. Someone who knew about the shadow world was sent eventually to interrogate the Turkish sailor. He was sent because the eighth gate had always been rumoured to be located in the Aegean Sea. What the Turk described – the fog and the golden light of the coastal city he thought he saw beyond its murky folds could not really be accounted for when his position was studied on a chart. That was the real apparent stroke of luck. He had been his ship's navigation officer and the fog had obliged him to calculate their exact position in the moments before the vessel was swamped by a series of massive waves.

McGuire, who had not been called McGuire then, had been the agent sent to interrogate the Turk. It had been almost a century ago, but the navigation officer's eyes had been characterized by the same ardent gleam he had just seen on the face of Martin Prior after insisting the young man remove his sunglasses.

The agent McGuire had boarded *Incomparable* a few weeks after her sea trials and subsequent mothballed seclusion among the inlets of Scappa Flow. The ship was not a resource of naval warfare. Not on earth. Not after the disastrous fate of the British battle cruisers at Jutland. Her armour was too thin; she was a seagoing liability. But the forces of the shadow world did not include torpedo armed U-boats and steel battleships bristling with gun turrets. The theory was that should she cross successfully, her pulverizing fire power would find its target and the great warship, despite her inherent weaknesses, achieve her vindication.

They found the gateway. The fog duly descended. The current strengthened under their hull into a whirling vortex. The waves, when they came, were gigantic. But so was the ship, with her thousand feet of length and 48,000 tons of displacement and the 180,000 horsepower of her engines, and she did not founder.

She emerged instead from this furious, elemental challenge into light and calm on an ocean on Endrimor and the fabled port city of Salabra glistened and preened well within distance of guns with an effective range of close to eight miles. The command was given, the guns were trained and the bombardment started, the steel flanks of the ship shuddering with the careening force of shells propelled towards their defenceless target.

The War Cabinet should never have been told about the shadow world. The secret should have been maintained among the few. Whose decision it had been to share the knowledge generally was a detail lost to time. There had been no cabinet minutes taken. The shared brotherhood of crisis, the camaraderie, had probably been to blame, McGuire thought. But telling men as vain as Lloyd George and belligerent as Churchill about the real cause of the war and the ancient enemy responsible for provoking it was simply foolish.

The first salvos shrieked through alien air. The city in the distance shuddered. The tars raised a spontaneous cheer that thrilled through the ship. Round after round tore through the vacant sky, the shells so enormous that their trajectory could be followed by the naked eye almost on to their target. And the man who had not been McGuire but someone else in that far-off time, studied the golden city they should have been destroying and had his first inkling that all was not as it should have been with their surprise assault.

The more he studied Salabra, the less clearly defined it looked. None of the shells were exploding there. The city in the distance seemed to swallow them. He swallowed himself, saliva acrid with the cordite he was inhaling as it belched forth from the gun barrels. And he realized with a sick lurch in the pit of his stomach that they were looking at a mirage, the illusion of a target.

Sulphur filled his nostrils and his senses reeled. The steel floor juddered under him. The metal sang. Beneath their hull the sea had begun to boil. A sailor passed him along the deck stiff-legged in his blues, walking only from memory, voyaged in his unblinking eyes to some destination from which he would never return. The barrage had stopped. McGuire, who was not then McGuire, looked about him through the thinning mist of their fire. Crewmen no longer toiled over martial tasks. They moved routinely but with the spasmodic stiffness now of marionettes about their purpose.

Escape became his sole imperative. He fingered the stolen charm worn around his neck as a precaution. He knew where they were now and, knowing, realized there was no way back for the great battle cruiser or its company. The illusion of land had become entirely absent, he saw. There was no stretch of coastline at the horizon. Salabra no longer glittered. The port city gleaming proudly in their gun sights had never been there to destroy. They were stranded in a waste of simmering ocean. They were adrift on the Miasmic Sea, that wilderness of enchanted water from which no sailor was ever freed.

He needed to get away. The command to abandon ship would never come aboard *Incomparable*. The captain and his senior officers on the bridge were spellbound, no longer capable of issuing commands. But it was every man for himself nevertheless. He muttered the incantation taught him by the Dowager Countess of Sarth, reciting the words as a dying man might mutter his last, beseeching prayer.

They executed the Turk who had baited the trap. Now it was clear that he had been turned by Endrimor and told God knew what beguiling lie about the reward that would be his in whatever afterlife they had inspired him to believe in. McGuire attended the execution. Its subject died with a smile, the light of anticipation only leaving his hopeful eyes in the moment of death.

That came with the drop and an audible snap of the neck that was no consolation to those gathered in secrecy to witness the event. The loss of the ship was a small thing in the context of the losses inflicted by the war, but the manner of that loss was hard to take. It was difficult to see the fate of *Incomparable* as other than the shadow world's ghastly joke.

'You violated the peace of a tranquil world with a vast weapon of war. Why on earth was the attack sanctioned?'

The words were spoken from behind him. The narcissistic boy

had returned to gloat. McGuire clutched the pier railings, the metal chill against his palms, his cane propped against his leg, a cold winter coming on and feeling every day of his considerable age. 'The tranquil world you speak of provoked the war that brought that weapon into being.'

'You are a liar.'

'Who are you?'

'I was one of Professor Stuart Grayling's students. I won't be going back. He perpetuates the Great Lie, as you do. I won't go back to Cambridge to be peddled myths about our history.'

'Dray told you about the Miasmic Sea?'

From behind him came only silence.

'What do you think happened to *Incomparable*?'

'She sank in a squall.'

McGuire laughed.

'What's funny?'

'I wish she had sunk in a squall, young man. But she did not. She toils still through the water, a vast and rusting hulk, her crew somewhat weathered and threadbare by now, I should think, shuffling as wooden as mannequins through their endless servitude.'

'That's insane.'

'You're an educated young man. You'll have heard of the siren song and the legend of the *Flying Dutchman*. Those myths originated somewhere. They were not dreamed out of nothing. You are right that what I suggest is insane. But Endrimor is a place where madness thrives. And you meddle with the shadow world at your peril.'

'Are you a man fit to speak of peril?'

'What does that mean?'

'Dray said you imperilled your soul when you evoked magic that was not yours to use. He says that doing so has guaranteed you a long life, the span a sorcerer might enjoy, but there will be a reckoning when you die and you have not the means to pay it.'

McGuire released his grip on the pier railings and picked up his cane, aware of the tremor in his right hand as he did so. He tucked the elderly weapon under his arm, resisting the temptation to unsheath the steel and turn and run this impertinent boy through, just to silence his gloating. He felt angry. The truth was provocative as well as painful. But he did not turn. He would not now willingly take another life. He had taken enough of them already.

'Where are you going?'

The light had gone out of the day. Darkness came earlier each afternoon; the nights were growing longer. 'I'm sick of hearing you parrot Dray's platitudes. I'm going home. I suggest you do the same. You might be able to shrug free of whatever enchantment they've worked on you. You'll come to a sorry end if you can't.'

'You won't see out the winter.'

McGuire stopped walking. Still he did not turn. 'Who told you that?'

'Jakob Slee did.'

'Then it is very likely true,' said McGuire. 'My, what company you've been keeping. There is no hope for you at all.'

Martin looked at his watch with a curse mouthed silently because the bloody thing had stopped again. It had not worked properly since his return from the shadow world and he did not share the precise gift he had witnessed there of knowing the hour to the second without reference to a timepiece.

The sea was orange under the descending sun. He breathed deeply of the cool, salty air and looked down, leaning over the railings, at the water rippling beneath where he stood. His watch was justifiably expensive and had functioned perfectly until his return from his recent other-worldly experience. He would send it back to his dad, who would get it repaired or serviced or whatever was done to restore complex mechanical objects. His dad was good at sorting out problems like that.

The sea was deepening to the colour of blood. Martin began to hum. He was unaware that he was doing this, so he was unaware of the tune he was humming. It was the old prog rock anthem he now listened to all the time on his iPod, the King Crimson track 'The Court of the Crimson King'.

There was something strange about the motion of the water below. The waves seemed to be moving backwards, like the mirror image of waves, in rebellious folds of brine that mocked normality and made Martin queasy at their perverse rhythmic retreat. He felt nausea swell in his stomach. Beads of sweat broke out on his forehead. He put his head on the top rail to cool his brow and gasped as bile rose, gushing into his throat. It scalded his nostrils, dripping from his nose on to the boards between his feet. He opened his mouth, leaned out and puked copiously into the sea.

A party waited to greet us when we arrived in Endrimor, and we were greeted in the most furious and hostile manner. Their warriors are tall and strong and, though I record this truth grudgingly, entirely without fear. Their size enables greater reach with a weapon than any among my own party possessed. They have the advantage in cut and thrust.

We also discovered them most skilled in swordsmanship, and with the battleaxe too, and the bow. Most advantageous to them in the fray, the quality they possess above all else, is their hatred of us. They fight with a fierce and gleeful loathing for everything of our world, which they seek only to destroy.

We matched them in strength, and in truth more, for they outnumbered us. But a company of thirteen cannot defeat the armed might of an entire kingdom. Left to the choice I would have fought as outlaws fight, as the terrier worries at the belly of the wolf when the wolf is distracted and its natural malice thereby for the moment diminished. My intent was to lie low and forage, and wait and watch and learn our enemy and how to pass among them while I planned the particulars of the strike. We were not there for the many blows of battle but for the one public and symbolic blow that would end a singular and loathsome life.

The cross is only the start, the alchemist Brandt had cautioned. The pass is the significant thing. The pass follows the cross and if you cannot pass, you will die in the shadow world, go to an unmarked grave there, exiled, obscure and unlamented.

You must copy their speech and manner and dress. You must eat and sleep and live as they do. You must learn even to think as they do to the point where it is as natural to you as your own instinct. You must do all of this, while never forgetting the secret of who you are and the one reason why you are there. Do thus or you will fail.

But I go before myself in the telling of the tale. I have never retreated in the field, but must do so now in my account. Unfamiliar with the construction of stories, I have neglected to detail the particulars of our arrival. The tale is straightforward enough, though. It requires no great craft or imagination to render my truthful recalling of real events. And my memory

of what took place is as sharp as was the edge of my sword
in that long-ago time.

The clear weather held through the second night and the
brisk wind made our progress swift. Fog was sighted by our
Hanover pilot as it began to get light and we found our voyage
had delivered us amid a cluster of islands so numerous as
to be beyond counting. We anchored shortly after dawn in a
thick, befuddling layer of this enveloping greyness. Our horses
were delivered on to the deck and we groomed and saddled
them as they fed from their feeding bags, then we mounted
and a gangway was dropped, splashing into the tide.

'North,' our captain said. His voice was no more than a
murmur as he held the bridle of my horse and raised his eyes
to mine in the grey gloom. 'It lies straight ahead of you. When
the sand turns to grass under the hooves of your mount,
when the mist thins, you are there, sire. Go and may good
fortune go with you.'

We clattered down the gangway and thundered over the
sand. The mist thinned and I felt the firming of the ground
under my mount as the very air changed in scent and texture
with sudden strangeness, and I sensed our deliverance into an
alien land. Then I saw the glimmer of armour between trees
in early light and heard the snort of steeds: a war party
positioned to guard against this rude breach of their world.

That welcoming fight was ferocious. We could let none of
them live beyond the moment to warn generally of our arrival.
Dead men would be missed, but the dead spread word less
quickly than the living. Reluctant to die, our foes were not
shy of killing. The clash of arms was a furious clamour amid
the trees of that small wood, sparks struck with the collision
of steel on steel as blade and mace ball struck breastplate
and helm. Horses whinnied and cried and bled in pumping
gouts of purple where they were cut. The maimed cried out
in pain and panic. I myself cleaved two men almost in half in
their saddles as the tide turned and battle descended into
slaughter.

We duly killed them all. We did so with the loss of four
most excellent men of mine own company. Before slaying the
last of them, a warrior grievously wounded, I listened for a
while to his speech to learn something of the tone and temper

of their language. The sounds seemed sympathetic to the tongue, not a difficult dialect to mimic and learn, I thought, as he cursed us until I wearied of his no doubt blasphemous wrath and performed the clean thrust that silenced him forever.

We burned their bodies on a fierce pyre to disguise as best we could the method of their violent end. But as the flesh melted off their bones, the wounds could still clearly be seen where they had been hacked in places to the marrow by our blows. Our own dead we took away with us.

Brandt had told me very little about the shadow world but did inform me of the whereabouts of the city state from which the land was ruled. There I would find the Court of the Crimson King. And in that treacherous labyrinth of magick and flattery, I would discover too Hieronymus Slee. The city was called Salabra. In relation to the gateway of entry, this city is located 200 leagues to the south. We laid-up until darkness fell and then headed north. We had our dead to bury, a language to master, a disguise to effect before we were discovered and outmanned, and then overwhelmed and slain.

By then we numbered only nine, but the mood among the nine survivors was defiant. We had won a battle and with victory came elation. I did not revel in this myself but was happy to feel its spread among the men I led. It lightened the hooves of the horses under us. It made insignificant the pain of our wounds.

We found a stream where the water appeared clean and untainted and we drank deeply of it and filled the light cask that was all we carried for the purpose, for we had brought with us nothing but the weapons we were armed with and the commitment in our hearts.

We saw no living person, only the odd corpse of men and women crucified at the wayside for the crows to pick over. They were nailed to their crosses upside down. Most curious were the parchments pinned above their pale, blood-drained feet. They bore characters writ bold but of course, we could not read them.

We saw no living thing but woodland birds and squirrels and some scavenging forest creatures, in appearance somewhere between foxes and wild dogs. We shot with bow and cleaned and then cooked various items of game on the spit once we made camp when night had fallen. The dog creatures were both fishy and tough. The birds and squirrels were succulent, their flesh tender and sweet.

The strangeness of the shadow world announced itself at night. Then it truly stirred, roused into a dark life it was a mercy and a curse at the same time to be denied the sight of.

It was on that first night we heard the great avian monsters wheeling through the black skies above us. The wind from their beating wings stirred the grass and stank most foully. Their cries were a ragged, piercing sound, a noise fit for hell itself that woke a sleeping man with a rude start of terror and confusion from his rest. The further north we progressed, the greater the profusion, it seemed, of these flying beasts. Yet it was weeks before I saw one.

What settlements we saw over those first weeks were heavily fortified. We travelled warily and stayed well wide of them. They were scant in number. Sentinels were not posted. At least, we never saw any and I do not believe we were seen. I came to believe that the fortifications were made not as a precaution against mortal enemies but against those great night creatures of which we were becoming more aware the more desolate the land around us became.

We scavenged and stole over those weeks to live but killed no one and destroyed nothing on our quiet northern progress. We had no wish to encourage pursuit. The land was bountiful enough to support life. The population of the shadow world seemed very thinly spread. Even after the affliction of the Great Pestilence, England was more populous.

It made me wonder whether envy might have been the urge that prompted the alchemist Slee in his foul industry. This land did not thrive in people in the way ours did before the plague, and the executions, though plentiful enough, could not themselves account for the lack. It was strange. But not as strange as what was to follow.

Towards the end of the second month, I allowed myself the belief that we had not been followed. We had put substantial distance between ourselves and the gateway through which we had entered Endrimor. I did not know what conclusion had been reached by our enemies about the battle fought there and the charred bodies we had left behind, but there seemed no general panic abroad, and I was sure I would have sensed even the stealthiest pursuit.

We still numbered nine. We had grown accustomed to the country. We had waited long enough for any general alarm to desist. We could achieve nothing more without the language. We needed a trade route, a crossroads. We required some place from which an educated man could be taken and used. I would befriend him and encourage him to talk on the promise of his eventual freedom. When I had learned their language fluently from him, I would kill him. I might do this with reluctance, but we could not imperil our mission and I knew that God would forgive the lie.

We duly discovered our crossroads. I dispatched four men to carry out the abduction. Their ambush did not go well. The caravan they attacked was guarded more heavily than my party supposed. There was an armed escort of four horses and more men concealed in the rear wagon of their train.

Only two of my patrol returned, one mortally wounded and with only hours of life left to him. They brought with them, bound, a native who transpired to be of affluence and education and great and surprising cultural accomplishment. But their hostage was a woman. And to complicate matters, Eleanor Bloor was youthful and comely. I knew the moment I laid eyes on her that I would never be able to do her violent harm.

My force now numbered six. It seemed expedient to go our separate ways. The carnage of the ambush could be neither concealed nor locally blamed, since the bodies of two of my men still lay at the scene as proof both of intrusion and hostile intent. The hunt for us was inevitable. We would be far more conspicuous prey travelling as a single company.

I told my men that they should try to return to the portal from which we had entered the shadow world. I would pursue my quest of vengeance alone. Their prospects of survival and escape were bleak, but none showed it in his face. I swore I would enrich any surviving man on my own return from the proceeds of my own treasure house. Plunder and reward had made me very wealthy and this was no idle boast. Alas, it was a promise that fate denied me honouring.

The attack upon my modest and reduced camp came an hour after I took farewell of my men. I had loosened the bonds securing my prisoner but with no common language between us had not established the terms necessary to release her from the confinement of the ropes binding her hands and feet. I was in the act of raising a cup of fresh water to her lips when she gave vent to a startled cry that warned me of assault.

They were three in number and had approached with not a sound, and their nimble footwork as they fought demonstrated how they were able to glide across the ground in near silence. They feathered the turf with their feet, and their mastery of weapons was prodigiously skilled. I was armed with my sword only.

It is difficult to fend off three without the play of a shield or the distraction of a dagger in your free hand. But these people had contrived the killing of my wife and daughter and they could not match the fury with which I subsequently fought. When I look back now, it is hard not to see myself then as a man possessed by my appetite for revenge. Certainly my anger lent my sword arm terrible strength.

I killed the tallest with an upward backhand stroke that entered his right side between the ribs and cleaved his heart in two. The second I ran through as his one surviving ally, to my astonishment, turned and tried to kill the woman as she knelt bound and helpless on the ground. In the last act of the encounter I pulled free my blade of his companion's flesh and took off his head with a lunging sweep that drenched my poor prisoner in gore. That said, the stroke saved her life, for he had his sword point at her throat and would surely have slain her.

She remained composed. Her tranquillity in the face of blood and murder was almost as astonishing a detail to me as the fact of the attack attempted upon her person. And then the third detail occurred which, of that day's turbulent events, has stayed most vivid in my memory. She spoke Latin to me and in the manner of a woman both modest and gentle. But the inference of her words was ruthless and cruel. She asked me if she was destined to be sold, or sacrificed. Or merely violated, she said.

I untied her, then. I unsheathed a dagger from the belt of the headless corpse at her feet and freed her from bondage. I told her I was not from Endrimor and from the subtle expression of her smile I saw that she had concluded this already. She had knowledge of the two opposing worlds.

'More men will be sent,' she said.

'I will be ready.' It was the simple truth.

'They will know you are formidable when these three do not return. We have a day or two's grace, I would say. Sit down and tell me why you have come to this awful kingdom. I can see from your face and know from your actions that you are noble. Tell me what business summoned you from earth.'

I told her nothing at first. There was a smell of the charnel house about that bloody pasture and so I insisted we leave the spot. We rode a dozen miles or so away from there with her before me astride my horse. Only when the faithful beast grew plodding and fatigued did we eventually stop. Then I asked her about herself. Firstly she told me her name, Eleanor Bloor. Then she told me about the circumstances of her travel at the time my men interrupted the progress of her caravan that morning.

She had been sold into marriage, a reluctant bride. Her hand in this union was the price of an accord between her father and a rival landowner who had long gained the upper hand in their bitter neighbourly feud. Though I said nothing, her account made me wonder what prize her father could have lost that he held to be of greater value than this most handsome and dignified daughter.

'You have not explained why that man tried to kill you.'

'They were assassins. Killing is what assassins do. I warned you of their presence when you pressed the drinking cup to my lips and so they failed. He tried to kill me because I warned you of them.'

'Was not your rescue the point of their presence there?'

'No one yet knows of my absence. Not my father, not the man to whom I am betrothed. Those men were there for you, not me. They were killers marked for the cross, men deprived of their tongues lest tortured if discovered. I do not know for certain, but I am sure that's what they were.

'They were seeking you. They came from the court of the Crimson King. They did not accord you the merit your strength at arms deserves. But if they cannot kill you with steel, they will resort to magick. Travelling north is no strategy for eluding them. They will pursue you to the very border of the Kingdom of Parasites, where awaits a worse death even than the one they would inflict upon you.'

'I do not seek escape, Eleanor Bloor,' I said. And then I told her truthfully of my mission and my strategy for its eventual accomplishment.

'I can help you pass,' she said. 'It will take time for you to learn the language and the customs. You might disguise yourself by growing your hair and beard. You can be costumed in the trappings of the court. If you are clever and brave enough, it might be accomplished. Already I think that you have the courage for the task.'

'Why would you help me?'

She was silent after I put this question to her for such a long moment that I did not think she was going to reply to it at all. 'We can assist one another,' she said eventually. 'We can hold one another to a bargain of sorts. I wish for my father and my intended husband to think me dead.

'We shall travel north together. I will not go further than the forest that guards the Parasitic Kingdom. I will not venture to where the Miasmic Sea laps at the edge of the land with the lure of enchantment. But while we travel, you will be my escort and guardian and I will be your teacher.' She laughed then, a liquid sound, the sweet splash of a pebble in a brook. 'And nobody shall know of our arrangement.'

'Why would you help me? Is to do so not treasonous?'

'I am one of those who would like to pass to earth,' she said, 'and not for the purpose of assassination.' She looked wistful. 'We cannot choose our worlds. But we can choose in ourselves those virtues to which we are loyal.'

'Where did you learn to speak and comprehend Latin?'

'It was my father's secret indulgence when I was the child for whom he still cared. It is a crime to learn earthly tongues on Endrimor. Though of course, most of the court is fluent in your principle languages.'

'Who taught you?'

'Someone killed since for the crime of the teaching. You may have passed him on your journey. He hangs from one of the crosses. A parchment above his nailed feet declares the nature of his offence.'

'I could not have read it. I lack the knowledge.'

'Knowledge I will give to you.' She stood. We had been seated on the ground. 'Come,' she said. 'Let me bathe and dress your wounds.'

'They are merely flesh wounds,' I said.

'No, they are not. I felt you wince behind me in the saddle as we rode. Let me help heal them.'

'Can you accomplish magick?'

She paused. 'It would do you more harm eventually than good. It would not be worth the price you would be obliged, when your time finally comes, to pay for its assistance.'

I had only said what I had in jest but could see she was entirely serious. She looked around at the fertile land about us. 'I shall make you poultices from herbs,' she said. 'The pain will lessen once they are applied and the healing will begin. Have you lost much blood?'

'Other encounters have cost me more.'

'Men,' she said. And she laughed again. 'In some ways you are all the same.'

Jane Dobb stopped reading. She was forced to, because she had come to the end of the new pages Grayling had provided them with. 'I can't believe you've done this to us again,' she said. 'Talk about dragging it out.'

'I want to know you are taking from it what you should,' Grayling said. 'I need to know that you appreciate the implications and importance of this material. It is a primary source.'

'De Morey speaks with an authentic voice,' Adam said. 'You just don't get that contrast between brutality and grace in the modern character. He's hacked six people to death so far but he's so lonely and traumatized by his own grief, he's on the point of becoming besotted with a woman he's taking totally at face value.'

'God, you sound exactly like Martin would,' Jane said. 'Eleanor Bloor was obviously principled and intelligent and totally deprived of the independence she craved by the feudal circumstances in which she was trapped.'

'Her surname is intriguing,' said Adam. 'I'll give you that.'

Grayling said, 'De Morey was raised according to the chivalric code. It did not give him a great deal of choice in the way he behaved towards a woman of noble birth such as Eleanor was.'

'That's a fair point,' Jane admitted.

Adam nodded his head vigorously.

Grayling raised an eyebrow. 'Having said which, he does seem to have fallen rather hard for her.'

All three of them were silent. Then Adam said, 'Are you both familiar with the term ring-rust?'

'It sounds vaguely obscene,' Jane said.

Grayling said, 'It sounds self-explanatory to me. What's your point?'

'King Edward could not conceivably have committed a large force to this mission of retribution. He couldn't spare the soldiers. The plague would have depleted the army as much as any other sector of society and besides, England had a war with France to prosecute. So he sends a champion, probably the best he's got excluding his own son.'

'I wondered that. I wondered if he ever thought about sending the Black Prince,' Jane said.

'No,' Adam said. 'He needed Woodstock's generalship for the war with France. He was not available.'

'Good,' Grayling said. 'You show signs of having a brain after all. Go on.'

'The warriors of Endrimor are physically bigger than their opponents from earth. They are very skilled with the weapons of the period. And yet they're bested by de Morey. That's where my ring-rust theory comes in. You can spar as many rounds as you like in the gym, but you're doing it in eighteen-ounce pillowcases compared to the six- or eight-ounce gloves laced on to your fists for a fight. Impact, timing, urgency, spiteful intent – everything is different. There's no substitute for the real thing and de Morey and his company were battle-hardened.

'My point really is about the effect on Endrimor their apparent invincibility must have had, so soon after the Black Death and earth coming so close to complete breakdown. The shock of de Morey's victories against them must have been seismic. They must have shaken even the court in Salabra.'

'In the scheme of things they are very small victories.'

'Not symbolically, they're not, Professor.'

'You are assuming efficient lines of communication.'

'In a place so authoritarian that criminals were publicly crucified on a mass scale? I'm assuming some kind of network of spies and informers. They would have found out and put two and two together.'

'I agree with you,' said Grayling. 'De Morey's progress would have shocked them.'

'Can we read the rest of it?'

'I'll fetch the pages for you now, Jane.' He frowned. 'By the way, has anyone seen Martin Prior? He seems to have disappeared off the face of the planet.'

NINE

I took my leave of Eleanor Bloor after three months and I confess with a sorrowful sense of loss. We resided for most of that time in a modest hut at the heart of a forest close to the Kingdom of Parasites. I felt we were safest in the great northern wood of all places while I practiced the craft that would allow me to pass undetected into Salabra and the court of the capering despot the land we do not dare name endures as its king.

We ate what we could catch and the bounty was plentiful. We caught game with traps such as the keeper on my father's estates taught me to make for amusement when I was a boy. I fashioned a bow from a branch of a tree similar to yew in its properties and Eleanor Bloor proved to be a most excellent shot, once I had made and flighted arrows and schooled her in the weapon's use.

Elsewhere, she did the teaching as she made me conversant and then fluent in the language I aspired to learn from her. It somewhat resembled Greek in its grammar and was not arduous to master fully. English possesses many words because the English are so passionate about speech. They are countless, growing all the time, filched from other tongues or merely invented. This language, by contrast, contained a paucity of them.

The great bird I had heard in the night when I travelled with my lamented company I learned was called a Vorp. They are carnivores and kill and mutilate for sport. They are avian monsters, in truth, as I earlier speculated.

A skilled and bold rider might kill one with a lance, blessed with great good fortune on the open plain. But they are predator, not prey. They did not frequent the forest, where the vast span of their stinking wings means they cannot practically put down to kill. So we were spared their rapacious sound in the nights.

We saw no men in the forest, either. The legend of the parasites deters them, Eleanor told me. Men of Endrimor will not willingly pass so close to the border with the Parasitic Kingdom and the dark fate awaiting them should they be taken there.

She assured me the legend was true, and once or twice at twilight I felt the velvet chill of one watched from seclusion and knew I was not abroad in the forest alone. But we did not stray out after darkness fell, and the fire was kept brightly stoked and fierce till morning with burning embers. I slept with my sword laid beside me, always vigilant to attack.

I wondered often at the truth of why they had not followed me. The legend of parasites seemed insufficient reason, however loathsome those creatures if they existed at all.

I felt that some or all the men of my company to whom I had been obliged to bid farewell, would have been captured since and put to the torture. They knew of only the one gateway leading home. Even if any of them should have reached it, it would surely have been guarded in even greater strength than before. They had not known of the nature of my mission but would have been pressed into surrendering the name of the man who led them.

'They might think you dead,' Eleanor said when I pondered this question aloud. 'You left behind the corpse of the man wounded in taking me. You left two dead at the scene of the taking.'

'Commoners,' I said, 'leaders neither in aspect nor dress. They would not have been mistaken for someone born gentle.'

'They might still think you dead,' she insisted. 'You were sorely injured in the affray with the assassins. They might think you died subsequently of your wounds.'

'But I did not, thanks to you,' I said.

Her modesty caused her to bow her head and blush at this compliment but I had only said what both of us knew to be true. Thanks to her ministrations I felt stronger than before the infliction of my injuries.

'They will wait for you,' she said. 'They are watchful and implacable and they are patient.'

'They are patient, madam? They do not seem so in the field.'

'They have the luxury of time, Robert. Their mortal span is above that which a man can expect to enjoy on earth. Where you are concerned, time is on their side.'

I nodded. The time had come and both of us knew it. My hair and beard had grown to make me unrecognizable to all but a few of my intimates. I carried a sword weal across my cheekbone that had not been there before. Few alive on earth but my son and perhaps my king would have known me at once, without shrewd study.

And I spoke the language I had come to learn fluently. I could think and sometimes even dreamed in it. The time had come and it was a moment thick with melancholy because it signified our parting.

She could travel no distance beyond the forest outskirts with me. Capture with me on the route to Salabra was too great and foolhardy a risk. It would lead to her crucifixion. I was confident I could pass but there was no guarantee of it. She was safer alone. In open ground, her expertise with the bow would deter any hostile approach. She had become a most accurate shot and I did not doubt had the fortitude to kill a man if necessary. Moreover, Endrimor was not England, hazardous with outlaws and banditry. The crucifixions deterred such petty acts of crime; Eleanor had told me so herself.

I escorted her to the edge of the forest and there took my leave of her. She had given me much to be grateful for. She had healed me and taught me and blessed me with her companionship. I would spend one more night in our modest accommodation and then in the morning take the route south myself.

I would be on foot, having gifted Eleanor my horse. I had buried my helm and shield and my armour too. I had kept only my sword to remind me of my true nature and status in the world from which I came. It was enough. I had not forgotten my purpose and would accomplish it now or die attempting to do so.

'This isn't ringing true,' Jane said. 'Where are you up to?'

'He's sleeping with his sword in their shelter in the forest,' Adam said.

'God, you're a slow reader.'

'I'm wondering if it was all he was sleeping with.'

Grayling made some sound in his throat but whether of approval at this suspicion or disgust, was impossible for Adam to judge. 'I stand by my belief that he was emotionally vulnerable, professor. It isn't revisionism to think a man in the Middle Ages prey to human feeling. This woman saved his life and he had lost his wife and daughter to the plague, and we know from his own words that she was physically attractive. The king had commanded him to kill a shadow world alchemist.'

'The greatest mass murderer in recorded history,' Grayling said.

'Granted, but it wasn't stipulated anywhere that he had to carry out the job celibate.'

'Except that Eleanor would have had her say in that,' Jane said. 'We know de Morey was brave and principled, but he could have been physically repulsive. Do we have any idea what he looked like, professor?'

'There are surviving likenesses,' Grayling said. 'He looked pretty much as I think one would have expected him to. He would have had Millais and Rossetti and the like very hot under the collar, I should think. Fair, is the expression they would have used in contemporary accounts. Robert de Morey was exceedingly fair, even before that rather dashing facial scar he's just acquired in the story. What isn't ringing true, Jane?'

'Just saying goodbye to her like that. It has the feel about it of abandonment.'

'Maybe he's simply liberating her.'

'It doesn't read like that, though.'

'He has his duty to perform. Nothing can impede or obstruct it. It's the reason for his being there. It's the reason for his existence. Without it, he is nothing.'

'Yes, I suppose.'

'Please read on, both of you.'

They came for me in the night. I became alert to some subtle alteration to the material world in the still darkness beyond the door of that forest abode. There was no noise. They did not disturb a single nocturnal creature. They did not snap a twig on the ground or stir a rustling leaf, for it was autumn in the forest now and nature was in decline.

I smelled an odour, faint but no less sickening to the spirit for its slightness. That was the only clue offered my exterior senses, but the hairs stood proud on the backs of my hands and prickled the nape of my neck in a warning both fearful and somehow dreadful to me. It was as though danger mingled with the basest despair in some abject trick of alchemy.

When I opened wide the door I did so on a silent multitude of still figures assembled patiently there in the darkness. They were the parasites of legend and they were legion. Their hunger, or more truthfully their thirst, was a devouring pull held wilfully in check, like some sucking breeze that plucked at clothing and flesh. They were black-clad in monkish habits and their heads were hooded and I could not see their features in the dismal absence of light. I had the curious sense that their scrutiny was blind.

This impression was confirmed when one of their number approached. He raised three-fingered hands tipped with black talons that were truthfully more like the claws of some scavenging beast. He pulled back his hood. His head was entirely bald and misshapen and the only feature it possessed was a maw, like the sucking orifice from which a lamprey depends, feeding on the fishy flesh of its unfortunate river host.

I confess the sword felt useless in my hand. The great temptation was to imagine myself in the sleeping grip of nightmare. But I knew I was not. I could feel the rough boards of the floor under my bare feet and the cold weight of the weapon I held.

I would fight. They were too many and I would be overwhelmed. My death would be quick and savage though I did not fear it, determined to account for as many of these nocturnal monsters as I could in the quickening fray. But I had failed my king. Hieronymus Slee would escape retribution. My wife and daughter would go unavenged. It was a conclusion to my quest as miserable as it was strange. I breathed deeply of the tainted forest air and raised the blade I held firmly in both hands before me.

And the creature before me raised its own horrid hands in a gesture of supplication. All of them did, as one, with a rustle of the rough hessian they wore to cover the obscene sight of their stinking flesh. I saw with amazement that they meant me no harm.

The offence of them lay in their look and their odour. They possessed no violent intent. The leading creature gestured with a finger and I saw that they wanted me to accompany them.

The thirst they shared for me had not abated. I was aware of its deep, unsatisfied strength. They were acting not on will but from duty, as wild beasts brought cruelly to subjugation by a skilled trainer for entertainment at a fair.

They led me to a tent. I saw this structure as the dawn broke in a clearing in the trees that gave on to open ground. We were obliged to cross a wooden bridge over a stream to gain the tent. There was no sound of birds singing to greet the morning.

The fabric of the tent rippled in a stiff breeze and my spectral escort melted away from me. They diminished in number rapidly, as the last grains of sand will rush down the aperture of an hourglass in the moment before you tip it over to record the time to come.

I could not have said where it was they went. They were there and then they had gone and I was alone before the striped livery of the large cloth structure dominant on the field. It was a generous width and the height of two tall men, this construction of timber-framed cloth. It was boldly coloured in purple and gold and its lavishness suggestive of nobility and wealth.

A man emerged from the tent. He was a little taller than I, dark and bearded, and the beard was carefully trimmed and his hair longish and smoothly combed. He was altogether fair in appearance.

So soon after enduring the grotesque company of those who had delivered me there, any mortal man might have appeared pleasant in aspect. But the count of Sarth, as I was to come to know him, was a man well-made in every particular. He was finely attired, and a dagger with a jewelled hilt hung in an embossed sheath from his belt. Yet I felt no martial threat from him. Had he wished me harm, his eyeless acolytes could have accomplished that long before the coming of daylight.

'Noble friend,' he said. 'I have followed your progress, intrigued. Will you breakfast with me? Will you tell me of your earthly ambitions for the benighted kingdom to the south?'

For a moment, so startled was I at what he had learned that I did not identify the language in which his words had been spoken. And then I did. And my delight at hearing my own tongue swiftly delivered sorrow to my heart at how long I had been away from home on this most curious odyssey of vengeance. I missed my own warm hearth and my own bed and the familiar fields of my own domain, and before all, of course, I missed Simon, my fine, strong and most beloved son.

'Where did you learn to speak English, sir?'

'I learned the tongue in England, the land from where you come.'

'How did you come by this knowledge you have of me?'

'Your armour and the saddle of your horse were of the English style. The length of the bow you made for the lady who accompanied you suggested archery in the English tradition. These are compelling clues.'

'You have been observing me?'

'I have had you observed, a paltry distinction.'

'Those creatures have no eyes.'

'No, sir. But there is more than one way of seeing.'

'How did you tame them?'

He looked at me for a long moment, then glanced at the sword buckled to my side. He stroked his beard and smiled. 'Break your fast with me. I will undertake to answer the questions you have. But it must be an honest and just exchange, sir, for I require answers also of you.'

I nodded and followed his invitation into the tent. I am sometimes rash to judgment, impulsive, headstrong in forming opinion. But despite the vile company he kept and the curious nature of his earlier summons, I confess that I liked the count of Sarth from the first moment of our encounter.

He did not strike me as a kind or necessarily merciful personage. There was in truth a glint of cruelty in his eye. But there was courage and amusement in him and I had felt the lack of both qualities most keenly. I had missed more than I had realized the company of considerable men. The count, I knew at once, was one such.

His table was elaborately laid. Autumnal fruits were piled ripe on silver plate and there were loaves of fresh bread and butter newly churned and cheeses and aromatic pies. I had subsisted long in the forest on rabbit and fowl, and sour berries and scarce wild vegetables boiled and near flavourless. It was a feast the count provided and I ate as heartily as any man would, only a night march from accepting that the moment of his death had come to call.

'How did you tame them?'

'They are not tamed,' he said. 'They are trained. I make their lives easier and so they accommodate my family and me. They serve.'

'You have their loyalty.'

'They are loyal only to their own appetites and needs.'

'Then you have their gratitude.'

'You fail to understand,' the count said. 'They tolerate servitude because I am able to satisfy their thirst. Were I to stop, you would soon see how loyal to me those creatures are.'

'Why do you tolerate them?'

'They keep me safe,' he said simply. 'Their legend is fearsome and well founded too. Were it not for the fear they inspire and the protection they provide, the Crimson King would send assassins from Salabra and I would be dead and my family and household slaughtered with me.'

'Why would he do that? In what manner have you offended him?'

The count looked at me for a long moment. 'Do you really not know?'

'I know little of Endrimor beyond the language. I am ignorant of its politics and history.'

'He would kill me because I am his brother.'

'I still do not understand.'

'I am his elder brother, sir. I am the rightful heir and the Crimson King a mere pretender.'

'Yet you do not rule. You do not even rule the parasites.'

He laughed loudly at that. He slapped his thigh with mirth at the bitter truth of the jest. 'Your lack of tact suggests the soldier more than the diplomat. But I knew that about you. Word of your prowess with the sword has spread even unto this baleful corner of our world.'

He lived in exile. That was his true situation. He had material comforts and the parasitic creatures provided him with some measure of security, but he was divorced from the place and status rightfully his. I did not pity him and it was evident to me he had no pity for himself. I wondered why he had summoned me there. I also wondered what to tell him when he asked about my rude presence in the kingdom that had been robbed from him. As I had with Eleanor Bloor, I knew I would elect to tell the count of Sarth the truth.

When I had finished telling him, he was silent for a while. It was a brooding silence but possessed no menace towards my person. The count was a sometimes dangerous man familiar with malice and capable of the darker furies, I was certain of that. But I was not his enemy and suspected his feelings towards me not dissimilar from mine towards him. Outside the sun rose in the clear sky and the tent warmed pleasantly within. Serving maids came in and cleared our spent dishes before he spoke again.

'Their pestilence was a decade in the planning. I am sorrier than I can say for the loss of your wife and daughter. I hope with all my heart you will live to see your son again, but I do not think that you will. I have little doubt you can inveigle your way into the court and even less about the fate of my brother's alchemist should you succeed. Sadly, though, I do not think you will escape Endrimor after you have slain Hieronymus Slee. It grieves me to say it but the seven gateways will be guarded vigilantly and in some strength. You would require the army you do not travel with to breach one of them.'

I nodded. I had anticipated this. But I think what I said next surprised my host entirely. 'What about the eighth gateway?' I asked him.

'Where did you learn about that?'

'In a bleak cell set in a chill cloister at an English abbey. I was told about it by a man who claimed to be an apothecary. His name was Brandt.'

'He was a liar, if possessed of that knowledge he claimed that lowly occupation.'

'Perhaps he was. But I believe he was telling the truth about the gateway. He told me it cannot be impregnably guarded because it is to be found on the open sea.'

In his breast pocket, Adam felt his mobile phone begin to vibrate. He had silenced it to incoming calls but when he sneaked a glance at the display, he knew that this was one he would have to take.

The call came from Rotterdam and Delilah's harbour bar. He looked apologetically at Grayling before rising and taking the call out in the corridor, leaving the file he had been reading on his chair and shutting the professor's office door behind him.

'Adam? I think your father's time has come.'

Adam ran a hand through his hair. 'I thought he had weeks?'

'The prognosis in such cases can never be exact. He is weakening rapidly and he is asking for you. You are all that he is asking for, your presence here.'

Was there a note of bitterness in her voice? He did not think that there was. She sounded only urgent, grave. He would have to leave immediately. He still had more than 200 Euros of McGuire's expenses money in his wallet. Perhaps someone, Jane or Martin, would give him a lift north to the ferry terminal.

He had not seen Martin in days. Grayling wanted Jane and Adam to go with him to Brighton. The dying never met death at a time convenient for those they left behind. He felt his eyes fill with tears. 'I'll be there as soon as I can,' he said into the phone, before severing the connection.

Returning to Grayling's office, he explained the situation to Jane and the professor as briefly as courtesy allowed.

Grayling nodded. He rose and took the file from Jane's fingers and the loose papers from Adam's chair.

'I can read it aboard the ferry.'

'No, you can't. This material does not leave this office. You don't drive, do you, Adam?'

'No.'

'Jane?'

'I'm a pretty good driver but I've never driven a Land Rover.'

'Nor are you about to start, far too slow.' He took a set of car keys from a drawer on his side of the desk and slid them across the polished wood. He coughed, 'I've a mid-life crisis vehicle that will suit perfectly. It's a predictably racy little sports model. You'll find it in the long-stay car park.

'It's a green Lotus, near the west entrance on the first floor. A few clicks of my computer mouse will insure you to drive it, Jane. For God's sake don't crash. I value my no claims bonus almost as preciously as I value avoiding litigation with your father.'

'Thank you,' Adam said.

Grayling waved away the sentiment, unwilling to meet his eyes. They reached the door.

'Adam?'

'Yes?'

'If you forgive your father, tell him so. If you love him, tell him that also. Don't let misplaced pride consign you to a lifetime of regret over what you did not say.'

And now he did look and his eyes were coldly blue and appraising.

'I won't,' Adam said. 'Thank you.'

Jane was at the wheel of the car with the engine running when she said, 'Where's your passport?'

'It's in my pocket. I only got back this morning. You met me at the station, remember?'

'God, it seems like a lifetime ago.'

'The world is a different place from what it was then. And we've travelled a long way back over the last couple of hours to have that proven to us.'

'You believe it all?'

'Your father wasn't stupid. He knew it was true when he found de Morey's account a quarter of a century ago. Grayling wouldn't have bothered concealing a forgery. He hid it because it was real and has only exposed us to the truth now because he has had to.'

Jane put the car into gear and released the clutch and Adam felt the power of the race-tuned engine as the acceleration pushed him back in his seat. 'We're sitting about four inches off the ground,' he said. 'Does this thing have any suspension at all? There isn't even a radio.'

'Grayling provides his own music. He sings to himself,' Jane said.

'I know. You told me. Coldplay.'

She turned her wrist and looked at her watch. 'I hope you get there in time.'

'I'm praying I do.'

They were a few miles clear of Cambridge before Jane spoke again. 'Grayling hasn't told us the whole truth,' she said. 'And neither did de Morey. He prepared Eleanor Bloor for the cross, didn't he? He coached her for earth, as she prepared him for his mission on Endrimor.'

'That's my interpretation too,' Adam said. 'De Morey was terrifying in a fight but there's another side to him along with the ruthlessness. He wasn't a psychopath. He was sentimental and loving. He was a widower who did not want to be without intimacy in his life. The key to it is that he thought he was going to succeed in his mission. He wanted to be reunited with Eleanor and he thought that she could successfully pass and it was a realistic ambition.'

'I think it was a bit more noble and selfless than that,' Jane said. 'But he definitely connived in her escape and by the time of their parting, he had probably come to love her.' She glanced from the road at Adam. 'Sometimes you can fall for someone very quickly.'

'And she didn't need a gateway, like he did. They use sorcery to cross to here. And she hinted that she was capable of magic after the affray with the assassins left de Morey badly hurt.'

'Does Grayling think we're so dumb we can't see the sub-text?'

'No, he doesn't,' Adam said.

'He might where you're concerned. The speed you read at would give most normal people serious doubts. Have you ever thought about the possibility of some kind of remedial therapy?'

Adam smiled at her teasing. But his mind was on Rotterdam and his ailing father.

They drove in silence for an hour. Jane was a fast and confident driver and the car was very quick. Eventually she said, 'Does the count of Sarth seem familiar to you? In de Morey's description of his appearance and character, I mean.'

'He's a younger version of the professor. They're the same type of man, physically and temperamentally. But de Morey isn't the most reliable of narrators, is he? He perjures himself on the subject of Eleanor Bloor.'

Jane was quiet again. The road unfurled before them. Night had descended. 'It might be the whole point of the deposition,' she said.

'What might?'

'I can't think of any other reason for his having written it. De Morey was a cultured and intelligent man, but he was a warrior, not a scribe. He seems to me to lack the personal vanity to bother to record a memoir detailing his feats in the shadow world. Maybe it was written to be discovered and believed by those sent to pursue Eleanor and punish her for the crime of crossing.'

'Or take her back,' Adam said.

'Either way, it would make sense, everything in the account written truthfully to conceal the one lie contained within its pages.'

'What a devious mind you have.'

'There's an old teacher I know,' she said. 'He's retired now, but he's very patient.'

'So?'

'I just thought he might be able to help you, that's all. I mean, with the reading thing.'

Adam yawned. 'Just so long as his name isn't McGuire,' he said. He thought about the artefact he had discovered in the forest, how, confronted with it little more than a week ago, he had thought that it might make him famous and rich. Now it resided in a locked cupboard in the old doctor's flat in Brighton and he did not care in the slightest what happened to it. Shortly after reaching this conclusion, he dozed off in his seat.

Jane drove. From time to time she looked at the young man asleep beside her. She didn't feel tired. She didn't think Adam had either. Sleep was a refuge for him from concern about the father he had just found and was shortly to lose. But she thought that he would need his sleep. She sensed the uneasy quickening of events. She had a name now for the man she had seen in the forest at Cree. He was called Rabanus Bloor and he was half-brother to Adam and he meant nothing but harm if the look of naked malice on his face was any guide.

She looked at the motorway lights, at the bright passage of high performance cars and the careening juggernauts and the dot matrix displays of information spelled out in red on steel and concrete gantries above the three pulsating lanes of rapid traffic. And she wondered at what it would take to bring it all crashing to a silent halt. Not much, really. The world was so complex now and so relatively small.

Chaos had been caused in the static universe of earth in the fourteenth century by a plague virus. It would be much easier now to provoke war and disease and to crush hope. Mankind was less fatalistic than it had been then, more fractured and agnostic. Faith was a virtue in short supply and the painful chronology of the planet did not inspire much optimism.

'We're ripe for it,' Jane said, to herself. 'And they bloody well know we are.'

Grayling travelled to Liverpool pretty much on a whim. His students had plenty to do in the aftermath of the dig, and his return from Scotland, earlier than scheduled, meant that he had no seminars or lectures planned until the following week.

He caught the train. The express was much quicker than the Land

Rover, and he could use his laptop and so avoid the journey being a waste of time. His destination was only a mile's walk beyond the Liverpool terminus at Lime Street Station. Aboard the express, he took a call from McGuire that explained where Martin Prior had got to and why. He had phoned McGuire from Canterbury to warn him that matters were accelerating, but the news concerning Martin still came to him as a shock.

It meant that this latest tilt at the world was gathering momentum. It meant they were comfortable with breaking cover. It signified confidence.

It was eight o'clock in the evening when he reached the port city of Adam Parker's birth. He walked to where his student's old boxing gym was located. The streets here were still, some of them, cobbled. The houses were terraced. The street lights were scant and the howl and barking of stray dogs a constant and threatening soundtrack, given the breeds favoured by the residents of the broken dwellings Grayling walked among.

The gym was an old factory workshop. As Grayling approached, he could hear the slap of leather against the floorboards as boxers skipped. He could catch the smack of the hook and jab pads and the thud of the heavy bags being hit. Closer to the door, he could smell sweat and leather and embrocating cream.

He pushed open the door. There were a dozen or so boxers going through their separate routines. Two were sparring fiercely in a training ring. Bags of various sizes and shapes hung on chains suspended from metal beams in the low ceiling. All of them seemed wrapped and patched and fortified by as much broad black sticking tape as remaining leather.

It was very hot. There were strip-lights screwed to the ceiling and their illumination was white and harsh. The ages of the boxers ranged from late teens to early thirties. It was an environment in which boys became men or failed to. Its rules were unbending and its regime tough and Grayling thought that altogether, he rather approved.

He was ignored until a four-minute clock on the wall clanged the end of the round and the minute of respite it gave. Boxers always trained in rounds, Grayling remembered. They skipped and even did their floorwork to the dictates of the clock.

'Can I help you, mate?'

'Are you Mick Yates?'

'You plainclothes?'

Grayling smiled and took out his university accreditation 'I'd like to ask you a few questions about one of my students. His name is Adam Parker.'

'Clever lad. Is he in bother?'

Grayling sighed. 'Does every conversation one has in Liverpool have to involve the law? Is it somehow obligatory?'

Mick Yates smiled. 'Mostly football talk is obligatory in this part of the world, professor,' he said. 'But I've no interest in that. And when someone comes here in a suit, it's usually because one of the lads has got off the lead, or gone on the lash, and it's ended in tears. Come to my office and I'll make us a brew and fill you in on Adam Parker.'

Yates's office was a sort of hut on stilts in the far right-hand corner of the gym, reached by a narrow staircase.

'Great lad, Addie,' Yates said, sitting and inviting Grayling to do the same.

'Addie?'

'What we all called him.'

'But it's not even an abbreviation. Addie is no easier to say than Adam.'

'No one called him Adam. Maybe his mum did – far too formal for us. This is a friendly environment.'

'Your friendly environment is somewhere people come to get hurt. Sometimes they get maimed.'

Yates shrugged. 'You'll get no apology from me for the contradictions of boxing. I'll leave the philosophizing to the educated likes of you, professor.'

'What kind of boxer was Adam Parker?'

Yates appeared to ponder this question for a long time. 'Problematical,' he said eventually.

'Glass chin? Fragile hands?'

Yates smiled. 'No real interest in boxing was probably at the heart of it. He just wanted to get the other feller out of there as quickly as he could. And he generally did that. In fact, he always did that. None of his bouts went beyond a round.'

'So he was a big puncher?'

'Not really. I mean, he could punch, don't get me wrong. He was a correct puncher, great balance, sound technique. It was his hand speed that was the wonder. He was phenomenally quick.'

The one window in the cheap wood of Yates's office was smeared with condensation. Grayling reached across and rubbed it clear, then looked down at the muscular young men going through their ritualistic drills.

'Good fighters almost never get caught cleanly,' Yates said. 'Watch them. Even when they get hit hard they are almost always sliding off the punch, taking the momentum out of it with head movement that comes from instinct and anticipation, from reading their opponent. You couldn't do that with Addie. The lads he tagged said it was like being hit flush with a lump hammer.'

There was a silence between the two men.

'Where do you stand on David Attenborough?'

'I'm a fan,' Grayling said. 'I love wildlife films. Is there any point at all to that question?'

'Have you ever seen a panther or a cheetah snatch at prey? He was like that, was Addie. He was that quick.'

'Why was that problematic? Didn't he rack up the wins?'

'We couldn't train him. He always went to war. Too much devil in him once the bell went. Lovely lad outside the ring, but he couldn't hold back. Addie kept knocking his sparring partners spark out. If he wasn't such a sweet-natured kid, I'd say God put him into the world to hurt people. I'd say that was his vocation, the task he was born for.'

'Maybe it is.'

'He fenced as well, you know. Not garden fencing, I'm talking about swords, like in an old-fashioned film. I rang his fencing master once. I was curious. Apparently there are two main schools, two fencing traditions, the Italian and the French. I hadn't known that, before phoning him. He told me swordsmanship was something Addie just had a gift for, like it was in his blood, so to speak.'

'Was he as quick with the foil as he was with his fists?'

'Épée was his weapon of choice, Mr Grayling. They filmed him once, his coach said. Pointless, he said, if you'll pardon the pun. They had to slow it down to single frames to follow some of his moves.'

Grayling detoured slightly before returning to Lime Street Station and his return train. He found the street in which Adam had been raised, the house his mother still occupied in her fictitious widowhood.

There was a net curtain over the one downstairs window and in the living room beyond he saw the flicker of a television screen. It would be on all the time, he thought. It would greet her in the morning and say goodbye to her at night, her gaudy, chatty window on a world to which her junk channel providers convinced her she belonged.

The professor knew that he was a snob, but he did not think snobbery a particularly sinful vice. What he thought, passing Adam's mother's house, was that the cunning of man was quite something and that maybe there was hope after all. He strode to the station and his late train with a positive spring in his step. He was very glad he had made the trip. It had provided him with a degree of reassurance he had hoped for but had not confidently expected to find.

Adam sat at his father's bedside aboard the barge and held his hand. He found the old callus, the one that had felt to his reaching fingers as a small child like a coin. His father's breathing was a faint sound, as though to breathe with more authority might offend. There wasn't much breath left in him. Adam had his eyes closed. He knew that if he opened them, he would weep. He did not want his grief upsetting his father and so his eyes stayed shut.

'Why did you change our family's name?'

'McGuire suggested it.'

'When was that?'

'He advised I should do it as I rowed him back to the ship, after that first visit to the other place.'

'Your entry into the shadow world took place by chance. McGuire picked you from the crew at random.'

'Nothing happens at random, Adam. Chance is how we describe events when we don't yet know their purpose. I changed our name for the same reason as I left. It was to protect you. It was a small thing. It was insignificant compared to the leaving of you.'

'We're bastard offspring, Dad. The blood of what you call the other place runs through our veins.'

His father tried to laugh, but the laughter turned to coughing and it was a while before he could compose himself and reply. 'Dilute by now, I should think, Adam. Anyway, it's noble blood, to port and starboard; there's pedigree on either side.'

'McGuire told you?'

'Aye, he did.'

Adam had worked it out on the ferry crossing. Jane could tease him about the speed at which he read, but there was nothing slow about the turn of his mind. He had identified the flaw in her theory about the de Morey deposition as the waters of the North Sea churned darkly beneath the hull of the travelling ship.

He had written it when he was old. So he had not written it to prevent pursuit of Eleanor Bloor from the shadow world. Had that been his intention in writing it, he would have composed it immediately on his return. Adam believed she had crossed. He believed she had successfully passed. They had lived happily together and at the heart of the vast estate royal patronage had endowed him with, de Morey and his willing sword had been the only protection she had needed.

But she had also borne his child. She had borne him a son, a half-brother to Simon. The conflict was dynastic, and de Morey, old by then and feeble, had needed to protect his younger son from the Crimson King's retribution.

So he had written the deposition, truthful in every detail but for the one lie that was the reason for its very existence. And the child had survived. Adam's own name was de Morey and it was the name his father had endowed him with and then denied them both, and he thought he now knew what Grayling had meant in that odd metaphor about clay fired in the kiln and its quality.

'How old are you, Dad?'

'Older than you might think, Adam. More tired than you can imagine.'

'Why did you go back?'

'I was a sailor in my soul, I think, as much so as that distant ancestor of ours was a soldier. I was always restless, always keen to be away on some voyage, the further flung the destination the better, if I'm honest. But there is always a yearning for home. It's the contradiction at the heart of every sailor's life, that yearning pull. And in a way the other place was home and I longed to go back there, and I suppose I answered that longing.'

'It sounds an awful world.'

'It's in your blood.'

'Dilute, you said.'

'I said noble, too. As to how awful it is, you will have to judge that for yourself.'

Nothing is random. Chance is how we describe events when we don't yet know their purpose.

'You should rest, Dad.'

'I'm dying, Adam. I have little time left and want to spend what's remaining of it with the son I love and have missed so dreadfully. I'm due a rest, granted. But it will be a long one and it will come soon enough for both of us.'

They were silent for a while. Adam trusted himself to blink open his eyes. His father, looking directly at him, said, 'I used to lift you on to my shoulders and carry you up those giant sand hills on the beach at Formby Point.'

'I remember.'

'It's hard to believe it, now.'

'Not for me. I remember your motorbike too, the Norton.'

'I'd forgotten about that old beast. If I had a pound for every time I changed the head gasket on the Norton.'

'You'd have a few quid.'

'I would.'

'I remember the fish and chips at Reilly's on Blackpool promenade. And Reilly's mushy peas.'

'They tasted green.'

'They did! You always used to say that, that their mushy peas were the greenest tasting in the whole of Lancashire. And you used to say their tea tasted brown.'

'Did the Tizer taste orange?'

'I'll give you the same answer I gave you then, Dad. Tizer's a very reddish sort of orange. And to me, to be honest, it just tasted of pop.'

'I came to see you. You were sixteen. I was five rows from ringside when you beat O'Grady for the area title. You flattened him in twenty-seven seconds.'

'I'd have held him up for longer if I'd known that you were there.'

'I'd have been there always, if I could have. You were always in my heart.'

'I know. I know that now.'

'They will come for you, Adam. You will need to be on your mettle.'

'I will be, Dad.'

'And I'll be watching you.'

He died about half an hour after this exchange. Adam raised to his lips and kissed the hand he held and then gently put it down and closed his father's eyes. His own were blurry with tears. His smudged vision took in the details of the cabin, the books and the brasses, the rigged model ships in dimple bottles and metal framed prints mounted in a neat row, the coffee pot cold beside its ring burner, the meticulous possessions of a single man.

Delilah Crane was standing on the deck in the darkness when he climbed the stairs to reach it. Her arms were folded across her chest and she was staring down at where the oily water lapped against the hull.

'You poor boy,' she said. 'I'm so very sorry.'

'There wasn't enough time.'

'There never is.'

Adam sniffed. Grief shuddered through him. He shook with it.

'Come here,' she said. But she went to him and held him. He sobbed on her shoulder, thinking that he might never stop.

TEN

The following morning, Adam breakfasted with Delilah. After the previous night, he had an appetite. She, by contrast, seemed to have a hunger only for cigarettes and coffee.

'They'll kill you,' he said, of the former.

'Eventually,' she said, exhaling.

'Were you my father's lover?'

'He was not always an invalid.'

'I know that. I remember his strength.'

'But he wasn't chosen for the fray as you are, Adam. There is strength and then there is strength. Did he warn you?'

'He said they would come for me.'

'They will. You cannot attend the funeral. It is too great a risk.'

Adam nodded. 'How old are you?'

'That question is ungallant.'

'I apologize for it. What would happen if they came for you?'

She dragged heavily on her cigarette and then sipped at her coffee, which she took black. She did not look dishevelled in the morning. She looked as seductive as she had the first time he had seen her. 'It would depend on who they sent. At the least, they would cut out my tongue. Actually, they would tear it out. They might make me consume it.' She crushed out her smoke in the ashtray on the breakfast table between them. Given what she'd just said, Adam thought the nicotine habit more understandable than he had.

She slid something across the table, an envelope, which Adam picked up, worrying at the glued flap with his thumb.

'He was renting the barge at the end from the man to whom he sold it. That was a practical arrangement well suited to both parties. This is your legacy.'

The envelope contained a cheque made out to Adam by his father in the sum of ninety thousand pounds. Adam put it into his pocket. When he got back to England he would bank the cheque and make out one for an identical sum to his mother. It would provide him with much relief to be able to do that and he felt grateful to his father for his inheritance. It was not proof of love. He had been given that already.

'I have a half-brother.'

She nodded. 'Rabanus Bloor. They would not send an assassin for you, I do not think. You are too important. They might think you too strong. They could send Bloor. He would relish the challenge and Dray would enjoy the symmetry. You might merit, in their thinking, the distinction of a blue-blooded execution. If they sent an assassin for you, it would likely be Proctor Maul.'

Adam observed as her face grew pale and her lips bloodless, and her fists clenched on the table top. She reached for her cigarettes. He would not ask her questions about this assassin, Proctor Maul. He would not put her through the ordeal of recalling him. Her pallor and the dread in her voice when she said his name had pretty much told him what he needed to know.

'Did my father help you cross?'

'He did. Your father found the eighth gateway. He was sailing alone, for pleasure, manning a yacht single-handed in the Aegean Sea. It was almost seven years ago. He thought he found the gateway by chance.'

'Chance is what we call events when we don't yet know their purpose.'

'Good,' Delilah said, 'you're learning.' She smiled. Her eyes narrowed and sparkled. Her teeth were very white between ruby lips. Her expression was sultry in repose. When she smiled, she was simply beautiful. It was the sun announcing itself at the centre of a glorious sky. 'Your father was immune to the charms of the Miasmic Sea.'

'Tell me what that is.'

'It is a wilderness of water where men become trapped, their thoughts frozen and their actions no more than a slavish routine. They are aware but have no will. It is a kind of hell for mariners. It is the effect of some spell conjured centuries ago. It was designed to protect the eighth gateway from intrusion, but the spell went wrong and a sort of contagion spread.

'On Endrimor it is treasonous even to speak of the Miasmic Sea. It is one of our world's shameful failures, a living, spreading symbol of the corruption of magic. The people of earth are not the only species guilty of polluting their world.'

'But my father was immune.'

'He was. It did not intrude upon his mind in the slightest. Though he saw some strange and haunting sights there, they did not impinge upon his sanity. Once he made landfall, he looked for the son he had fathered. Not a happy discovery, though he spoke little about it. He found me. And in him, I found my escape.'

'Do many cross?'

'No more than a handful, Adam. It is very dangerous. And I have told you of the penalty once discovered and confronted, if you are successfully pursued.'

'The shadow world sounds a terrible place. All cruelty, corrupt magic and political tyranny, and that's without its natural monsters.'

'They are not really very natural.'

'I am surprised more people don't try to escape from there. They wouldn't have that much trouble. On the contrary, looking like you.'

Delilah studied him for a moment, as though careful of how much to confide. She said, 'Some people are drawn to darkness. The traffic, slight and secret as it is, runs both ways and always has.'

'Who is this Dray?'

'Sebastian Dray is a politician and plotter, a diplomat and disseminator of what passes in the shadow world for news. He takes responsibility for the gateways. Bloor would not have been able to come here without seeking Dray's permission.'

'Bloor didn't use a gateway, did he? He turned up at the place where I received the clarion call. He was seen in the forest at Cree, in Scotland.'

'He would not need a gateway, you are right. But the sorcery that delivered him to where he was seen would not have been accomplished without Dray's consent. His presence there, however brief, was a signal of the escalation.'

'Not very clever of him, was it, to warn us?'

'He arrived after the clarion call. It was after you found the artefact, which warned your professor and resulted in you coming here after McGuire told you to. His purpose was not to warn but to intimidate. He was flexing his muscles.'

'He sounds like a wanker.'

'You don't run a harbour bar without gaining some understanding of English slang, Adam, so of course I'm familiar with that insult. But you should not underestimate him. He is cunning and brutal and he can fight. You are a taint to him, no more. Do not expect sentiment from Rabanus Bloor. You will not get brotherly love.'

'That's all right,' Adam said. 'He won't be getting any in return.'

They were silent together for a while. She had seen him unmanned in his grief of the previous evening. She was glamorous in a way that was so exotically potent he thought that it should have felt dangerous, but actually he felt very comfortable with her. He liked her enormously. He had thought her particularly attractive the first time he had ever seen her and nothing had happened since to make him feel any differently.

'Will you attend the funeral?'

'I dare not,' she said.

'Will anyone?'

She shrugged, but did so with her eyes averted.

'I will go,' Adam said. 'I will honour my father. I will not have him go to his grave alone, unlamented.'

'He does not go unlamented. Please don't go to the funeral.'

'I'm nothing if I don't.'

'You sound like a de Morey.'

'Well. I am one.'

'Bloor might be there.'

'We have to meet eventually.'

'Jesus, Adam. They might send Maul.'

'I'm going. I'll not be scared away from the funeral of the man to whom I owe my existence. I loved my dad. They can send who they like. I might not win, Delilah, but whoever they send, they'll know they've been in a fight.'

Martin thought building a website the best method. He could have gone to the press, but in the first instance it would have to have been one of those crank publications that survived by publishing sensational conspiracy theories.

His new friends were averse to technology, but the internet was a necessary evil. What did they expect him to do, hawk hand-printed pamphlets on street corners? He was not some agitator from the eighteenth century. He was charged with treating the world to some select revelations about the Great Lie and he would quite reasonably do so in the most effective way possible.

The web designer he was paying for the job had finally finished his tweaks. They were ready to launch the site. Martin scrolled through the pages feeling quite proud and satisfied, with a mounting sense of excitement at just how convincing it all was. Well, of course it was. Sensational and shocking as it appeared, it was the truth. He gave the techie his three hundred quid in cash, considering the money well spent, and showed him to the door.

He was back in London, in his father's house. His father was away on a round-robin business trip to Brussels, Monaco and Berne. He had told his father by phone of his decision to leave university. He had not been precisely honest about the reason. His father had sounded philosophical.

Martin looked at his title page. He liked his picture byline: it made him look like one of those dashing foreign correspondents from the golden age of newspaper reportage. He scrolled through the story, trying to view it as objectively as he could and considering, as coldly as he was able to, the sensational claims it endeavoured to substantiate.

The Spanish influenza epidemic that had followed the Great War and devastated Europe was the consequence of a scientific blunder. The virus was a mutant strain created in the medical facility at Fort Bragg in North Carolina shortly before the Americans entered the conflict as participants.

They had been concerned about tetanus. It was a common problem among the wounded in the filth of the Western Front trenches and once contracted, it was almost always fatal. The infection spread quickly and the patient died of shock before he could receive effective treatment.

Sebastian Dray had isolated the outbreak of infection to a carrier from Chicago, a volunteer called Harry Doyle who had survived the war. He left Fort Bragg in July of 1918 having been given his inoculation on the sixth day of the month. He had a fever on the crossing, but it was not thought a matter of concern when the ship's doctor examined him. He was fine when he reached Le Havre on 17 July, from where his unit marched through the lanes of a dusty Flanders summer to Ypres.

They were involved in heavy fighting, during which Doyle's infantry unit distinguished themselves. They were physically robust men, mostly from the Midwestern States of America. They were well trained, well equipped and for the most part, saw the war as something of an adventure.

It wasn't until after the Armistice and the return aboard troopships to the eastern seaboard of the United States that doughboys began to become ill and die rapidly and in bewildering numbers. Aboard some of the vessels, the mortality rate was sixty per cent. The men died drowning on their own phlegm in the twenty-four hours following the appearance of the first symptoms of what history came to call the Spanish flu.

'An existing tetanus vaccine was first made available as early as 1890,' Dray had told Martin. 'But the American Department of War did not want to pay for stocks of it on the scale that would have been required for their soldiers in 1917. Their mistake was to make responsible for the manufacture of their own serum a second-rate chemist called Oscar Freemantle, working out of a third-rate medical facility at Bragg. Their sin was to administer what Freemantle had concocted before carrying out the necessary trials.'

'Hubris,' said Slee, 'or penny-pinching. Either way, what the Americans did cost fifty million lives in Europe alone. Imagine the grief, Martin. Imagine it.'

Martin had looked at the documentation spread out on the table in Dray's library, at Freemantle's research log, at the formula he had concocted described in a chemical equation, at the pattern of infection, at Doyle's corresponding movements and the smiling image of the uniformed infantryman, photographed in black and white at the centre of his happy troop. It was convincing, but it was still circumstantial. It wasn't solid proof.

'They would have to exhume Doyle to provide the most damning evidence of all,' Dray said. 'He prospered in the peace, becoming one of Chicago's leading business figures, and he was buried with some ceremony in a lead-lined casket. He carried a mutant virus that for several weeks and perhaps even months of his life was horribly virulent. Its exact character is a mystery to which his well-preserved remains hold the key.'

'We think your world ought to know the truth,' Slee said.

And Martin had nodded, because he did too. He had nothing against America as a nation. He had little appetite for conspiracy theory generally. But he did think a deliberate attempt to conceal such a vast and significant historical truth an insult to anyone with any intelligence.

The truth would out. He would tell it. To do nothing would be to perpetuate the Great Lie. When he made this parting observation to Dray, he could see the pleasure in the man's face and it made him feel proud to see it. In the shadow world, he was in no doubt he had enjoyed the company and confidences of two great men.

After launching the site, Martin waited for an hour before counting the number of hits it had scored with curious browsers. The number was modest, at twenty-five, but the comments were encouraging. His room at home occupied the attic. His dad was not due back for three more days. He went down to his father's basement den and rooted around among his old vinyl albums until he found the one he was looking for. The album was by King Crimson and its title was *In the Court of the Crimson King*.

His dad had a stereo system worth several thousand pounds, with a turntable precisely engineered by the Scottish high-end audio company, Linn. He put the record on the plinth and switched the power on.

It was over an hour before he went back up and discovered he had registered 500 hits on his site. Almost all the comments were approving of his having exposed a shocking truth. Very few questioned his findings.

That was at three o'clock in the afternoon. By seven o'clock, the site had scored almost half a million hits. Hostility to its claims was marginally higher, but the general tone of the comments was complimentary. Some he was obliged to translate from Arabic languages to read. It was clear that not everyone held the world's most powerful nation in great regard.

At eight o'clock he went to the Flask on Flask Walk, a few hundred yards from his father's house, for a pint of beer. He thought that he might enjoy a couple. He was feeling pretty good about himself. He'd sunk most of his second when his mobile rang at eight forty-five and he gave his first considered comments to a national newspaper.

He had done all the research himself, he said. For an amateur historian, he acknowledged it was quite a coup. Yes, he agreed, it had happened almost a century ago, but that did not invalidate the facts.

Just wait, he said, until he revealed his findings concerning the hushed up nuclear disaster in Tashkent in 1973. That was a lot more recent, and its impact was still being felt. Because the Russian Cold War scientists who had devised the hasty serum used to strengthen the immunity of those exposed to radiation had in fact achieved the opposite. They had given the world AIDS. Could he prove it? Watch this space, said Martin. My friend, just watch this space.

In the severest moment of the winter, in the last week of January and the first of February, the Miasmic Sea would very likely freeze. It had done so every year for more years than men could recall. When it froze it lost its potency and I would be able to walk to the eighth gateway across its petrified wastes in happy solitude, my senses unimpaired by the madness sewn within its depths as I escaped from the Crimson King's court with my duty accomplished.

The count was a gracious host. I could not have wished for a better companion. To my utmost delight, he was truly a champion at arms. He was spry, skilled, cunning and exceptionally strong. He was in the habit of schooling his sons, Arthur and Morgan, and it was my pleasure to vary their practice at combat with frequent tests against myself. He believed the variety would make them better accomplished and the proof of this was plain to see after a few weeks, which brought the count evident pleasure and pride.

It is ruefully said and often by some men in England that the poor are always with us. So it was in the count's domain with the parasites that protected him. They were not generally abroad by day, but once night fell their cold and menacing presence could be felt. Since the nights in winter grow longer and encroach upon the days, awareness of them became ever more acute as the season progressed.

This was their effect on me. I did not discuss them with the count. They were a necessary evil and I did not want to offend him or slight his hospitality. I was his guest and grateful to him for his advice, his shelter and his most welcome company.

They fed on Vorps. They lacked the wit to hunt down the feathered creatures for themselves, but the count had lures and traps placed at intervals to catch the great birds. He told me this himself, saying that both breeds were the consequence of sorcery gone wrong. The notion of monsters nourished on monsters appealed, I think, to his ironic turn of mind.

'Don't the feathers impede their capacity to feed?'

'They have become adept at plucking feathers. Nothing interferes with the satisfaction of their thirst.'

I assumed the birds endured this ordeal still living. Blood in a dead creature would thicken and congeal. Plucking would not kill them. Having seen the dimensions of the Vorps in flight, the size and sharpness of their beaks and talons, it sounded a hazardous way to feed. But I did not pursue any greater detail from the count.

He raised the subject only once. 'They are an aberration,' he said, to a question in my mind I had not asked of him. 'They know this. They are doing what they can to adapt to the world in which they abide, but their thirst prevents the kind of advancement of which men seem capable. Their physical and intellectual progress is painfully slow, and their failure encourages anger and frustration. They are not capable of independence. Anger is no ally, though, of subservience.'

'You fear they might rebel against you?'

'Do not credit them with the intelligence for rebellion. They would turn on me gleefully, however, if they could think of a way to live independent of what I provide them with.'

At the end of January's second week I took my leave of the count and his household. I bade a fond farewell to my host and his goodly wife and held and kissed the boys to whom I had become close and whom I would miss most grievously, thinking my own son Simon would do well to find such boon companions back in the land I hoped to see once again. Firstly, though, there was my duty to discharge.

Lastly, the count approached me and gave me a pendant to wear about my neck.

'No magick,' he assured me, 'simply a charm that might bring good fortune. Your adversary is clever and watchful and an alchemist of great potency. Promise me, sir, you will wear the charm.'

I put it about my neck and swore that it would remain there. Finally we embraced, as ardently as brothers might, and I mounted and turned about the horse he had given me with tears pricking at my eyes. I felt I had lost a family anew, the second to be sundered from me in one lifetime. I rode on from that spot believing my spirit and character the better for having met and shared the weeks and months I had with that one true monarch of the shadow world. Writing this, in my dotage, I believe it still. And I still think often of that noble friend.

The southern latitudes brought no increase in warmth. The count had provided me with a cloak of something that resembled sable and fur-lined boots and gauntlets. The steel of a helm would have frozen to the flesh of my face in such conditions and a sword been stuck useless in its scabbard by the frost, but I rode warm enough with a hood of fur about my head and a heavy blanket for the sturdy steed I rode. So hard was the frozen ground that when we travelled at dusk I saw sparks brightly struck about our progress by her iron-shod hooves.

The city, when I reached it, was ice-bound. In character it reminded me of the great cities of antiquity described in scholarly books. The vaunting dimensions of its surrounding wall and principle buildings gave the whole a cold and haughty grandeur. It lacked entirely the populous bustle of a great metropolis. At the edge of its frozen sea, the great waves paused and petrified beneath the harbour wall.

They had games in Salabra, martial in character, somewhat resembling the gladiatorial spectacles of ancient times. My strategy was to achieve prominence in these, all the time encouraging a rumour concerning my prowess and the reason for my successes. I duly entered the lists and distinguished myself.

My manner and tone, my voice and appearance, marked me by now as an Endrimorian of northern extraction. I passed with ease and conviction.

My opponents were successively more skilled and testing. My notoriety grew. The nobles of the court attended. After a dozen combats the Crimson King himself was drawn to the arena, curious to watch me. I had beaten all of their champions but one and the king rose to acclaim my skill. I bowed deep in secret mockery and it was announced I would fight, if I would agree to the match, a man called Edgar Maul.

'It will please me to kill him,' I said, the first true words I had uttered since entering the city. 'The man has yet to be born who can defy the power of my sword.'

I am no friend of rhetoric. No sword is mightier than the arm that wields it, not even Arthur's Excalibur, the legend of which was the inspiration for my scheme. But this was my plan: to make them believe that my sword was possessed of magical properties so potent that Slee himself would be curious to examine the weapon and question me on its power and provenance.

I prayed on the night before the duel. I had seen this Edgar Maul. Brooding and gigantic, he was like the city of Salabra made flesh, the muscles shaping his physique as sculpted and solid as marble itself. I did not fear him. I did not in truth fear death. I feared only failure. I prayed for the souls of my dead family and I prayed too for success on the morrow.

The arena was full. The air was raw with cold. It made sound brittle as the shouts of the spectators rose in it to encourage their man. I looked at the cobbles, sanded to absorb the gore, and thought that it would be a desolate place for a man from my world to die. No lonelier or more forlorn spot could be conceived, I thought, gripping my sword and gathering my strength within me for the fray.

He came at me boldly with a battleaxe between his brute fists. I have never encountered a man stronger but he was subtle also, carving at the air with short sweeps to limit the space allowed for counter-blows.

He was expert with the weapon, agile and quick, a smile like a leer stretching his mouth in relish as he fought, drawing first blood with a cut to the shoulder so powerful I could only half-parry it, steel clanging in collision on honed steel, my blood dripping down about our capering feet, sparks struck as we engaged our violent craft.

There is about a duel something similar to debate. It is an engagement, a dialogue that becomes more fluent the more skilled the two participants are. But it was not like that with Edgar Maul. It was more in the nature of trying to endure a tempest. I was bloodied after five minutes. In ten I was tired. I had never been obliged to fight at such a pace only to avoid the sundering of my own limbs.

The sword was lead in my grip and his two-headed axe the raging of a metal storm about me. He struck again, slicing open my right side, and stepped back to admire the work before closing for the kill.

The mind dictates what the body responds with in emergency.

And in that brief moment of respite I pictured in my mind my daughter dead and unresponsive in my loving arms and found the venting fury of revenge from somewhere in me.

It roared and bellowed out of me and in this rally Maul withered under a ferocious rain of blows as I fought possessed by hatred, mad with it, filled with appalling strength, finishing him with a side-swipe that cut the shaft of his blocking weapon clean in half before burying my blade so deeply in him it stopped against the juddering bone of his spine.

He sank to his knees, trying to put back the guts spilling out of him, bright and blue in the cold air, with both hands. The expression on the large face under his shaven head was curious. He had not expected to lose this fight.

I freed my sword from him and as he knelt there on the cobbles used it to part his head from his body cleanly at the neck with my final blow of the morning. Blood gushed steaming from the great wound and I felt the heat of him dissipate as his life ceased.

The crowd was entirely silent. Pain from my own wounds began to throb through me. I skewered Maul's head on the point of my sword and held the weapon high. This last was a gesture for Slee to observe and for him to ponder on.

The sword was taken from me as my wounds were dressed. I did not think to try to recover it. The mechanics of its confiscation were of no interest to me. I knew to whom it would have been delivered. I made for the lodgings I had taken as the scant population of that great marble mausoleum of a city pointed and stared at me.

I was sore and weary, and the recent, vivid memory of the daughter lost to me had brought a great, melancholy emptiness upon me. I took no pride in my victory over Edgar Maul. He was an obstacle removed from my path. No more.

The summons came on the afternoon of the following day. I was to present myself at court. Hieronymus Slee would receive me in his chambers. There were questions he wished to learn the answers to. I was not made aware by the herald of what subject they might concern. I thought I knew but it mattered not.

The audience was the thing. All that mattered to me was the alchemist's proximity. I speculated on how he would appear.

I could not imagine the countenance and manner of a mortal man responsible for the catastrophe he had willingly engineered. But I would know him when I saw him.

The royal palace was a gloomy labyrinth. Wood torches smeared with burning pitch lit its long passages. All the things that bring life to a building of distinction were absent. There was no music, no laughter, no conversation, no bustle of urgent business or vivid parade of great men attired in their finery. Instead it answered best my grandfather's description of the catacombs he saw while wearing the red cross of a Crusader fighting in the Holy Land. Dreary and forbidding, the palace of the Crimson King felt like a place of death.

The alchemist slouched on a wooden throne at the centre of a vaulted chamber with my sword between his hands. He was dark-haired, thin and spectral pale. 'Steel,' he said. 'Finely hammered and honed and prettily engraved though this object is, it is merely fashioned metal of a base sort, is it not, sir?'

'Wield it in battle, sir,' I said to him. 'Its strength will confound and delight you.'

With the hilt held between delicate fingers, he turned and studied the blade. It was well balanced and finely tempered and had served me proudly. But it was little to look at, notched with the scars of old battles, worn and wearied now like the knight it had armed.

'Tell me how you came by it,' he said.

He was in the habit of command. He was the king's favourite, after all. He knew nothing about my name or station and cared less. I did not answer him.

'Have you crossed?'

'No, sir, I have not.' *But you have,* I thought, *to do your awful misdeed to my world.*

'Yet this sword was fashioned on earth,' he said. 'It is crafted in the English style. I knew it from fifty feet distant the first time I saw you in the arena. There is no magick on earth, sir. There is much superstition. But the miracle of your fight against Maul was not achieved for this weapon there; it was done here. I wish to know, by whom?'

He believed in the power I had claimed for the sword. Why not? In that warped world, a spell was the likeliest explanation for the outcome of the fight he had witnessed. This was my chance.

I turned my head slightly, to either side, as though wary of the guards behind me eavesdropping on what I might reveal and Slee motioned me towards him with an impatient wave. I bent close. He gave me his ear. I pulled open my doublet and groped for the hilt of the dagger concealed beneath the dressing wrapped thickly about my wounded body.

He recoiled like a snake. Something in his eyes changed. My limbs were frozen by the look, as stiff as the rigging I had seen on the ships in Salabra's ice-bound harbour. But he had seen something when I'd torn open my doublet and doubt troubled him and then horror dawned, so that he could not sustain the petrifying glare. It was the pendant the count had given me. Slee had seen it and knew it from somewhere and it delivered a terror to him that broke his mesmeric spell.

I pulled the dagger free of my bandages and plunged it to the hilt into his right eye. I took my sword from his shuddering grip and turned and dispatched the guards. It was nothing to accomplish. After the speed of Edgar Maul they moved like men dazed. I turned my attention back to Slee. He was in the grip of some manner of seizure, having slipped from his throne on to the floor. I pulled the knife free and drew it across his throat to sever the cords of his voice so he would not be heard screaming. I whispered into his ear why I was there and at whose command I had come.

The brain is a great and complex puzzle. I was concerned that perhaps my injury to his had deprived him of the gift of pain, but it was not so. I carried out the king's command and slowly butchered him. He sobbed. He tried to beg. His death was hard and long drawn and I am sure that he felt every cut and mutilation till the stroke that gutted him and put him beyond feeling for eternity.

I escaped the dread confines of the palace and trudged across the frozen sea in the direction the count had counselled I take. My wounds had opened in the combat with the guards in the alchemist's chamber. I was careful not to bleed on the ice and leave a trail by which I could be followed.

I think I might have bled more grievously from such deeply inflicted wounds as Maul had given me, but the cold prevented it. The cold was my ally. It left no scent for pursuing dogs and of course, I left no tracks in my progress over that slippery waste.

What happened on my return to our beloved world is a tale for another time. This story is the proof of my survival. I commit it to the page in truth and in humility. It has been my privilege to serve a great sovereign and to be as beholden to my God as a sometimes hot nature allowed. Since He, in His infinite wisdom, endowed me with that nature, I hope He can find it in His merciful heart also to forgive me for its less fortunate consequences.

Adam and Jane finished reading the de Morey account in the stately comfort of McGuire's sitting room. She was silent, pondering its implications. McGuire and Professor Grayling were on the other side of the spacious room, studying Martin Prior's new website on Grayling's laptop.

The professor had breached his own condition of confidentiality in allowing the de Morey pages to leave his office. Adam and Jane had not been told specifically why, but they thought the decision had probably been provoked by what Martin was up to. The tabloids were full of him and he had booked a berth on the forthcoming edition of 'Question Time'. Events had taken an urgent turn.

Jane stood and neatened the pages she held, then placed them precisely on the arm of her chair. 'I need some air,' she said. It was three-thirty in the afternoon. She had perhaps an hour before dusk descended. The pier would not close until darkness fell and she thought she might stroll along its bracing length and breathe in some sea air. She had to get out of the flat. It was very comfortable, but she thought that if she did not get away for a few minutes she might scream or puke or tear at her hair like somebody mad.

It was not the de Morey account. That was bad enough. She now knew that Adam was his direct descendent, the bastard offspring of two conflicting worlds, a young man made a sort of fugitive by genealogy and the vengeful insult to Endrimor of an execution carried out centuries ago.

But it was not the de Morey deposition or the dreadful reach of its implications that had sickened her to the stomach. It was Delilah Crane and the thought that Adam had spent the night with his father's glamorous and seductive lover.

'Excuse me,' she said.

Adam glanced up at her from where he sat. He had almost finished the story. She remembered her jokes about the speed at which he read, made in the cramped cockpit of Grayling's Lotus on the way to the ferry terminal at Hull. Her teasing jibes had felt intimate between them then.

Now they rang hollow in her memory after only a couple of days – but it wasn't the days, was it? It was the night she was concerned with, and the comfort in Delilah Crane's voluptuous embrace she believed he had found.

She limped across the room and fumbled at the door.

'Are you all right, Jane?'

The question came from Grayling. She ignored it and went out. In the lift she closed her eyes. It was the mirrors. She was not in the mood for study unto infinity of her own familiar reflection. She knew that she was pretty. Some men thought her beautiful. Evidently she was not beautiful enough.

She smiled to herself. It was a shame. She tried for sympathy, imagining how lonely and raw Adam must have felt in the aftermath of his father's passing from life. But sympathy did not arrive. Instead, she thought what a shame and a waste it was that in such circumstances he could think only with his dick.

The pier was brisk and breezy, busy with late visitors, Wurlitzer music and bright lights assaulting the senses, burger grease in drifts meant to entice but which Jane found sourly stomach churning.

It was the English seaside. It was all of a piece. She thought that she should sit down and drink a cup of tea and try to compose herself. She did not know, after all. It had not been confirmed to her that Adam and the Siren of Rotterdam had shared a bed; it was only her supposition. He had described her with some relish after his first visit. He had also claimed she wasn't interested in him.

Did it even qualify as infidelity? Jane had rejected his advances. They had not actually made love. At what point did a couple become such? She had thought in that desolate moment, for him, on the bank of the Cam, that they had become truly close, a real couple. Perhaps she had been wrong.

She had thought it right and natural to wait. Feelings of magnitude required a degree of respect and caution in how they were acted upon. Such emotions were too important for haste. But men and women were differently wired emotionally. Everybody said so. Popular books had been written on the subject. Adam Parker had just provided her with the proof.

She went into one of the cafés at the end of the pier at random and bought her cup of tea. It came with a complimentary biscuit, vacuum-wrapped in cellophane. There was a view through the western-facing window of the descending sun amid flushed frills of cloud. She sat at a table. Coldplay were oozing through speakers concealed in the ceiling. It would be fucking Coldplay, she thought. It was a very pretty sunset. Coldplay were yellow and the sunset was pink. She did not know when she had ever felt more desolate in her life.

Someone sat in the seat opposite hers. She did not look up from where she grappled with the cellophane. It was a café. People were entitled to sit where they liked. Someone with a taste for sunsets, she thought, or a thing about vacuum-packed biscuits, or just a Coldplay soundtrack. The biscuit broke between her fingers in its wrapper and she gave up on it, dropping it on to the lip of her saucer.

It was his stillness that made her look up. His size and his absolute stillness compelled it, eventually. It breached her Adam misery and her general indifference to where she was. Her human alertness to what was not natural summoned her attention and she was obliged to look at the man who had placed himself opposite her. And when she did, she was looking into the grinning, gleeful face of Rabanus Bloor.

He was dressed in conventional clothes. He wore jeans and a pea coat and a blue cotton shirt that highlighted, in the low, slanting sunlight, the alert blue of his eyes. There was a thin silver chain around his neck. His long hair looked more stylish than anachronistic in Brighton. It quite fitted in. Brighton was that sort of place. The angle of the sun made a dark crevasse of the scar beside his eye.

'Dora,' he said. His voice was Adam's, deeper, vastly less innocent, only slightly accented.

'Dora?'

'She's your twin, my dear.'

'Yes.'

'I know her.' He winked. 'Remember me to her.'

'We don't really speak,' Jane said. The words sounded hollow and inadequate. She was so consumed by terror, by the sheer recumbent menace of the man lounging in the seat before her, that she trembled and was hoarse with it.

He pondered for a moment. His eyes did not leave hers but they dulled in thought before their bright focus returned. Something had amused him. 'She's the darkness to your light, isn't she,' he said, 'the night to your day.'

He rose smoothly, turned and walked rapidly out, beyond sight.

ELEVEN

S ebastian Dray had as little appetite for the tests as he had for the executions. But this one was slightly different. They had caught one of the leaders of the Parasite Legion. He was sighted and possessed honed reflexes and an alert mind. He had been schooled in the rigours of combat. His rank had not been achieved by fluke, but was hard earned. Sarth did not suffer fools, especially among the monsters he bred. He would naturally cull the dull-witted and the weak. This was a specimen that would tell them much about the threat they faced from the north.

He would have the news by now about the public death of his wife. Dray was sorry that the king had thought it necessary. She had been of far more practical use as a hostage than as someone whose execution would provoke an intense and quite natural desire for revenge. Her execution just perpetuated the seemingly endless war. Making it a public spectacle simply made the count of Sarth more resolute in his hostility. The conflict had been going on for centuries. It was Dray's secret ambition, one of many secret ambitions, to bring it to a peaceful and mutually acceptable conclusion.

In the meantime, he thought the test useful. What was done could not be undone. The countess could not be brought back to life. The test would indicate the progress the count had made in the selective breeding of his soldier slaves. There was a wonderful economy, Dray thought, to the paying of one's warriors in blood. Defeat inflicted thirst. Their reward for victory was visceral and immediate. Their impulse to fight was constant. They were a cheap and willing army.

He would not have shared these conclusions with Slee or with the king. They were too close to open admiration for the count and what had been achieved by the Parasitic Kingdom. He was philo-sophical and objective in a way that his ruler and the alchemist were not.

Dray was surprised Slee had seen the point of using Martin Prior and the other three spreaders of mischief on earth he had recruited. At first, of course, he had not.

'Why not simply tell the people of earth the truth about the Great Lie?'

'They would think it too fanciful; they would not believe it. And if they became convinced, what good would it do? They would be alert generally against us; they would strive for retribution.'

'Remind me, Sebastian. What is the point of the stories to be spread by this boy you wish me to enchant?'

'They are well made and difficult to refute,' Dray said.

'Granted, but to what end have they been so carefully forged?'

'They will sew disharmony and distrust and encourage turmoil,' Dray said. 'Faith in the noble motives of other nations is the foundation upon which earth's goodwill is based. We will shake it.'

They had a moment to study the parasite before the arrival of Maul and the test. It was manacled to the wall of the testing vault. They viewed it from behind the safety of bars through a high window, so they looked down on it. And it looked up at them when it scented the sweet warmth of their blood, almost immediately they took their seats.

They had been pale and flaccid once. The pictures and engravings of the past proved it. They had been eyeless too, the maw their only distinguishing feature, though they had been able to smell and feel, and capable of orientation and the efficient hunting and killing of men. This one was not like that. The maw had been muzzled in precaution by a heavy arrangement of leather and steel. The eyes above it were small and black and alert. The creature was naked. Its skin was translucent and taut over a musculature so hard it seemed almost brittle, like an insect carapace. They moved like insects too, Dray thought. The sudden, spasmodic speed of them in attack was quite shocking if you had not seen it before.

'Have you handicapped or maimed it in any way?'

'No,' Slee said. 'It is as you see it. It is a healthy specimen.'

'It will be thirsty.'

'Very.'

'Maul will have his work cut out.'

'It will be a proper test,' Slee said. He grinned. Dray was reminded that the alchemist enjoyed this sort of thing.

The keepers entered the vault. There were three of them. Two were armed with barbed steel harpoons they held from either side pointed at the creature's throat while the third man unfastened the manacles. The work was done swiftly and their backwards retreat to safety was equally rapid.

Freed, the creature did not move at all at first. It stood with its long and muscular legs still splayed and its long arms aloft in the attitude in which it had been restrained by its iron fetters.

There was no warning before it leapt. The leap was too rapid for the eye. It was just there against the bars, pulling at them, tearing free and tossing back the muzzle, stretching for Dray and Slee as they scrambled amid the plumped cushions of their box to escape its groping reach. There was the dead flesh stink of the maw. Dray felt a talon graze his shoulder as they wrestled their way through the door and down the steps to elude it, hearing behind them the groan of iron under strain as the parasite tried to rip the bars from the stone into which they were rooted.

Maul must have seen what had happened from the spyhole in the vault door. He stood outside it when they reached the ground, grim-faced with a rifle between his hands. There would be no test. The creature was vastly too dangerous for sport. Its strength and speed were sobering, Dray thought. How many more had the count bred like this in his dark domain to the north?

The features under the purple ink of Maul's facial tattoos wore an expression Dray had not seen there before. He never betrayed emotion. But for once the assassin looked conflicted.

On the one hand he was a purist who liked his killing to be intimately accomplished with weapons of cold steel. On the other, he was a pragmatist and an expert at killing, and the size and ferocity of the creature made the rifle only practical.

They heard a sound from it, then, from high on the wall of the vault where it crouched and writhed against the bars of the spectator box. It could have been a parched grunt of thirst or a roar of defiance, Dray thought. But as Maul raised the rifle and took aim through the hole drilled for observation in the door, he thought it sounded much more like a chuckle of contempt.

Adam found Jane seated before a cold teacup in a café at the pier's end. She looked a pale, almost broken figure, her fingers interlinked on the table top in front of her, he thought to stop them trembling. It was dark and they were clearing up and trying to close.

Jane seemed unaware of the busy, pointed fussing of the waitress and the loud pantomime of the bloke cashing up at the till. She raised her eyes to him. They looked blank with shock. He put a gentle hand under her elbow, raised her to her feet and steered her out into the exposure of the night.

'They hate us because of what de Morey did to them,' she said.

'They gave him ample reason. They hated us before the few of us aware of the conflict hated them. And what de Morey did was only a symbolic retaliation. The body counts hardly compare.'

'Most of the Black Death victims were peasants,' Jane said. 'They would not really have signified in feudal times. De Morey laid waste to the elite of the shadow world. He befriended the king's rival for the crown and trained his sons in combat. He killed the king's champion and butchered the king's favourite and defied the Miasmic Sea.'

'He wouldn't have been flavour of the month there,' Adam said. 'I'll give you that.'

'I wish you had not slept with Delilah Crane,' Jane said. 'I wish it with all my heart.'

They had been walking back towards the promenade. Adam stopped. 'Why do you wish it?'

'I want you to myself. I mean, I wanted you to myself.'

'I didn't sleep with her.'

'I don't believe you.'

'It's the truth.'

'Weren't you tempted?'

'Yes, I was tempted.'

'Did she want you to?'

'Yes, she wanted me to.'

'Why didn't you?'

'It's really simple, Jane. And it's really obvious. I love you.'

'Hold me,' she said. His embrace was warm and the strength of him solid and comforting. 'Bloor was here,' she said. 'He knows my sister. He must pass, Adam. He implied he knows Dora well. I think I understand now the look he gave me in the forest at Cree.'

Chance is how we describe events when we don't yet know their purpose. Adam was thinking of something Delilah had said over their breakfast together, about how the secret traffic ran both ways and always had.

Jane raised her head. Her face was pale in moonlight. 'Do you honestly love me?'

'Yes. And now I have told you so.'

'And how does that make you feel?'

'Oh, you know, foolish and vulnerable.'

'Don't feel that way. Feel loved back. It's much more sensible.'

They kissed and then laughed together. They were nineteen and resilient. They were like buoys bobbing unsinkably on the tide. Adam thought that they would need all their resilience. Bloor's appearance was a gloomy portent. But he felt elated at what he had told Jane. He had wanted to tell someone the truth of how he felt about her. She was the person he had wanted most to tell. They resumed walking, arm in arm.

'It would be Brighton, wouldn't it?' Jane said.

'What do you mean?'

She punched his chest and then pulled him towards her. 'Dirty weekends in seafront hotels, is what I mean. This is the classic location for booking into somewhere with groaning bedsprings and a dodgy landlady as Mr and Mrs Smith.'

'It isn't the weekend.'

'Don't be deliberately dim. We're not waiting for the weekend. I don't think time is really on our side. I don't want to be gloomy or pessimistic, but I'm not going to spend the rest of my life regretting that I didn't ever go to bed with you. And I need you tonight, Adam. I need you asleep beside me.'

'Well, I suppose we might go to sleep,' he said, 'eventually.'

They went back to McGuire's flat. Grayling and McGuire were still studying Martin's website. The four of them sat together in chairs facing the doctor's desk.

Martin thought about the two-headed abomination fashioned in Babylon, snarling at itself in its dark cupboard over against the wall. He thought about the bird kept in flightless confinement along the corridor. He looked over at the shelf where he had seen the Sarajevo swordstick, but the weapon was no longer where it had lain in its dusty retirement. Recommissioned, he thought, shivering at the memory of the nauseous stink of the bird.

'Martin appears to be one of four bright new conspiracy theorists duped into spreading corrosive lies about history,' Grayling said. 'Their work has the hand of Sebastian Dray all over it. He has turned a Mexican who communicates in Spanish and a Hong Kong native writing in Chinese. The fourth of his little helpers is a Hindi speaker based in Calcutta.

'So that's the world's four dominant languages neatly taken care of. The stories are well fabricated. Their narratives and visuals seem very authentic, but they are fundamentally untrue. Their job is to make the world a more uncertain, fearful and divisive place. They are a part of the undermining.'

'I don't really understand,' Adam said. 'When I first came here to see Doctor McGuire, he told me that the conflict is kept secret from most people on earth because if they knew about it, they might lose hope. Why doesn't the shadow world just turn to open hostility?'

'They want us to turn on ourselves,' Jane said, 'that's why. Maybe they don't dare tell the truth because they think us more resilient than the people here sustaining the secret do. Maybe they fear revenge.'

'If that's the case,' Adam said, 'our obsession with keeping the conflict secret plays into their hands.'

'It's a bit more complicated than that, philosophically,' Grayling said, 'geopolitically, too.'

'Explain,' Jane said.

'If all the world's ills could be blamed on Endrimor, unscrupulous leaders of delinquent nations would take full advantage. No country would be obliged to face full responsibility for its own actions. They could claim interference.'

'The shadow world would become their get out of jail card,' Adam said.

'Exactly,' said Grayling.

'How do you think they made a believer of Martin Prior?' Jane asked. 'I know him pretty well. At least, I knew him pretty well before he became all evangelical on the internet about the apparent sins of the superpowers. He was clever and witty. He was also vain, cynical, superficial and self-serving. The only things he was really passionate about were partying and clothes.'

'And he was your friend,' Adam said. 'On the basis of which, I'd really hate to be your enemy.'

'I think you're mistaken,' Grayling said, looking at Jane. 'Actually, I think he was pretty passionate about you. I think he might still be.'

Jane coloured. 'What a horrible idea.'

'He's been indoctrinated,' McGuire said. 'If you like, he's been brainwashed. We know that Jacob Slee is a very powerful mesmerist and with the other, dubious tricks they've perfected down the centuries, it would be easy to bend a boy as malleable as Martin Prior seems to be to their will. They are shrewd judges of character. They would have exploited his vanity and ambition.'

'You sound as though you've met him,' Adam said.

'I have, very recently. He had carried out an impressive piece of background research on a catastrophe he could only have learned about from them.'

Jane looked at him. 'Would you care to tell us about the nature of this catastrophe?'

McGuire glanced towards Grayling. Grayling nodded almost imperceptibly. But Adam wasn't falling for it. He thought McGuire the real manipulator here. The man who had exiled his father and insisted he change his family name was the man in charge. Without McGuire's say-so, he was sure they would never have seen the de Morey deposition.

He told them the story of *Incomparable*, without disclosing the fact that he had been witness to and part of it.

'My father was immune to the Miasmic Sea,' Adam said. 'I wonder why that was.'

'There are a number of possible explanations,' McGuire said. 'His ancestor de Morey walked across it unscathed.'

'That was a consequence of freezing weather.'

'He did so after killing the man who had enchanted that ocean in the first place. Perhaps the slaying endowed immunity.'

Adam shrugged.

'Or it could have been the charm that the count of Sarth insisted he wear. We don't know what that was.'

'Whatever it was,' Jane said, 'it was no mere charm. The count lied about that. He did so for a selfless reason, I think. He wanted to protect the man from earth he had come to love as a brother. But that pendant possessed the power to terrify the king's alchemist. Without it, I actually think de Morey's mission would have failed.'

'There was no altruism in the offering of the charm if it did possess occult power,' Grayling said. 'The count was ruthless. De Morey, a sentimental man who liked him, nevertheless admitted as much himself. It was in the count's interest for de Morey to succeed.'

Adam was having difficulty keeping his mind on all this. It was important and possibly even crucial. The detail concerned his own ancestor and he did not think he had ever come across a man in history braver or nobler or more determined in his duty than Sir

Robert de Morey. But Adam kept thinking of the prospect of Jane, naked between cool and spotless cotton sheets.

Her composure had returned. She reclined on her chair with her long legs crossed at the knee, curling a stray lock of hair with a finger. She was pale – her colouring made her naturally pale – but she no longer looked like she had in the pier café. The bright red blush of her lips and the sparkle in her eyes had reappeared.

Adam looked at the two men in the room. He was sure that both of them had deliberately killed other men. They might not be killing machines, the guided missile of the medieval world his ancestor de Morey had been, but they had taken lives with skill and premeditation, he was certain of it. He did not want to dwell on the fact. On the whole, it was much more pleasant to think about the prospect of making love to Jane.

McGuire stood. 'I'll make some coffee,' he said. He looked at his watch. It was just after six o'clock. He turned to Grayling. 'And then I must tell our two young guests what really happened at Sarajevo.'

Jane glanced at Adam. He winked at her and said, 'Could we have a proper drink, Doctor McGuire?'

'Of course you can,' said McGuire. 'Firstly, though, I shall give you good reason to need one with a short preamble to the tale I am about to tell.'

His tone of voice had changed. They both sat up, alert in their chairs.

'I was born in Aberdeen in 1882. I have lived for far too long. My name when I was born was Angus Robert Haydn Grayling. My father was a physician. Stuart there is my great-grandson – a finer forebear, no man could reasonably wish for, but that's by the by. My first proper occupation was as an espionage agent working in the service of the Crown. I first became aware of the existence of the shadow world as a student member of an occult brotherhood at Edinburgh University in the autumn of 1910.'

Adam let out a whistle. Jane merely stared.

'Now, I'll fetch those drinks,' McGuire said, making for the kitchen and the fridge.

'You lied about him,' Adam said to Grayling.

'At that stage, you would have thought me mad if I'd told you the truth. Doing so would have been self-defeating.'

'I think you have a talent for deceit.'

'Given the circumstances, it's as well that some of us do,' Grayling said.

'Stop it,' Jane said, 'both of you.' She looked at Grayling. 'You should have fenced, as Adam did. You would have been good at it.'

'I did,' Grayling said. 'And I was.'

McGuire came back in, carrying a tray bearing little cans of mixers and a bucket of ice, and a chilled bottle of white wine and a beer for Adam.

Jane had taken a sip of her Chablis when she said to McGuire, 'You were aboard her, weren't you? You were on the gun deck of *Incomparable* when she was lured into the Miasmic Sea.'

He had his back to her, over at his drinks cabinet, pouring whisky for himself and Grayling. He stiffened. 'I was.'

'You used magic to escape. It's why you are still alive. You called upon something very potent to save you.'

He turned to face her.

'It means we have allies there,' Jane said, 'in the shadow world. We must have. You were able to call upon their help.'

'I'll begin at the beginning,' he said. 'It began for me, as I've said, in the autumn of 1910 in Edinburgh. That was a bitter winter in Scotland.' He smiled at the recollection. 'No global warming at the start of the last century, not as I remember. The snow was already thick and heavy on the ground.'

Her name was Alabaster Swift. She was studying chemistry. It was rumoured that she had mounted a framed photograph of Marie Curie on the wall in her rooms but of course none of the male students knew that for sure because for men to go there was strictly forbidden by the college rules. What was certain was that she was a confident and extremely capable student. She was also strikingly beautiful, with violet eyes and a sensuous mouth and an unruly mane of auburn hair.

Its clandestine nature was the sustaining force of their occult society. They called it the Hades Club. McGuire did not think that any of them actually believed in occult goings-on, much less attempted their practice. But meeting by candlelight over a log fire at the inn room they hired under an assumed name was exciting.

They would scare one another with ghost stories and tales of curses and ancient prophesies of doom. The inn itself was supposedly haunted. With its gothic turrets and open blazes in great stone and iron grates, with the wind howling at its high, narrow windows, it was certainly properly atmospheric.

Because the Hades Club members were mostly students on the science courses, they were progressive generally. They were drawn to magic in the way that the computer geeks of a century on would be drawn to cyberspace fantasy games about witches and warlocks. They were secretive about their club, but not snobbish or misogynistic in the way that the equivalent society at Oxford or Cambridge certainly would have been at that time.

Nobody knew how Alabaster Swift found out about them. Or none of the members confessed to knowing. McGuire suspected someone had simply told her, pleased with themselves and showing off. When she made discreet enquiries about joining the Hades Club, they were delighted and flattered. Everybody who knew her knew of her intellectual accomplishments, her skill in the laboratory. But she was also enigmatic and distinctly glamorous. She would add to their exotic character and mystique.

She seemed to enjoy their stories about malevolent beasts of bosky legend and galleons struggling through hostile seas burdened by a pirate's curse. Scottish and Scandinavian folklore intrigued and evidently also amused her. She was openly fascinated by stories of the Highland witches and their trials and persecution in the time of Oliver Cromwell. They did not really notice that she did not contribute material of her own. They were too busy trying to impress her, jostling conversationally to be the one to treat her to a monologue about a ghoul or a disturbing claim about some apparently blighted location.

They met once a week, on a Thursday evening. At the conclusion of the meetings they took turns to walk her home. Her college curfew was earlier than theirs and while the male students would linger over a late beverage, she would be obliged to leave punctually.

After the fifth meeting she attended, it was the turn of McGuire to escort her back. More accurately it was the turn of Angus Grayling, the young medical student he had been back then. For most of that particular evening, the dominant topic of discussion had been reanimation. They had strayed on to the zombies of Haitian voodoo and the vampire undead of Eastern European folk tradition. This latter mythic species had seemed to particularly fascinate Alabaster, and she continued to discuss it on the walk back.

Perhaps that was why they got lost. Alabaster was absorbed by the subject of nocturnal drinkers of blood who slept by day in their coffins. McGuire was flattered by the attention paid his words by a young woman far more attractive and engaging than any other in his youthful experience.

Then there was the snow. It made everywhere look the same. The city was featureless under its white uniformity. They only realized they had strayed into the rough area of the town when a party exiting a seedy-looking tavern turned and appraised and then began to follow them.

McGuire was three years away from beginning the habit of carrying a concealed blade in his walking cane. He was unarmed and unprepared physically or psychologically for a fight with half a dozen street toughs.

He thought that robbery was the likely motive for the pursuit but knew enough about crime in the city to think that violence would certainly accompany it. Should he resist, or would that only increase the severity of the beating? Would it endanger Alabaster even more than the situation already did?

He glanced at her. She seemed serene, unperturbed. Behind them, the gang members were closing the distance, packed snow on the pavement squeaking ever closer under their boot leather. Snow flurried thickly through the air. The streetlamps were few and their light scant in the lane into which they had strayed. And the weather meant that there was no crowd to take refuge in, no witnesses to deter a brazen attack.

'You must promise me to keep what you are about to see from our fellow club members,' Alabaster said. Her words were delivered in a murmur so low McGuire thought he might have misheard them.

'What?'

'Promise me.'

The gang was almost upon them.

'I promise.'

'Good.' She turned. McGuire turned almost with her. There were seven or eight of them. They wore caps and overcoats and complexions made raw by whisky and cold. Two of them carried short wooden cudgels and there was the matt gleam in the snow of a brandished blade. The closest of them was near enough to have begun to raise, for the blow it would deliver, the heavy, leather-covered sap gripped in his right fist.

Alabaster lifted both hands and extended them. She flexed and folded her fingers in what looked to McGuire like the rapid parody of a pianist's exercise. And on a hoarse intake of breath she made a rhythmic sound in a language he had never heard before and he thought, *she is incanting something*. The gang stopped as one man, as though petrified into stone. There was a half-blink of time when nothing happened. Their last exhalations of breath cleared from their frozen faces. And they toppled rigid to the ground.

'I have not killed them,' she said.

'But you could have.'

'They will remember nothing. They will awaken frozen and bruised, which is the least they deserve. You must keep your promise.'

'You are capable of magic.'

'Yes, I am.'

Snow fell on to the faces and clothing of the men on the ground. Their mouths lay open and their eyes were wide and senseless and the descending flakes did not make them blink. 'Where did you learn it?'

'You are far better not knowing,' said Alabaster Swift.

She told him just the same. Her life was solitary, the more so because of her secret. Confiding in McGuire made it less so. She had crossed and she could successfully pass. But she missed things about the world she had been born and grown up in and she missed the trust and intimacy of friendship. In her new confidant there on earth, she rediscovered it.

They did not become lovers. McGuire hoped, but in a fairly hopeless sort of way. He was small featured and of slightly less than average height. On his optimistic days he thought he might possess a boyish charm. She was tall and imperiously beautiful.

Perhaps that would not have mattered to her. He did not know. Curiously, he knew that the age difference between them did not matter to her either. He was twenty years old on the evening of the spell cast upon the robber gang in the snow. Alabaster, she told him, was by then already fifty-eight.

'Callow in our years,' she said. 'It's an age that barely puts me beyond adolescence.'

'Is it the same there for everyone?'

'It is always so for those born with the gift of sorcery. It is not so for everyone, though the lifespan there is naturally longer than it is here. That is often cited by our rulers as a symptom of our superiority to you people.'

'You do not accept the argument?'

'Sea turtles live to a great age, Angus. So do certain birds of paradise and some species of whale. It is an anomaly of nature only. Longevity requires no talent or special aptitude. It can be a gift or a curse but is not an attainment.'

'You speak my language wonderfully well.'

She shrugged. 'I speak it precisely.'

'Will you teach me yours?'

'Yes, I will.'

Two things made him more open to her revelations about Endrimor than he might otherwise have been. The first was his youth. The young are accepting of new concepts and the student mentality encouraged the acquisition of knowledge. He was more open than cynical and had no prejudice against possibilities he had not previously entertained.

The second characteristic predisposing him to believe was his own interest in matters mysterious and unexplained. Once told about the shadow world, about the great conflict and its spiteful architects, much of what had puzzled him about human history made clearer sense than it had.

And this process worked both ways. The Vampire mythos was obviously inspired by events on Endrimor. Though the count ruling the Kingdom of Parasites was human, the nocturnal bloodsuckers protecting him were not.

Nothing about his relationship with Alabaster Swift troubled McGuire as much as her abrupt abandonment of it. She vanished suddenly and completely. Months went by. A full year passed. There was no word or mortal trace of her. He immersed himself in his studies. Then, in the early December of 1911, he received the summons to London and to Whitehall.

From the start it was unconventional. He would sign no visitors' book and fill out no forms. His attendance was not logged. The fact of it went completely unrecorded. Instead he was ushered into a side door on a narrow mews and taken through a labyrinth of corridors, the heels of his carefully polished shoes clacking along what felt like miles of parquet. Eventually his elderly, frock-coated guide paused outside a door. He knocked upon it lightly, once.

'Enter,' commanded a muffled voice from within.

McGuire walked into the room and closed the door carefully behind him. He was in a small study. A coke fire burned in a little grate. After the frozen ordeal of the London streets and the chill of the endless corridor, it was warm in the room. The man with whom he shared it stood with a hand on the mantelpiece. Leather easy chairs were angled before the fire and he gestured for them both to sit. He was tall and slender and very distinguished looking. His hair and clipped beard were white and his eyes had the glint of steel in winter sunlight.

He did not say anything immediately; nor did he look at the young man summoned there to see him. He stared over the steeple of his fingers into the red heart of his little fire. Finally, he spoke: 'Chance is the name we give to events when we don't yet know their purpose.'

McGuire swallowed. The Whitehall man had spoken the words in Endrimorian. He did not know how to reply. Finally, the man looked at him. And he said, 'You understood that sentence, didn't you?'

'I think you know I did.'

'Do you agree with it?'

'I don't know. What happened to her?'

Again, there was a long silence before any reply was forthcoming. 'She committed a grave crime in coming here. She compounded it in studying a subject with the scientific rationality of chemistry. I can see the logic of it for her, the lure if you will; but it was a terrible risk for her to take.'

'Why?

'They abhor science. They despise technology. It mocks and threatens every warped principle on which their society is based.'

'So what happened to her?'

'We cannot be certain. Her nerve may have failed her and she may simply have fled. They may have located her and sent an assassin. If they did, he would have torn out her tongue and made her swallow it before killing her. Her death would have been drawn out.'

'That's barbaric.'

'Barbarism isn't far away, my young friend. It laps at our shores and the tide is strengthening. A storm gathers. A deluge looms and a flood threatens us.'

'That all sounds very apocalyptic.'

'I do not exaggerate.' He smiled. 'Let me have some tea fetched, Mr McGuire. Do you like toasted teacakes?'

'Yes.'

'With marmalade, I'll warrant, since you're a Scot.'

'Marmalade would do very well.'

'We will have our tea and we will discuss your career ambitions. I can always find gainful employment for a man of talent and the necessary discretion.'

By the high summer of 1914, much had changed about the young fellow who would eventually come to be known as McGuire. He was by then a qualified doctor. But there were other, less likely accomplishments.

He was an excellent swordsman and a skilled practitioner of the oriental martial arts. He was an expert shot with both pistol and rifle. He had learned to transmit Morse code. He was a very good driver and a capable mechanic. He could sail a boat single-handedly and navigate the route to any seagoing destination. On a clear night he could do this without instruments, by the light of the stars.

He thought that his old Hades Club colleague and confidante, the exotic Miss Swift, might find him a figure of greater substance and appeal by then. The diffidence had gone. He was capable and confident and decisive.

He would have said the weight of his responsibility to the world had made the change in him necessary, but he might concede privately that his experience of fighting and killing had brought gravity and seriousness to his make-up. How she might react to him he could only speculate. He hoped she was alive and happy somewhere, but he never saw or heard from her again.

The Sarajevo intervention had failed for a number of reasons. They had intelligence that the shadow world had sent Darius Maul, their fabled assassin. The agents of earth had been concentrating on the hunt for him. They had not thought the Black Hand capable of orchestrating anything really dangerous. They were fanatical, but they were badly organized amateurs. Fanaticism rather than professionalism was the qualification that earned their active members their decisive rolls.

It had not helped that the intervention was an international initiative. French and Italian agents were involved along with the Scotsman sent by Great Britain. Languages and egos inevitably clashed. The obsession with Maul was the key to the failure, though.

His rumoured presence was a distraction that occupied too much attention and absorbed too much manpower. And the fluke of Princip's ambling into the perfect position to take the shot was a piece of bad luck they could not have provided for. They had not known the identity of the five young Black Hand gunmen. Had they done so, they would have hunted down and discreetly eliminated them in the teeming anonymity of the Sarajevo streets.

'The Maul distraction was clever,' McGuire told Adam and Jane. 'The murder of the archduke itself was a masterstroke. But what if it had been averted? I have often asked myself this. Could war by then have been prevented? Did any of the great nations really want diplomacy to prevail? Sometimes it seems to me they have needed little prompting from the shadow world to rush gleefully towards self-destruction.'

'I've seen the photographs taken in the immediate aftermath of the Sarajevo assassination,' Adam said. 'I looked at them after coming here and speaking to you the first time, with the artefact. There is one capturing the moment of Princip's arrest, and he looks dazed, almost hypnotized. Do you think there is a possibility that he was?'

'I do and always have. I don't think Maul was sent, but they sent somebody with another set of skills entirely. Someone with the power to enchant people infiltrated the Black Hand. I think all five of those young men were mesmerized. You will see a similar look on the face of your erstwhile colleague Martin Prior, should you see him again. And I think you will. I also think you should be very much on your guard, both of you, when you do.'

'They may not have needed to send their mesmerist from the shadow world,' Jane said. 'There was someone already on earth who was capable of magic and who could successfully pass. What's more, she possessed a proven gift for learning earthly languages.'

'And speaking them precisely,' Adam said.

'She was running,' Jane said. 'She had taken flight in Edinburgh and eluded them. By the time they caught up with her, they had a scheme requiring someone with her skills, so they offered her an opportunity to redeem herself. And, of course, she took it. And pardoned, she was then obliged to go home. Does that strike you as a plausible scenario, Doctor McGuire?'

'It had occurred to me, of course. It's a question of whether their pragmatism could outweigh their spite in the balance. If she did do it, she achieved something momentous for them. But she would have needed guarantees concerning her safety to go back willingly and the Crimson King is nothing if not capricious.'

'You do not want to believe she did it,' Adam said. 'You loved her.'

'More than that,' McGuire said, with a wan smile. 'She was the only woman I ever did love.'

TWELVE

They left McGuire and the professor just before eight o'clock and went to a seafront bar. Grayling had booked them into separate rooms at the same boutique hotel. It was only half a mile from the doctor's promenade flat.

Brighton was a city and a very famous resort with a colourful history, but physically it was much smaller than most English cities. It would have been a cosy sort of place, Adam thought, if it wasn't so self-consciously edgy, so drugged-up and heavily pierced and beaded and tattooed.

Their conversation was a bit stilted in the bar. Adam tried for carefree, but his dialogue didn't take off, let alone soar. Partly it was the sobering magnitude of what McGuire had confided. His age alone was a quite terrifying revelation when you thought about how much he must have done and witnessed over that turbulent life of his. Partly it was nervousness over what was to come. He had never been nervous prior to a sexual encounter before, but he had never experienced sex with anyone about whom he felt the way he did about Jane.

He wanted things to be successful between them. He wanted everything to be perfect. You could not choreograph the mechanics of sex. You could not rehearse it mentally. It happened pretty much spontaneously and was good or bad, felt right or impossibly wrong, indifferent to what you hoped for it.

They had come close before to making love. It had seemed right then, on her sofa in her Cambridge flat. But there was no knowing, was there, until it was too late, if it was to be a failure or an anti-climax.

Jane said, 'Are you as nervous about tonight as I am?'

'No. More so, I should think.'

She stood. 'Let's go back to the hotel.'

'You want to get it over with?'

She smiled. 'No, Adam. I just can't wait a moment longer to get started.'

In the event, neither of them need have worried. In one another's arms, as the night unfolded, they discovered ecstasy and then a blissful refuge in one another.

They were woken in the morning by the bedside radio, which had come on automatically at eight o'clock. It must have been set to do so by the previous occupant of the room. Jane had her back to Adam. The duvet had wriggled down in the night and he looked at her back, from the splayed tangles of hair that covered it between her shoulder blades, along the creamy skin of her spine to the cleft at the top of her bottom.

The radio was on her side of the room. It was a talk station and people were phoning in with shrill opinions about the Congressional Hearing the Americans were holding over what was now called the Fort Bragg Vaccine Exposé. It seemed surreal to hear Martin's name reverentially mentioned on a national broadcast. It also seemed miraculous to be lying beside Jane after the naked passion of the previous night. He reached for her and stroked her hair, then pushed the strands away to kiss her neck, reaching over her to switch off the shrill row erupting over the airwaves.

'We can't hide from it,' she said drowsily.

'We can for a while. We'll be forgiven.'

She laughed into her pillow, her shoulders trembling against the touch of his lips. Her skin was warm and smooth. She smelled of shampoo and Shalimar perfume and sex. 'Who will forgive us? Martin won't.'

'Fuck Martin.'

'Ugh. No thanks.' She laughed again. Then she rolled towards him to return his kisses.

They showered together and shared a late breakfast on their balcony. There was no wind and the sun shone from a clear sky. Their room overlooked the sea. From their balcony chairs they could hear the breaking waves hissing into the shingle. The pier was a distant, spindly, abbreviated bridge.

'Back to the usual routine next week,' Adam said. 'Lectures, seminars, essay topics to pick.'

'Nothing will ever be normal again,' Jane said. 'That's the point of our night in this hotel. It's Grayling's treat, our last before the serious business begins.'

'You think he knew we'd sleep together when he booked the rooms?'

'When it comes to reading people, on a scale of one to ten, he's an eleven. He's very shrewd and alert to situations. It's why he's still alive.'

'Do you still think he's gay?'

She shrugged.

'I wouldn't put it past you to think Robert de Morey swung both ways. He was awfully fond of the count.'

She smiled. She enjoyed being teased. 'I don't think de Morey had issues with his masculinity. I suspect he was fully in touch with his feminine side.'

'You should share that insight with the professor, in exactly those words. It would go down really well.' Adam looked out towards the pier. 'I had a kind of hallucination out there the first time I came to see McGuire. I realized last night when he was talking that it was about *Incomparable*. I know it sounds a bit bizarre, but I sort of saw what happened to the sailors aboard her, the state they were in on the Miasmic Sea. It was nightmarish.'

'I dreamed about it,' Jane said. 'I fell asleep in the front passenger seat of the Land Rover on the road back from Cree to Cambridge and I was aboard her. It must be a sort of telepathy or shared vibe between us all. I thought about it when Grayling quoted what that Whitehall mandarin said to him.'

'Chance is how we describe events when we don't yet know their purpose,' Adam said. 'My dad quoted that line to me on his deathbed. We don't have a choice, do we, about any of all this?'

'We don't have any choice about being involved,' Jane said. 'We have to believe, though, that we can affect the outcome. We have to think we can stop the undermining. If we don't, the future will be very bleak. Are you still determined to go back to Rotterdam?'

'There'll be nobody else. If I don't attend that funeral, he will have gone to his grave unlamented. I'll regret it for the rest of my life.'

'It might *cost* you your life, Adam. I couldn't bear that.' She reached across their table for his hand.

He squeezed hers. 'It won't,' he said.

'Grayling was attacked in Canterbury.'

'Opportunistically, I think. He was being watched, observed. He made the mistake of straying on to isolated ground and his stalker saw his chance. That's my reading of it. There's been no second attempt. He hasn't given them the chance.'

'When will you go?'

'I'll leave this afternoon.'

'I'm not going to sit in Cambridge waiting for you to come back. I'm going to go and see my father. And then I'm going to go and find Dora and ask her a few questions about her romantic life.'

'You don't much care for your dad, do you?'

'It's more that I've never believed he greatly cared for me. But what Rabanus Bloor said about my sister makes me think I might have misjudged my dad rather badly. I can be a complete bloody idiot at times, it's very annoying.'

'I'll remind you that you said that.'

'Don't bother,' she said. 'I'll just deny it.' She reached over and ruffled his hair and kissed him. 'And I'm such a good liar, you'll believe me.'

He crunched over ground he couldn't see under the night cloud cover, in the absence of the neon which had flashed over the door with lurid optimism the last time he was here. The door was slightly ajar. He went inside. There was a smell of stale cigarette smoke and beer. There was stillness and cold and neglect. He skirted items of bar furniture and found a power switch in a back room. He switched it on and the strip lights buzzed and flickered and came alive.

She had fled, funded by his father's money. She had stayed to care for the man who had delivered her from Endrimor until his death. He was gone now, but he would have left her something, wouldn't he? The bar would have provided only a subsistence living, Adam thought. The money left her by his father would be needed to enable Delilah to travel. The bar felt and looked dismal in her absence. She had endowed even this drab place with a desperate sort of glamour. It had departed with her. He wondered where a woman with her impact on men could successfully conceal herself. He wondered also whether her abrupt disappearance signalled a specific threat.

He helped himself to a bottle of beer from a cold shelf puddled with melted ice. It was cool rather than properly chilled, but it would do. He opened it and raised a silent toast to absent friends. There it was again, that feeling of lost intimacy, of someone he knew well and cared for deeply, gone.

It was an emotional response the facts did not really justify. He had known Delilah for only a couple of weeks and spent only a matter of hours in her company. Yet the strength of feeling couldn't be denied. He did not know what it signified, unless it meant that there was something unfinished between them and they were destined to share some future encounter.

He saw the letter, then. Or rather, he saw the pale envelope on the bar, the letter shoved hastily back inside it as though by doing so, the message it contained could actually be undelivered. It was not good news, Adam knew with a feeling of cold dread, as he put down his beer and picked up the envelope. He opened its contents.

It was a single, thick sheet of paper, folded into four. Unfolded, he saw that it contained no written words. In that sense it was blank. But it was heavily embossed. A large bird with outspread wings and fierce beak and talons stretched in flight in raised relief from the centre of the sheet.

It looked like something mythic, like some heraldic beast dreamed up by the craftsmen who decorated warriors' shields in the time of his own noble ancestor. But he knew that it was a representation from life and he knew too where it came from. It was a Vorp. And it was also a warning. They had located and were coming for her.

Unless, that was, they had come for her already.

Adam refolded the sheet of paper and put it into his pocket. He sniffed at the air. He could not smell violence the way that McGuire had claimed he could. Blood smelled coppery and fear was a sour secretion, and he could detect neither odour. None of the chairs or tables had been knocked over in a struggle. No glasses or bottles had been smashed. He opened the till. It was empty. She had not been abducted. Her departure might have been hasty and fearful, but it had been escape rather than capture. That was something.

Why had they warned her? He thought that he knew. It was an established protocol, a formal beginning to the punishment ritual. The dread it provoked was the point of the warning. The slow process of her execution had begun with the letter's delivery. But it was as much a boast as a threat, wasn't it? It told her that she could not elude them. The tongue would be torn from her head and she would choke on it. Her fate had been decided and her attempts to avoid it would be futile.

He switched off the lights and walked out of the bar. It had a derelict look already. He could walk the few hundred yards to the creek and take a last look at his father's barge, but the barge was no longer home to his father. His stuff was neatly crated and packed safely away in a storage facility until Adam decided what to do with it.

The barge had been sold to someone else. He would be a trespasser aboard her. Two lives he had only recently learned of had now gone from here. He would walk instead to his hotel. In the morning, he had a burial to attend.

Pages of a discarded newspaper blew on the ground around his feet. He flattened a spread with the sole of his boot, his eye caught by something there. There was a banner headline he could not read because the language was Dutch. Under it was a picture of a young man standing at a podium addressing some kind of formal gathering.

Adam's first thought on seeing the photograph was that Martin Prior looked good in a suit. His second was that there was something that had not been there previously in the expression in Martin's eyes.

Jane visited her father in Canterbury. She thought that he had lost weight. They met at a restaurant for lunch and after their casual kiss of greeting, once she had sat down and ordered a glass of sparkling water, she sneaked a look over her menu at him and thought him definitely thinner and paler than she remembered him being the last time, back in the late summer, before the start of the term.

It was odd, because he was almost always tanned. He would travel to somewhere in Africa or the Middle East to oversee some critical period of construction of something and come back with his face brown and his famously shaven head burnished. But he was pale today.

'This fish is very good,' he said. 'I can recommend it with my conscience clear.'

'I need to talk to you about Dora.'

'I've been worried about you. You read the document I found?'

'Once Grayling had transcribed it, yes, I did. I don't share your scholarly fluency in Latin.'

'You could, dear. You picked up Greek in about a fortnight, as I recall.'

'I think Dora might be in trouble.'

Sir Rupert put down his menu and looked at Jane. 'Dora *is* trouble,' he said. 'She always has been. You are opposites.'

'Like darkness and light?'

Her father blinked. 'Who suggested that comparison?'

'Someone from the land we dare not name. The same man I saw in the forest at Cree. The one I'm sure Professor Grayling told you about when he broke it to you that I would need to read the de Morey to prepare me. I think she's been there, Dad. I think Dora might have been to the shadow world. The Siren of Rotterdam said the traffic travels both ways and always has.'

'Who the bloody hell is the Siren of Rotterdam?'

'It doesn't matter.'

'I understand you are courting, Jane.'

'I am. His name is Adam. He is directly descended from de Morey.'

'Yes, well, I suppose he would be, wouldn't he?'

'You're not shocked?'

'Stuart Grayling said the struggle was dynastic. I don't suppose I found the deposition by accident at all.'

'Chance is how we describe events when we don't yet know their purpose,' Jane said.

'There is something malign in your sister. It has been there since she was born, I think, by which I mean she was born with it. It repelled me. In trying to treat you both equally, for the sake of fairness, I treated you with the coldness and disdain with which I treated her. But I always loved you, Jane. I love you very much. God forgive me, I love your sister too.'

She reached for his hand across the table and held it. 'You don't have to explain, Dad.' She could afford the generosity of saying that, she thought, now that he had done so.

He coughed. There were tears, unconstrained, leaking from his eyes. 'Tough love, your mother called it. She convinced me it would work. But it punished you and left your twin indifferent.'

Their waiter arrived. They ordered their food. They ate their starters. Jane could not even have said what it was she was having. 'Did you ever wonder why de Morey wrote the account at all?'

'I've had twenty-five years to think about it. He wrote it as a double-bluff, a long and truthful litany of events concealing the lie at its heart. I am convinced Eleanor Bloor crossed and they were reunited. If I'm right, the blood of more than one world runs through Adam's veins.'

'I think you're right and so does he. Why do they hate us so much?'

'It's gone well beyond whatever original motive they had. They haven't solved the problem of the Miasmic Sea, I don't think. I expect its polluting sickness has spread. And I suspect the Kingdom of Parasites is a bigger problem to them now than it's ever been. They seek a fresh start. They want our world, but they want it unpopulated.'

'Do you think the undermining can be stopped?'

Sir Rupert seemed to ponder this question for a long time. Then he said, 'They do things in a particular way. They have a feudal predilection for single combat, for champions. They appear to be capable of some kind of sorcery. Beyond that, they like the volatile nations of the earth to do the dirty work on their behalf, as the events of the twentieth century demonstrated so bloodily. We barely survived that.

'The truthful answer is that I don't know, Jane. In some ways it seems the shadow world is very predictable and that's to our advantage, if we're clever. But the complexity of our world makes it a far more volatile and fragile place than it was in the time of the Black Death. The Cold War came much closer to destroying us than the pestilence.'

'A nuclear war wouldn't be to their advantage. It would destroy the new home they covet, the world they want to colonize.'

'There is far less chance of any war being nuclear now than there was fifty years ago. The old balance of the superpowers is gone. Wars are won with anthrax vials and improvised roadside bombs and suicide vests. The world is far more fragmented now, and there is a great deal of latent hostility. Have you noticed the international impact of that poisonous nonsense Martin Prior is peddling on the internet?'

'Not really.'

'Believe me, Jane. We're more vulnerable than we've ever been.'

Their main courses arrived and for a while they ate in silence. Jane was aware that this was the most grown-up conversation she had ever shared with her dad. After what he had said to her, she could barely taste the food. The texture of the flakes in her mouth told her that she was eating fish. It was a waste, really. It was probably delicious.

'Where's Dora?'

Sir Rupert smiled. 'You've never been close, have you?'

'I don't even know where she's living. So there's your answer.'

'She rents a flat in Chelsea.'

'You mean that you rent it on her behalf.'

He shrugged. 'She is my daughter. I do not like her and never have. But I think that an unadulterated regime of tough love would have lured Dora into crime or prostitution by now. I tell myself that helping her out economically encourages what little morality she possesses.'

'How does it do that?'

'By providing her with stability and a measure of domestic security and earning her gratitude.'

'I see.'

'It's a small price to pay.'

For a man with her father's wealth, Jane thought it certainly true that it was a small price. She also thought it a dubious investment. From what she had heard, Dora's lifestyle choices were dodgy enough without a subsidy to encourage them.

The Siren of Rotterdam would have enjoyed the irony of this appellation, had Delilah been aware of the nickname Jane had given her. She had her charms and they were sensuous and potent, and they would do nothing at all to protect her from the deadly attentions of Proctor Maul.

She remembered him at court, when her job had been to teach music to the son and daughter of the king. She had seen him almost daily and though it was said, at least on earth, that familiarity bred contempt, she had not become contemptuous of him.

She had feared him, as she was supposed to do, as everyone did. Uncertainty was the currency of the court and fear was what underwrote it and maintained its value.

She had enjoyed teaching the children. Her escape had been more forced on her than planned. They had pleasant natures and were both clever and gifted. But when they reached the age when they began to be taught their lessons in ethics, when their deliberate corruption began, she found that her fondness for them made that an unbearable process to witness.

She resigned her position and went north. Disguising the natural refinement with which she spoke, she opened a tavern and the tavern prospered. She discovered there just how popular she was with men.

It was said that the king never forgot. Probably it was true. Certainly it was true that he never forgot anything he might perceive

as a slight. So she was not at all surprised when the letter from
Sebastian Dray arrived, saying that it was the king's wish for her
to return to her music teaching duties at the court. She was only
really surprised that it had taken two years for the missive finally
to come summoning her back.

Dray was a courteous man. He was very careful not to show it,
but she also thought him instinctively kind. He disguised this
tendency, which would have been construed as weakness, but she
thought it was there. He was considerate and compassionate. It was
the reason, she thought, that his letter allowed her a month in which
to frame her response. If it was time enough to prepare for returning,
it was also time enough to plot her escape.

She was sure the melancholy sailor with the kind eyes was from
earth. Once in a while he would come and sit and drink alone in
the tavern. Once he had been careless with one of the sleeves that
covered his arms and she had caught a glimpse of some motif inked
there. On Endrimor, only assassins wore tattoos.

The sailor was not an assassin. He spoke little, only to order a
drink and pass a comment about the weather, but the tongue had
not been rent from his head to guarantee his silence. However reticent, he was capable of speech.

One evening, very late, a week after the letter, she saw her
opportunity. He had drunk a little too much. Melancholy had become
moroseness in him. Men in such a condition always liked to talk
about what was laying low their spirits. She fetched him a beer he
had not ordered and joined him at his table. The candles were
guttering. The rain hammering at the panes had deterred her trade.
The place was almost empty. Her serving girl would cover in her
absence from the bar.

'What ails you?'

He blinked and looked at her before replying. Then he told her
that he had two sons. Fate had deprived him of the presence of the
one he loved. The other, he said, he had been given cause only to
fear and fret over. He had failed at fatherhood. He had failed at
everything in life. He had achieved nothing remarkable and was
sorrowfully confident that he never would.

'You could take me back to earth with you,' she said, so quietly
that she hardly heard herself say the words. 'Once there, you could
help me pass. That would be remarkable. It would also be very
brave.'

'It would be foolhardy,' he said.

'It would be my salvation.'

He did not reply. He sipped from the pot of beer she had brought him, then wiped his lips with the back of his hand.

'Are you thinking about it?'

'I am thinking about the Miasmic Sea and my immunity to its charms,' he said. 'I am thinking of something an old man once said to me when he said chance is how we describe events when we don't yet know their purpose.'

'Does that mean you will help me?'

'Yes, I think it does.'

Possibility rose and just as swiftly sank in her. 'But you are drunk.'

'In the morning I'll be sober. And I won't have changed my mind.'

Delilah expected that Maul would find her because he had found her already and she did not think now that she would be able ever to lose him. She would hide nevertheless.

First she would post the letter to the son of the man who had gifted her with seven years of carefree, earthbound life. She thought that it might be of help to him in what he was trying to do. She had never known a man who could resist her once they had tasted her kiss. He was remarkable, if only for that. But he was remarkable in more important ways. He had been chosen to fight in a noble cause and she would assist him if she could with what she knew.

His father had paid for a funeral mass. Adam was surprised his dad had retained his Catholic faith. The six candles burned in their big brass holders, three each side, flanking the coffin. Catholic churches were scarce in Rotterdam. Holland was proudly Protestant in its national religion. But the Dutch were a tolerant people, were they not? Apart from the Jews they happily surrendered under occupation in the Second World War, he thought. Apart, too, from the nation's million Muslims now.

He supposed such thoughts were provoked by what he had seen and heard the previous evening. His interest stirred by the discarded newspaper featuring Martin's picture, he had watched the Sky News channel in his hotel room.

He had discovered that the descendants of the victims of the Spanish flu epidemic in several North American cities had launched a class action seeking damages against their own government for the deaths. Legal experts said the compensation claim could run into billions of dollars. The United States had already struck a compensation deal with the major European nations affected, which did run into billions. The exact figure would remain undisclosed. Great Britain, Ireland and France had been the major beneficiaries. The president was to deliver a public apology for the Bragg Fiasco.

Adam thought fiasco a frivolous word to describe a blunder that had cost millions of innocent lives. Then he watched in disbelief as the channel ran footage of the sacked and burned-out Russian embassy in the Zimbabwean capital, Harare. The Russian embassy in Cape Town was besieged.

There was nobody inside the embassy to be concerned about that, because South Africa had expelled the embassy staff and severed diplomatic relations with Russia altogether. Moscow wasn't dishing out compensatory roubles, though. Nor did an apology seem likely. The Kremlin had strongly denied and continued to deny the Tashkent story about the mistaken creation of AIDS.

It wasn't just a question of Martin's face popping up on television. The medium required sound bites. And Adam had to concede to himself that Martin was very good at giving them.

He sat open-mouthed at the incredible detail concerning Martin's bodyguard. There had been death threats against this fearless crusader for truth. The British security services were providing him with twenty-four-hour protection at the taxpayers' expense. He was pretty good value, Adam thought, in terms of what Britain had just gained in dollars for the Spanish flu. But the bigger picture was that his antics were stirring up resentments that could have terrible consequences for international relations and for the moral authority of the nations his stories besmirched and scandalized.

There was almost nobody in the church. He was the only mourner, the sole occupant of the front pew. A couple of elderly mass groupies sat somewhere towards the back of the church, missing out, Adam thought, on the smell of the incense the priest coaxed from the burner when he swung it over the coffin.

He did not personally care for the smell. Nor did he care for the smell of burning candle wax. They reminded him of poverty and loss. They were the smells of too much of his childhood when his prayers had gone unanswered and his own faith unrewarded by events.

Eventually the service concluded and the coffin was wheeled out into the rain and slid into the back of the hearse. His father's remains were to be cremated. He had not cried during the funeral mass and would not do so at the crematorium, he knew.

The body in the hearse was his father's but was a cadaver only, cold and dressed. His father had gone on the afternoon he had grieved, watching him slip from life aboard the barge a few days earlier. He was here to honour his passing formally but had done his mourning already, elsewhere. He would maintain the family dignity. He had recently discovered he possessed a great name. And now he was the last of his line.

Waiting to climb into the funeral car, Adam became aware that he was being watched. It was a sensation like the trickle of an icicle between his shoulder blades. The cold discomfort of it could not be ignored. The two-car convoy occupied a circle of gravel outside the main entrance to the church. The scrutiny came from behind him. He turned. Grass stretched beyond the gravel to a wooden fence. Over one section of it was a small stand of trees. In the wet and gloomy light under the boughs, a lone figure stood.

He was heavily built but poised, his considerable weight balanced perfectly on the balls of nimble feet. He was entirely still but looked restless, as though this motionless attitude was an act of will, unnatural to him. He looked powerful and quick, a human weapon cocked and lethal should the discipline restraining him fail and the trigger of his temper be pulled. Adam knew immediately who it was.

He had never been in the proximity of anyone more dangerous. He felt no fear at all. That was odd, he thought, even illogical. But it was true. He walked across the grass. The air thickened with impending violence the closer he got to the man. It was like wading through static. The atmosphere grew gravid with threat, heavy, immense. It was a struggle to breathe it in. Silence spread outward from the well-dressed figure in the shade of the trees. Rain fell on to the grass around him in a respectful whisper. Adam stood before him.

'You would be Proctor Maul,' he said. 'Have you come here to pay your respects?'

The assassin did not reply. He could not.

Adam did not feel respectful towards Maul. 'Cat got your tongue?'

Maul still stood entirely still, his eyes concealed by black sunglasses. He was around six feet tall, bald-headed and attired in a beautifully tailored three-piece suit. The cloth was brown and had to it a slight sheen. He filled the suit, Adam observed, as solidly as someone might if sculpted from marble.

He raised a hand, took off his sunglasses and stared Adam in the eye. His face was tattooed. The ink made deep recesses of his eyes, which were almost black. His skin was roughly textured and had a reddish quality to it. His exhaled breath smelled sharp like vinegar. He bowed curtly, just his head moving on his thick neck, and when it was raised and still again the hand not holding the glasses snapped up in a blow that Adam raised his own arm instinctively to block.

Maul smiled. His teeth were uniformly capped in gold.

It was like being clubbed with an iron street bollard. Maul had been testing him and he had passed the test. The expression on the assassin's face told him he had been expected to. It had been a playful strike. They would not fight today, on the day of his father's funeral; decorum would rightly prevent it. But their day would come, he knew. When it did he would need to be stronger. The block had rocked him on his feet. The bruise to his arm would likely put the limb beyond practical use for days.

Maul turned and vaulted the fence. He put his shades back on and walked away, dusting his hands drily together, not looking back.

Dora sat smoking and chewing her nails on a park bench. There was a febrile quality to her that Jane thought was probably to do with too much coke. Not now – she was not coked up at eleven o'clock in the morning – but she had been the night before and was suffering her narcotic hangover now. She had an appetite for life. And the life she chose to live was edgy and excessive. She partied hard. Partying was the point. Accomplishment was what her father had already done on her behalf.

That was Jane's opinion, anyway. That was her summation of her sister as she studied her for a moment before approaching to greet her. She had pretty much written Dora off. She was not usually an intolerant or ruthless person but she had been both of those things with her twin. Then again, Dora had been pretty consistent in earning her disapproval. Jane had concluded a couple of years ago that change would never come. Dora dismayed everyone close to her. She dismayed everyone, that was, except herself. But she was very happy with who she was and would remain contented as long as the parental allowance continued to bankroll her ramshackle life.

She smiled and stood when she saw Jane, flicking her cigarette away and treating her twin to an extravagant hug. Jane saw that her teeth were becoming discoloured and that her roots were showing. She dyed her hair an uncompromising black that hardened her features, and her nails were bitten crescents of chipped scarlet polish.

She was well dressed. She spent a lot on clothes and had on a red wool coat of asymmetric cut. She had inherited their mother's interest in fashion. She had no talent for it but good taste. The coat was teamed with black leather boots cut tight on the calf to compliment the length of her legs. The day was mild and the coat open, and under it she wore a grey sweater and a short grey pleated skirt. Her tights were the red of the coat. Jane thought she had probably dressed down as a back-handed compliment to her student sister.

They sat down together on the bench. For the first time since Scotland, Jane craved a cigarette herself.

'I hate you for looking so good,' Dora said. 'You always look fantastic, you bitch.'

'I want to talk to you about a man you've met called Bloor.'

'Jesus,' Dora said. 'Why don't we just cut right to the chase.' What little colour her face possessed drained from it. She looked uncomfortable. 'This is not something I can talk about.'

'He talks about it. He boasts about you.'

Dora's eyes flicked right and left. She looked trapped. She must have hammered the coke the night before, Jane thought. Up close her breath smelled thick with tar from chain-smoking and she lacked her usual breezy indifference to what was being said to her. Then again, Jane imagined that Adam's half-brother might be a handful.

Dora lit another cigarette. She did not offer the pack to Jane. Jane was grateful for this, because she knew she would have taken one.

'You don't wake up one morning and realize your life is empty,' she said. 'There's no Paul on the road to Damascus moment, Jane. At least, there wasn't for me. There's just this sort of corrosive scooping out of you until you feel quite hollow and know that you are a shell with nothing inside it. Oh, you look the same. And provided you are very careful and don't actually crack, no one really notices. But it doesn't feel good, emptiness. It really doesn't.'

'Bloor is not a therapist,' Jane said. 'He's not one of Mum's self-help gurus. He doesn't come from a very nice place, Dora. I can't see where this story is going.'

Her sister looked at her, held her gaze. It was uncharacteristic.

She usually had evasive eyes, the fugitive look of someone concealing something. When she held you like that, by contrast, Jane thought her eyes actually rather compelling. She still had time to be beautiful, if she could discover the inclination and cut the long list of self-destructive vices.

'I met him in a bar. He's tall and strikingly good looking and he has this dry wit I found appealing. And he told me about a place where there's no bullshit or consumer greed and where lives are not sacrificed on the altar of material gain. The population are not robotic servants to technology. It's a serene and unspoiled place with real and proper human values.'

'He brainwashed you.'

She laughed. 'No, he didn't. He fucking well took me there. And I loved it. And I want to go back and live there because this is my chance not to be hollow and to have and be someone of real substance.'

'The shadow world is not Utopia. It isn't Goa or Marrakesh, somewhere on the old hippie trail you tune in and drop out to. It's alien and evil.'

'Have you been there?'

'No.'

'Well shut up, Jane. Take your talent for sermonizing off to somewhere it's welcome. Don't pass judgment on something you know nothing about.'

'I know about Bloor. He's bad news.'

Dora shrugged. She was looking away again, down at the grass of the park, at the path the bench faced, at anything but her sister's expression. 'Maybe he's bad news for you,' she said. 'But I honestly believe he could be my salvation.'

'Think about this. Please.'

'Your interference isn't welcome, Jane. Fuck off.'

THIRTEEN

D elilah had hand-written her letter to him. Adam was more touched by this than he would have expected or even imagined. She had written it in a neat hand in the English he presumed his father must have taught her. She had done so after receiving the message from the shadow world confirming that she had been found.

He thought it selfless of her to have taken the time and courageous too to write what she had to him. He had no doubts about the significance of the letter's contents, about its possible ramifications and the chance it gave them. He told Jane about it straight away and together they told Grayling. And with the professor, they made the trip once more to Brighton to seek McGuire's counsel on this new and crucial revelation.

Dear Adam,

The purpose of these pages is to recount a true story. I hope that it will be of help in arresting matters. It may be too late to halt the speed and repercussions of the undermining now. Events, once set in chain, have their own momentum. But in all conscience, I must do what I can to intervene and offer whatever modest assistance I can to the cause of earth. The knowledge I am about to impart is secret. It is said that knowledge is power. We shall see. You can be the judge when you reach my concluding words.

This account involves your great and terrible ancestor, Sir Robert de Morey. You cannot know the impact his marauding adventures had on the world into which I was born. I know you have read his personal recollections, but they will not describe the baleful legend he left in his bloody wake. To refer to him there is to invoke a demon's name. Mischievous children are still harried to bed at the threat of his visitation. He is both devil and phantom. The shock of his outrages still lingers in folktale and song.

A decade ago I was a teacher at court. I taught music to

the young children of the king. It was a pleasant life in some aspects, but women are more servile creatures in Salabra than in Rotterdam. They are not considered the equals of men. Birth, beauty and brains can achieve a woman privilege, but nothing is hers really by right. It is often oppressive and sometimes disappointing. It is a situation that makes allies of women who might on earth more naturally view one another as rivals.

So it was that a woman named Alabaster Swift became my friend. She was an assistant to the alchemist, Jakob Slee. She was principally what you would call a chemist. She was very clever and gifted at this craft. I sensed that she was unhappy, which, once we knew each other well enough, she did confirm. She felt compromised, sullied almost, by the use of magic. Her inclination was to pure science rather than to the bastard trickery of Slee's tradition. An opinion such as hers was heresy there and I felt flattered that she trusted me with it.

She was the lover then of the courtier, Sebastian Dray. He was and remains a skilled and powerful politician. My world is autocratic and the king capricious, whimsical and often simply cruel. But he trusts Dray and relies on his talents as he relies on the gifts of very few men. Dray's achievement in remaining influential cannot be over-stressed. It is the measure of his brilliance and ability to read more shrewdly than anyone the moods of his monarch.

Dray is a handsome man, charismatic and charming and sometimes even kind. Mine is a harsh and spiteful world and it takes more courage to show kindness there than you would easily comprehend. No distinction is made between kindness and weakness, certainly not at court. But Dray has the courage and the confidence to indulge it. They were a good match, Dray and Alabaster. She was considered very fortunate to find favour with such a man. She was nobly born and beautiful. He was civilized.

When he was in counsel in the evening at his home, or in the company of great men, and this was often; it was her habit to spend that time in his library. He has amassed one of the great libraries of the world. Many of his books are priceless. He owns volumes of which there are said to be only the one copy existing. His library is half secret, played down in its magnificence, lest it incur the envy of the king. I do not think this is a very likely eventuality. The king is not much interested in books.

Of principle interest to Alabaster were the volumes on the subject of science. Dray is much more interested in poetry and history and art, and she found the section of the library devoted to science to be a chaotic jumble of spell books, alchemical tracts, formulae, principles of physics and general theorizing. She decided that she would catalogue it, bringing some order to the chaos and learning what she could of its contents at the same time.

Thus did she stumble upon what she very quickly realized was the laboratory notebook of Hieronymus Slee. Two things occurred to her immediately. The first was that the contents of this elderly volume were so secret that merely to read it would be a capital offence. The second was that Dray was unaware of its presence. It must have been bought in a job lot of old papers only carelessly examined. He was far too cautious a man to have something so sensitive stored on an open shelf.

Alabaster studied it. She could not help herself. Her scientific curiosity was too great to allow her to do otherwise, and she thought the risk of discovery slight. She had found something only she knew still existed in the world.

Slee was a magician by birthright, choice and obligation. But he was also something else, Alabaster discovered. He was what earth would call a virologist. And at this aspect of his discipline, he was nothing short of a genius. She found his formula for the plague bacillus. She found the vaccine he had formulated, a simple yeast variant baked into Endrimor's bread to prevent the spread of the pestilence to our world. It was chilling, she told me, to see them described in the hand of their creator.

There was something else, though, some virus he was working on that seemed to have a very specific genus. In the notes, Slee claimed success for it. It confused Alabaster. It killed by encouraging body temperature to a level the host would find intolerable, but it seemed to be predicated on the assumption that the host would be cold-blooded. She stared at the formulae until the scrawled figures and symbols swam before her eyes. Then she turned the page. And she saw a precise anatomical sketch of a parasite on which dissection had been performed.

There were to be two plagues, Adam. There was the one de Morey was sent to avenge. And there was the one intended to wipe out the legion of parasites on which the count of Sarth depended for his protection. That is the real reason the count was so anxious to assist your ancestor. It was not friendship. His spies at court had told him about what Slee was working on. Or someone from Slee's laboratory had boasted in a tavern and the rumour had spread north. What can't be denied is that when de Morey killed Slee, he stopped this pestilence before it began.

It was Alabaster's belief, in her phrase, that Slee only had the skill to transmit the formula from the page to the petrie dish. When he died, the disease he created to all intents and purposes died with him. Certainly it was never used.

The present count is much more powerful than his ancestor. Selective breeding has made the parasites less the ghoulish, leech-like creatures they were then, than true and formidable monsters in his service. He owes earth a great debt of gratitude. It is my belief that now is the moment to make him honour it. Earth has always had allies on Endrimor. I am the proof, an ally of earth when I am from there myself. The count of Sarth could be your greatest ally in your moment of greatest need.

You should appeal to him personally. Without the bravery and fortitude of the great knight whose blood and name you share, he would never have been born. Petition him. He owes you his life.

My Love to You,
Delilah

Adam read the letter aloud. McGuire was the first to speak when he had finished it. 'The parasite bacillus could not have been ready. Either that or it was not fully formulated. If it had been, they would have unleashed it.'

'The present count of Sarth is not to know that,' Grayling said. 'For all he knows, it is complete and intact and highly virulent. It gives us a lot of leverage.'

'You don't have it,' Adam said. 'It exists only as a formula in a laboratory log from the Middle Ages on a shelf somewhere in Sebastian Dray's library. And I don't see the need for leverage, as you call it. Why threaten the count? Why blackmail him into becoming our ally? Why not just do as Delilah suggests and petition him?'

'Appeal to his better nature, you mean?' Grayling's voice was heavy with sarcasm.

'If you had seen one of his parasites, you would not imagine him generally very charitable,' said McGuire.

'I agree with Adam,' said Jane. 'The parasites have been bred to engage in a guerilla war that his family has been forced to fight for centuries. If you want a guard dog, you don't buy a poodle. He's been practical. He's followed the family tradition. It doesn't necessarily mean he's a sadistic or dishonourable man.'

Grayling looked at Adam. 'You can appeal to his sense of obligation, his integrity, if you wish. It might work. If it doesn't, then threaten him with the pestilence. Regard it as the ace up your sleeve.'

'Me?'

'Well of course you, Adam. Or would you rather stay here and wait for Maul to come back and pull you apart at his leisure?'

He had told Jane and the professor about his confrontation at his father's funeral. By now he expected that McGuire would also know about it. The sense that they were all being toyed with had only been increased by Jane's account of her meeting in London with her sister. Delilah's letter, the information it contained, presented the opportunity to do something positive, to act rather than to react all the time to events. He should welcome it, he thought. But there was one serious objection.

'I don't speak the language,' he said.

McGuire laughed out loud at that. 'You'll probably be devoured before you get an opportunity to speak,' he said. 'The niceties of linguistic protocol are unlikely to be required.'

'I'll go with you,' Jane said. 'The doctor here speaks it and I'm good at languages. He can give me the rudiments. We'll do a crash course. When do we go? Where do we go to get there?'

Grayling said, 'There's a gateway in the high Alps, above the monastery which contained the atlas in which your father found the de Morey deposition.'

'That's right,' Adam said. 'They were coded and you said you broke the code.'

Grayling nodded. 'It means that the gateway has not been used since medieval times, so it will not be guarded, even if it is still known about there.'

'Do we know where it will bring us out?' Jane asked.

'Further north than south, I believe. That's a practical advantage. But you will need luck, both of you, to succeed in this mission. It is vastly more dangerous than anything either of you have ever done in your lives.'

'I'd like to talk to Jane about this privately,' Adam said.

'You won't talk me out of going,' she said.

'I know that.'

They crossed the road and walked the length of the pier. It was a bright autumn afternoon, the sea vibrant under a blue sky, the air cool with a candyfloss tang, the Wurlitzer music so exuberant it almost sounded funny. They went into one of the coffee places they had not tried before, one free of sinister associations.

'Did you really not sleep with Delilah Crane?'

'We kissed.'

'I bloody knew something had gone on.'

'It was just a kiss.'

'With the Siren of Rotterdam, I don't think there's any such thing.'

Adam thought Delilah was by now probably dead, her corpse lying at the bottom of the harbour with her tongue half-digested in its stomach, a remote and pitiful distance beyond seducing anyone. He looked out of the window behind him, in the direction of the doctor's flat on the promenade. 'Did you notice they weren't exactly queuing up themselves for this vital mission?'

Jane picked up her tea and blew on its surface. 'McGuire's too doddery for the physical stuff. But I've got a theory about that.'

'Go on.'

'The conflict is kept secret. The thinking is that we'd lose heart if it was generally known about, so it's all hushed up and deliberately misinterpreted.'

'Thus the Great Lie.'

'Exactly that, but a network of people are in on it. They were probably recruited the way McGuire was.'

'Then there's the dynastic element, which is how Grayling became involved.'

'There must be some international, orchestrated campaign, like there was at Sarajevo,' Jane said.

'Sarajevo failed.'

'I know, but just the same. There will be a network of people like McGuire and Grayling globally. There must be. They will be planning strategies to lessen the damage to international relations Martin and his three apocalyptic pals are doing. I think Grayling wouldn't think of going himself because he's too important. I doubt he's thought of as dispensable.'

'He was important enough to try to kill in Canterbury,' Adam said. 'They were keeping tabs on him.' He rubbed his tender arm. 'That said, I was important enough to merit a personal introduction to Proctor Maul.'

She smiled at him. 'Yes, Adam, you're very important. Is that what you wanted to tell me in private?'

He looked at her. She was very beautiful in the sunlight through the café's picture windows. He thought the love he had for her infinitely rare and precious. He did not want anything to happen that would stop her looking at him in the way she was at that moment, and yet he thought he was about to jeopardize completely the tender feelings that she had for him.

Quietly, he said, 'When we cross, Jane, I will not be deterred. If Bloor tries to stop me, I will kill him. That is not rhetoric. It will be ugly. I don't want you to think of me as someone with blood on his hands. It will ruin what we have between us. For that reason if for no other, I'd rather you didn't come.'

'You won't be deterred. Neither will I.'

'It isn't about you being a woman. I've no objection in principle to women going to war if that's their choice.'

'I know that.' She looked down at her hands, linked in her lap below the table surface. 'When I went to see my sister, I noticed some discoloration on her face. It stretched from her cheekbone to her ear. It had been very skilfully concealed with make-up, but I saw it. I asked her if Bloor hit her.'

'How did she reply?'

'She said that though she was improving, she was not perfect. She was a work in progress, and she needed occasional chastisement.'

'Has he done anything else?'

'I didn't ask. I didn't have the stomach.' She raised her eyes to look at him directly. 'Remember your father's old saying about chance?'

'They all say it. I'm getting sick of hearing it.'

'You were born for this, Adam. And if you have to kill to succeed in it, then that's what you have to do. It won't make me feel about you any differently at all. We didn't pick this fight, but we can't afford to lose it.'

Jane was given her crash course in the language. Adam brushed up on his fencing technique against Grayling. It felt odd initially, naked, not to fence in a mask. He was also wary at first about the thrust and parry of the contest with weapons keen and edged. He adjusted quickly. By any objective standard, Grayling was very good. Adam, though, was infinitely better.

'Why can't I take a gun?'

'If they catch you with a gun they will kill you straight away.'

'That's the whole point of the gun. It will prevent them from killing me.'

'Start leaving bodies lying around with bullet holes in them and they will hunt you down before you get anywhere near the count's domain. Kill them with a sword thrust and anyone could have done it. Swords are not just less conspicuous there than automatic pistols; they are a great deal quieter.'

'People actually go about there armed with swords?'

'Of course not. Don't be bloody silly. You will take the doctor's cane. If anyone looks at it suspiciously—'

'Stab them.'

Grayling raised his eyes to heaven. 'Lean on it. Walk as though you are afflicted with lameness and a slight limp.'

McGuire told them something about the customs and landscape. The first thing they would notice, he said, was that there were very few people abroad. Travel was not encouraged. Settlements were scarce. Most of the population of the south lived in the hovels, a sort of vast shanty town spreading outwards in the hinterland beyond the walls of the city of Salabra. There were several hundred thousand slum dwellers, despite the frequent and savage culls carried out on them. There were no ethnic distinctions, just strict caste divisions between those born noble and the peasantry.

'Maul's complexion is that of a Native American,' Adam said.

'The pigment is applied. It's a decorative thing, like the facial tattoo.'

'So he possesses a certain amount of personal vanity.'

'Presumably so,' McGuire said. 'He was immaculately attired

when you saw him. But I don't think his vanity is a weakness that's going to assist you in a fight with Proctor Maul.'

'Cheers,' Adam said. 'You have a real gift for positive thinking.'

The civilian population lived with only the most rudimentary technologies. There was no electricity. Their homes were lit by candles and heated by fires fuelled with wood. The more prosperous had gas lanterns. A volatile gas could be harvested from natural toxic marshes to the west of where the hovels petered into scrubland. This fuelled the vehicles the king's army was equipped with. By earth standards these vehicles were almost comically crude, but they sufficed because civilians were obliged to rely on horse-drawn transportation. The soldiers were also trained in the use of rifles and artillery pieces, but did not have routine access to weapons except in time of war.

'Don't tell me,' Jane said, when McGuire informed them of this. 'The king fears a coup.'

'I don't think fear is an emotion the Crimson King has ever felt,' McGuire said carefully. 'But he is cautious and distrustful and suspicious of everyone.'

'The army is quite small numerically,' Grayling said. 'You must remember that the king has Jakob Slee and Slee's magic, and he is anything but reluctant to use sorcery against his enemies.'

Far less was known about the count of Sarth's domain to the north. There was reason to believe it had expanded, Grayling said. Aerial reconnaissance was not possible. There was no aviation. It might be possible to rig a hot air balloon. But a Vorp would certainly bring it down. The forest in that part of Endrimor was in places impenetrable. It was believed that cities thrived under the count's patronage, but no one from earth had ever visited them.

Jane said, 'Could you not send spies?'

Grayling and McGuire looked at one another. Grayling said, 'Until I broke the atlas code there were only two gateway locations known to us. There was the one off the coast of Scandinavia and the one in the Aegean that puts you in the Miasmic Sea. The former was hazardous. The latter was deadly.'

'You cracked the code a quarter of a century ago,' Adam said. 'You must have sent people.'

'We did,' Grayling said. 'But no one we sent north ever returned.'

'It sounds a very small and parochial world,' Adam said.

'It is the same size as ours physically,' McGuire said. 'But most of it is ocean. There is only the one land mass, so in a sense it is small. But it is also a much stranger and more exotic place than earth. Spells that somehow soured or were corrupted account for the Miasmic Sea and the parasites, we think. And the wildlife there is best avoided. Predators have thrived on a civilian population prevented from being able adequately to defend itself. The animals are deadly and strange. The people are cowed. The hovels teem with filth and hopelessness. The sea grows daily more poisonous. The rulers are capricious and cruel.'

Jane and Adam, listening, nodded as one.

'Try to come back safe.'

The weather in the high Alps was harsh. In one way that was a blessing. Adam did not like heights. Jane had actually climbed and abseiled. She had done some bouldering in Colorado and even some free climbing and was an experienced off-piste skier. Grayling, who led them, had become a crack rock climber at school and an expert mountaineer in his army days. Adam was just grateful that he could not see how far they could fall in the blizzard they struggled through, walking upwards with the deliberation inflicted upon them by the crampons they all wore.

Finally, mercifully, they reached a plateau. They huddled on the flat snow in a white-out so severe it was not possible to see further than your own extended arm. Grayling took off his gloves and retrieved a pocket flashlight and a compass from the pouches on the equipment belt buckled around his waist.

In his hooded canvas smock and goggles he looked to Adam more the World War Two commando on arctic patrol than a modern Alpinist. They were all three of them attired in these drab, old-fashioned waterproofs.

Modern fabrics in bright colours would make them as conspicuous as zoo exhibits where they were going, McGuire had warned. Their concession to the conditions was the crampon friendly modern climbing boots they were all equipped with. They would swap these for the plain boots in their packs in the moments before the cross.

Their plateau ended abruptly at a vaunting rampart of solid rock. They edged left along it until the granite surface was breached by a fissure just wide enough to squeeze into. They followed Grayling into a cave. It widened sufficiently to accommodate them beyond the entrance.

He lit a lamp once a few feet inside and Adam was able to see that the cave narrowed again in the gloom where it deepened beyond the pale bloom of light. Grayling rigged a stove to make them a last drink before departure. It was very cold in the cave and Adam thought Jane would be as grateful for the warmth of the beverage as he would. He would heat his hands on the mug and change his boots when the numbness had left them.

'That way,' Grayling said, nodding into the darkness, a few minutes later. He paused, standing there. They hesitated. He looked down and brushed something imaginary from the front of his smock. And then he raised his eyes again and strode across and embraced each of them in turn.

They emerged into weak sunlight. The cross was an assault on the senses. The ground felt different, softening under their feet as the cave walls fell away into a limbo of space and the rich smell of an autumnal wood hit their nostrils in bark and ferns and windfall apples and pine resin. They were only aware of the loud shriek of the alpine wind beyond the cave entrance when it was gone, replaced by the busy chorus of birds in the branches above them competing in song. Jane felt the compulsion to crouch and gather herself. When she did, she saw that Adam had done the same, on his haunches beside her, the trickle of a stream nearby gurgling pleasantly, moss feeling cool and rough under them when she spread her hands on the earth.

They stood. 'Look at the sky,' Adam said.

Jane did. It was cloudless and blue and looked strange for a reason that would not quite clarify in her mind. Something was weirdly empty about it.

'No con trails,' Adam said. 'There hasn't been a sky like that on earth in our lifetimes.'

They tightened the straps on their packs and trekked steadily north. Jane occasionally took a compass reading to see that they had not strayed. The ground was lightly wooded and gently undulating and they made good progress. They had rations in their packs but snacked on apples and pears and damsons plucked ripe from the trees they passed.

Jane's only immediate concern was about the great carnivorous avian creatures that blighted the shadow world. They would get plenty of warning of the beast's approach in the clear sky above them but the odd wild orchard or copse would not shelter them from attack. They would not be safe from the Vorps until they reached the cover of the count's forest and one threat was swapped for another, even more menacing, in the bloodthirsty shape of the parasites.

'What are you thinking about?'

'About how drab these retro outfits we're wearing are. We could be kitted out head to toe in that Roam stuff you designed. I'm pretty sure we could have got it at cost price.'

Jane shuddered. She did not appreciate the joke. 'Martin Prior wears Roam.'

'He makes your stomach turn, doesn't he?'

'It's really strange. We were good friends. I never fancied him but could see how someone could. Now I think he's a loathsome creep.'

'Next time he's on television, take a good look at his eyes,' Adam said. 'He doesn't look much different from the sailors I daydreamed about aboard that dreadnought. He's been interfered with, charmed in some way. I'd hate to be inside his head.'

'If we're successful he won't be on television for much longer,' Jane said. 'He won't have any new sensations to reveal.'

They sighted the forest towards the late afternoon of the second day. When it first came into view, on the horizon about ten miles distant, Adam took it for a lake. He was judging what he was looking at by its darkness and density. But as they got closer it became green and they realized they were looking not at water, but at a vast expanse of trees.

'Do we really want to be in there at nightfall?' he said.

Jane looked at him. 'Do we really want to be out here for a second night?'

It had not been discussed between them, but they had both heard the territorial cries of what sounded like large and predatory beasts in their tiny tent in the darkness. Their shelter had been fragile and they had been almost pitifully vulnerable inside it. And towards dawn, she had heard the flap above her of enormous wings, and the fabric over her head had rippled inward with the draft they stirred.

Full darkness had descended by the time they reached the forest. It was a clear night and the moon shone brightly. The forest was coniferous and its foliage thick and still, unchallenged by seasonality. It was totally silent. Pale toadstools littered the loamy forest floor.

Jane did not think it could have contrived to be less inviting. Then she remembered the size of the single fallen vaned feather she had found at the site as Adam folded their tent after breakfast. The shaft had been the thickness of her arm and tipped in gore. She recalled the feral stink of it.

They had no choice. She walked forward into the trees, gesturing for him to follow her.

She could not have said how far they had travelled before the suspicion that they were being observed began to grow in her. Soon it became overwhelming. So strong was the sense of scrutiny that it became difficult to walk normally. Jane felt self-conscious, as though their movement was less progress to a destination than a performance. This was not an encouraging intuition. All it encouraged was fear. Every step felt more disheartening, as though it lured them nearer to a trap.

She glanced at Adam and he glanced back and nodded, and telepathy was not necessary between them to know that he was feeling the same skin-prickling instinct that she was. Nothing apparently moved other than the two of them. There was no sound. But the observation and pursuit were skilled, stealthy realities. They were not so much intruders here as prey. Their mission had been misconceived, their efforts futile.

The attack was very quick. There were three of them and they had waited for the space on the ground in which to fight. The density of the forest had slightly lessened at this point, and there was some clear space between the trees. They were pale and naked and powerful in the moonlight and moved with insectile suddenness. They were slightly taller than a man. Their assault came from three sides as though from the points of a triangle towards Jane and Adam at its centre.

Jane bit on a mouth full of loam as Adam shoved her off her feet and on to her stomach and she heard the shriek of escaping steel as he drew the swordstick's blade and then a sort of gasp as he struck home with it. She turned her head and looked up to see him weaving out of the way of blows so fast they cut the air audibly.

He was fighting two of them. He was making them pay for every miss with clusters of blows of his own. She had never seen reflexes like those Adam was gifted with when he fought. His fists travelled through space at the speed of crudely edited movie footage. It was faster than some jump-cut trick. But his punches were bouncing off the creatures he fought. His knuckles left blood in black, moonlit smears on their carapace hides.

Where was the third? She twisted her head. He was lying against the trunk of a tree with McGuire's lethal toy protruding from his chest. She looked at the creature's face: alert, tiny eyes over holes for nostrils and a maw which receded in complex rows of needle-like teeth. He was not dying. He did not even seem to be in pain. He pulled at the pommel of the weapon he'd been skewered with and it exited his body with a metallic shriek.

Adam was losing the fight. They were slowing him. Against one he might have prevailed, but he was matched against two and they were very strong and quick, and the third had rallied and was joining them with the blade that should have killed him held in the grip of what passed for his hand.

She saw Adam's eyes glance down to look at her and saw only concern for her in them and loved him for his courage as he ducked under a sweeping lunge and responded with the smack of a solid headbutt to the temple of the creature's head. It staggered. He kicked it to its knees. His hands were ruined, she realized. They were finished. He followed the butt with the point of an elbow and the creature flopped earthward. Jesus. He'd actually beaten one of them. The parasite holding the sword chittered out some awful, triumphant sound and bore down upon him.

'Enough,' said a voice. 'Bravo,' it added. The creatures stopped and stood entirely still.

'You speak English.'

To Jane's ears, Adam sounded spent. But the voice *had* spoken English. She did not dare look to see who had spoken. Her hands were soiled, filled, fists squeezing out what they contained between her fingers with tension. The voice had brought hope to hopelessness and she felt the more fraught for the optimism it delivered her.

'Do not move, for the moment,' it said. 'Remain still, both of you. Do not speak again, young man. You are brave and able. But if you wish to survive this encounter, you would be wise to curtail your words. This is not the moment for defiance. You have demonstrated quite enough of that. Be quiet. Follow me humbly.'

The creature Jane had thought rendered unconscious by the point of Adam's elbow unfolded abruptly off the ground. The parasite holding the sword surrendered it to the man with a bow. While he examined it, she examined him. He looked about thirty-five and could plausibly have been a far closer relative of Professor Grayling than Doctor McGuire, who claimed to be. He was silver-headed in the moonlight and austerely handsome.

'Come,' he said. Jane got up and Adam wiped the blood from his knuckles on his smock and put an arm around her. They followed the man a hundred yards to where a carriage waited. Harnessed to it were a team of two blinkered horses. The parasites had disappeared, Jane saw, as they climbed into the carriage, the forest silently absorbing them. They had seen no driver, but the horses must have been well schooled. They set off as soon as the carriage door was closed. The wheels groaned on their axles with the twists and turns of their route.

Jane wore no watch – Grayling had forbidden it – but she thought that the journey took about half an hour. The interior of the coach was leather and luxurious, deep piled animal pelts draped warmly over the seats. It smelled richly of hide and some heady, floral perfume.

'The scent is that of my late wife,' their host said. 'This is her carriage. She was murdered just over a week ago.'

'You are the count of Sarth,' Adam said. 'We are very sorry, sir, for your loss.'

'And you are a descendant of de Morey, I believe.'

'Believing that,' Jane said, 'why did you try to have us killed?'

The count laughed curtly. 'They were an escort only, instructed to disarm you. Had they been instructed to kill, you would be dead now and an empty vessel. They overreached their instructions. Sometimes their exuberance is difficult to contain. It does not greatly signify. They provided me with a useful measure of our friend.'

'How long have you known we were here?'

'You ask a lot of questions, madam. Since your arrival, is the answer to that one. My question is, why have you come?' The carriage stopped. 'We are here,' he said. 'You can satisfy my curiosity over dinner. The exertions of your young champion will have given him an appetite.'

'His hands are ruined.'

'Yet he is very fortunate. He has your devotion. His hands shall be repaired before we eat.'

When they alighted, Jane half-expected it to be before a gothic

castle fit for Dracula. But the count's residence was more a grand
hunting lodge in the style of the dachas of Imperial Russia, the sort
of country refuge enjoyed by the Czar and his nobles before the
Bolshevik Revolution. It did not appear fortified. This was no
stockade or keep. His parasite legion was all the protection he
required from the hostile nation to the south.

He insisted they bathe and change. Clothing was provided for
them. A woman was summoned from somewhere who applied a
salve to the torn skin of Adam's knuckles. The flesh began to mend,
to regenerate and heal so fast he could see the process taking place.
The cream must be some agent that enabled rapid cellular recon-
struction, he thought. It was very powerful, whatever it was. It eased
out the bruising before the worst of the pain he expected had even
arrived. By the time he sat down with Jane at the count's table his
hands were completely restored.

They explained their mission. Their host listened with a look on
his face that betrayed nothing of what he thought. Then, addressing
Adam, he said, 'It is true I am greatly in the debt of your ancestor.
And of course mine knew of the pestilence on which Slee was
working to eradicate the parasites. But the parasites have evolved
so far since then I doubt the bacillus would have the effect on them
today it would have then.'

'We are not here to blackmail you with threats of plague,' Jane
said. 'We are not here even to accuse your family of exploiting de
Morey centuries ago. Your ancestor enabled him to fulfill his obligation to his king. What he did was of mutual benefit to them. There
was no exploitation. But there is, as you have just said, a debt of
gratitude to be repaid.'

He seemed to ponder for a long time. He had more wine poured
for all of them. He ran a staff at the lodge that seemed large. He
lived well. Then she remembered that his wife had been murdered
only a week ago.

As though reading her mind, he said, 'My wife suffered a genetic
condition. It required her treatment, twice annually, by a skilled physician in Salabra. She enjoyed these clandestine trips.' He shrugged.
'Salabra has its mercantile charms and she was a woman. She was
betrayed. Perhaps it was only a matter of time. Perhaps I was naïve.
I always thought that if she was found out, a ransom demand would
follow. It breaches the protocol to feed a woman of noble birth to a
giant bird of prey trained in the practice of execution.'

Jane and Adam swapped a glance. Silence seemed the tactful response.

'I have been musing on my revenge. But I am not mobilized for war. My army of parasites, my thirsty horde of monsters, numbers at this moment scarcely twenty.'

Adam could not conceal his frank astonishment. 'Why?'

The count smiled at him. 'Practicality is the answer. Their thirst is relentless. They are self-sufficient, feeding on the men sent from the south by the pretender. They are as formidable as they are voracious and alert. It is enough. I maintain a stock of captive beasts as food for when their own prey becomes scarce. If I bred an army, only a war could sustain it. So I keep twenty.'

Jane said, 'How long would an army take to breed?'

'They breed rapidly. They come to maturity with the swiftness of insects. In three months I would have the numbers. In six they would be trained.'

'I don't think earth has six months,' Adam said.

'And I have no intention of breeding an army.'

'So you won't help us,' Adam said.

'On the contrary, my young friend.' He smiled and leaned across the table to squeeze Adam's shoulder. There were jewelled rings on his fingers which glittered in the light of the candelabra, and Jane wondered how old they might be.

'We will halt the undermining with a bluff. You will take a letter to the pretender from me. In it I will threaten war unless their dabbling stops. For all they know, this domain of mine contains twenty thousand parasites. My letter will promise to unleash a horde from hell. They will meet my terms.'

'It will not avenge your wife,' Jane said quietly.

The count looked at her. Adam thought the look openly appreciative of Jane's qualities; her brains and beauty and her courage, too. 'Nothing will avenge my wife,' he said. 'Come.'

He rose and led them to one of the dining room's several doors. It opened upon a library. Logs blazed in a great fireplace. Above it was a portrait in the medieval style of a man of noble aspect attired in armour, seated bareheaded astride a warhorse. The knight was caught in profile.

Jane turned to Adam. 'When did you sit for that?'

The count chuckled. 'Yes, madam, the likeness fair reflects the bloodline, does it not? The whole of Endrimor knows of the debt owed by the house of Sarth to the house of de Morey. I would not be the man to deny or dishonour it.'

They met Sebastian Dray in a tent erected for the purpose in a field with the towers and turrets of Salabra a distant smudge to the south. Adam had expected a glittering power display to offset the defeat of accepting the count's terms. The undermining took time and planning and orchestrated effort. The conflict was ancient and bitter and the ultimate ambition perhaps closer to realization than it had ever been. But it was Dray and Proctor Maul only. Maul for protection, Adam supposed. Dray looked physically capable. But he was a diplomat, more schemer than warrior.

He and Jane had travelled to the site on horseback. The journey had taken them five days. The parley had been arranged by a fast courier dispatched on the evening of the count's decision to help. He had communicated the threat of war, the demand for safe passage and the proposed location of this conference.

They had arrived dusty and ripe. It didn't matter. They sat across from him and Dray read what the count had written. If the contents of the letter made him angry or frustrated him, it did not show in his expression. Adam stole a glance at Maul, wondering whether Delilah Crane had yet perished in the man's inhuman grip. He looked back to Dray, hoping that they would never connect the dots and that Alabaster Swift was a woman capable of keeping a secret.

Dray smiled at them. It was an engaging smile. He had aimed it in Jane's direction. 'How many parasites do you think he commands?'

'He is a student of earth history,' Jane said. 'He is a great admirer of Imperial Rome. He boasted of having raised nine legions.'

'It's my understanding that the Ninth Legion disappeared,' Dray said, 'somewhere beyond Hadrian's Wall, in the land where you so recently grovelled in the ground without reward.'

Jane shrugged and smiled back at him. Adam saw that Maul was staring intently at her. 'That would leave him commanding eight legions. Have you seen his parasites fight?'

'Have you?'

'An exhibition bout,' Adam said. 'One of them briefly toyed with me. I ran it through. It lived to sport at full strength before the count was obliged to call it off to spare my life.'

Maul's eyes turned to Adam. He frowned.

Dray said, 'I did not think they were capable of play.'

'They are capable of whatever he instructs them to do,' Jane said.

Dray shrugged. He put the letter down on the round table at which they sat. Autumn sunlight had raised the temperature in the tent and there was the smell of canvas, slightly musty, and the sharp, vinegary smell of Proctor Maul breathing heavily – Adam supposed to control his fury.

'It ends,' Dray said.

Jane said, 'As easily as that?'

'How can we trust you? Trust is earned,' Adam said, 'not gifted.'

'We are as patient as we are implacable,' Dray said. 'A war on the scale threatened would not benefit our world. I see no alternative but to end our involvement with yours. I speak for the Crimson King.'

The public execution of the count's wife had been a spiteful miscalculation. Tactically, it had been a disaster. Adam looked from Dray to Maul and knew that they both appreciated that. And so would their king, and someone would pay for the blunder. Salabra would not be a pleasant place for them to return to. It would not be a comfortable place for any of its citizens in the face of the king's petulant wrath. That said, it would be worse in the hovels, where disease held sway and the culls thrived and the scapegoats endured whatever caprice delivered.

'Hostilities end forthwith,' Adam said.

'They do,' Dray said, with just a subtle note of exasperation.

Adam nodded at Maul. 'So if he hasn't yet killed Delilah Crane, he cannot return to do so now, can he?'

'He cannot.'

'Does she live?'

Dray did not reply. The look on Maul's face was enough to give Adam his answer.

'We are free to leave unmolested?'

'You enjoy the protection of the count. Go now.'

They reached their gateway at dawn. Adam's thoughts were muddled by the fatigue of their having been in the saddle for so long and the spent adrenaline cost him by Maul's proximity in their tense conference.

He thought about the warrior whose blood he shared, smiting Edgar Maul in a lonely arena with his dead daughter in his arms summoned for strength to his mind. He imagined McGuire, watching as Alabaster Swift sent a gang of thugs sprawling in the Edwardian snow with only a vindictive thought. He pictured that colossal battleship and its slavish crew marooned in their collective madness on an ocean poisoned by magic. He heard the words his father had rasped out during that bedside vigil on the afternoon when the breath at last departed him. *Chance is how we describe events when we don't yet know their purpose.*

Finally they arrived at the place. Jane reached out her hand and Adam held it. He kissed her. She said, 'It isn't the end at all, is it?'

'It's the end of the beginning,' he said.